# About the

Philip Wilding is a journalist, writer and radio producer who lives and works in London. His debut novel, *Cross Country Murder Song*, was described, variously, as 'like a worm inside my brain' and 'compelling and sophisticated writing'. He ghost wrote Carl Barat's acclaimed autobiography, *Threepenny Memoir*, and helped launch the BBC 6 Music network as producer and co-presenter on *The Phill Jupitus Breakfast Show*. He currently spends his days producing at talkRADIO. And when not sat near a microphone, he dreams about running a half-marathon in less than two hours.

# THE DEATH AND LIFE OF RED HENLEY

# THE DEATH AND LIFE OF RED HENLEY

## PHILIP WILDING

Unbound Digital

This edition first published in 2018

Unbound

6th Floor Mutual House, 70 Conduit Street, London W1S 2GF

www.unbound.com

ISBN (eBook): 978-1-912618-27-9
ISBN (Paperback): 978-1-912618-26-2

Design by Mecob

Printed and bound in Great Britain by Clays Ltd, Elcograf S.p.A.

MIX
Paper from
responsible sources
FSC
www.fsc.org
FSC® C018072

*For a badge-hoarding, poetry-writing, tifter-sporting, Renaissance man: always working, always angry, the incomparable Phill Jupitus.*

Dear Reader,

The book you are holding came about in a rather different way to most others. It was funded directly by readers through a new website: Unbound.

Unbound is the creation of three writers. We started the company because we believed there had to be a better deal for both writers and readers. On the Unbound website, authors share the ideas for the books they want to write directly with readers. If enough of you support the book by pledging for it in advance, we produce a beautifully bound special subscribers' edition and distribute a regular edition and e-book wherever books are sold, in shops and online.

This new way of publishing is actually a very old idea (Samuel Johnson funded his dictionary this way). We're just using the internet to build each writer a network of patrons. Here, at the back of this book, you'll find the names of all the people who made it happen.

Publishing in this way means readers are no longer just passive consumers of the books they buy, and authors are free to write the books they really want. They get a much fairer return too – half the profits their books generate, rather than a tiny percentage of the cover price.

If you're not yet a subscriber, we hope that you'll want to join our publishing revolution and have your name listed in one of our books in the future. To get you started, here is a £5 discount on your first pledge. Just visit unbound.com, make your pledge and type HENLEY18 in the promo code box when you check out.

Thank you for your support,

Dan, Justin and John
Founders, Unbound

# Super Patrons

Aaron Aedy
Suzanne Amos
Sharon Archer
Lauren Archer
Rosie Austin-Webster
Steve Ayland
Nick Azinas
Alan Bambrough
Pete Barlow
Andy Bass
Tim Batcup
Brenda Bent
Carl Bigmore
Lynwen Birch
Zaki Boulos
Stephen Bowyer
Stephanie Bradley
Jennifer Bradly
Terry Brown
David Burgess
Alex Burrows
Sarah Christie
Samantha Collins
Steve Collins
Jon Collins
Alex Constantinou
David Cummings
James Cunliffe
Marti Davidson Sichel
Mona Dehghan
Robin Dewson
Willie Dowling

Charlotte Duncanson
Emma Duyts
Elaine Edwards
David Edwards
Darren Evans
Mikey Evans
Russell Fairbrother
Steph Farrer
Sarah Faust
Brendan 'Fucky' Fish
Ben Ford
Justine Fox
Karen Gable
Drew Gallon
Nick Gillett
Eleanor Goodman
Richard Goodman
Rebecca Gowers
Steve Hammonds
Shahid Haq
Emma Hatcher
Keith Hide
Steve Hill
Richard Holmes
Andy Hunns
Andrew Hunt
Simon & Helen Hutchinson
Eliza & Dexter Hutchinson
Matthew Ingham
Charlotte & James Isaacs
Louise Johnson
Laura Jones
Michael Joseph
Solly & Jude
Phill Jupitus
Phil & Keely

Paola Kellman
Jo Kendall
Michelle Kerr
Dan Kieran
Kevin King
Kate Ksiazkiewicz
Neil Lach-szyrma
Linda Lach-Szyrma
Pippa Lang
Piers Leighton
Damian Leslie
Fraser Lewry
Alex Lifeson
Shelley Lindley
Sian Llewellyn
Lee Mann
Paul Mapstone
Chris Marlowe
Phil Martini
Emma Masip Font
Clarry McDonald
Billy McMillan
Tim McMillan
Iain McNicol
Stuart Mcnicol
Viki Merrill
Rowan Messingham
Alexander Milas
Nicola Miller
John Mitchinson
Willie & Monika
Grant Moon
JC of the Muffin
Emily Mules
Chris Myers
Anne Newman

Kristin Nielsen
Kevin Nixon
Stewart Noble
Ady Packham
Steve Page
Freddy Palmer
Ben Pester
Cameron Pirie
Nellie Pitts
Justin Pollard
Madison Pollard-Shore
Frances Porter
Elspeth Potts
Anita Procter
Hamish Rankine
Jennifer Reddington
Rodolf Reed
Bob Ripperdan
Clare Robinson
Scott Rowley
Paul Rowlston
Tina Saul
Jevan Shepherd
Deborah Skelton
Lewis-Jon Somerscales
Matthew Spoors
Chris Staples
Steven Stephenson-Taylor
Matt Stevens
Ian Synge
Gwennan Thomas
Richard Thompson
Richard Todd
Jonty Vane
Adam Ward
Dominic Ward

Rose Watt
Gus White
Adrian White
Kate Wiles
Helen Williams
Steve Williams
Rich Wilson
Lisa Winn
John WN
Ian Woods
Matthew Wright
Nancy Young
Rachel Zager
Azra Zakir

# January 1956

*'A daughter?'*

His shrill damnation blotted out the noise of the newly born baby as she wailed her way into the world. She didn't yet know it, but her father's ire was aimed at something indistinguishable that sat far above the roof of the hospital wing and delivery room they were in: his Lord.

'A daughter?' he asked again, imploring the ceiling's glare. 'A daughter,' he said again, but this time his voice was softening, with something like acceptance creeping into it as he stared at the bloody, vacant gap of his daughter's sex. He was trembling and quiet now, glaring at the midwife holding his daughter out towards him, apportioning blame, his eyes murderous and dark, and by the time the nurse had turned to the washed-out face of his wife there on the operating table and back again it was to the silent flapping of the delivery-room doors, the memory of his shape scything through the air.

As she grew up he dressed her in boy's clothes; people would stop and tousle her hair and coo things at the little boy seated in the pram before them. Her father never corrected their mistakes: he grinned broadly and then his face would register sadness and disappointment as the truth focused his thoughts and the trilling women walked away. Her mother had died when the girl was barely a year old, a red station wagon mounting the sidewalk and snatching her away while her hand still played lightly on the pram. She remembered laughter and her mother's face glancing in at her, softened by a golden light, her features glimmering in a halo and then the revving of an engine, a car screeching out of control and suddenly her mother was gone as if she'd been pulled into the sky, and in a way she had been. The car came to rest against the corner of a women's clothing store, her mother caught between the shining veneer of the hood and the ruddy brown of the building's bricks next to a large picture window advertising that season's latest styles; she was broken almost completely at the hips, her back pressed hard against the wall,

1

her mouth a surprised circle, there was steam rising from the car's ruptured radiator, a horn keening loudly, the day was shattering, coming apart like a jigsaw that had fallen to the floor.

Her name was Rose, but her father called her Red, because, he said, her colour was the same hazy copper shade as her mother's had been when they first met. She grew up in plaid shirts and shapeless jeans, her father took her from school and taught her at home as soon as he could, they spent all their days together, he kept her hair cut short, and one day she found a painting of Joan of Arc among her mother's things, the flames rising from the wooden logs at her feet to claim her, her hair austere, almost brusque, but somehow right for someone who had spent her short life caught in a fight. Joan was staring upwards, her eyes filled with a brilliant light, and though her mouth was open, Rose didn't think it was in fear or a cry for help from her God, to her it looked like jubilation, like she was exultant, as if she were finally going home. She liked her own hair a lot more after that, it made her feel that she too was fighting the good fight, though she wasn't sure for who or against what.

As Rose grew, she learned to play basketball, began to enjoy the high metallic sound it made when she bounced the ball against the concrete of their drive, comfortable with the ball in her hands, enjoying the swish of the chains hanging from the steel hoop tacked above the garage door. She played with her father, one on one, learning to dip past him and climb towards the rim, momentarily weightless; she imagined cameras flashing as she slammed the ball to score, her father's delighted whoop reverberating behind her as she fell back to earth, the sound of her trainers slapping hard as she landed. She developed calluses on her hands tossing a football back and forth in their back yard, snatching the spiralling torpedo out of the fading winter light. Summer she swung bats at curving baseballs and felt the tendons tighten in her arms, the muscles harden, her father's pitches coming faster, the strike reverberating in slow shocks along her bat.

When Rose thought back on her father she had to concede that he was probably never the giant she thought he might be. There was bluster and the banging of doors, but when he turned his back to her it was with small, round and inexpressive shoulders – she'd never seen him stand up straight

2

since the death of her mother. In his silent moments, which grew longer like shadows as the day draws to an end, he looked like gravity had become too much and was slowly pushing him down into the earth. Grief's monstrous weight, she thought, as his glistening eyes settled on her from somewhere deep inside his skull.

In his never-ending quest to free her from her own sexuality – to have the son he'd always wanted – he'd taken her into the mountains one morning with a surprising, frantic glee. He harried her out of bed and into her indeterminate outfit (she was twelve and hid her period and slowly emerging body like Victorians used drapes to cover the legs of their pianos) and told her they were going to spend the day together in the mountains that sat in neat peaks in the distance; with a flourish he produced an old BB gun that she'd never seen before. He brandished it before her with a zeal missing since her mother's death. It was a long piece of varnished, chipped wood with a sleek, dry-looking, matte black barrel. It came in a canvas bag with a shoulder strap and excited and scared her equally.

They set off into the rain that came at their car at an angle; it fell from a sky that was all drizzle and paunch and clung to the serrated face of the hills, the low cloud looking like it might roll down the incline at any moment and land like a deflated parachute in a tangle at the base of the mountain. They parked up the car and walked past the lake with its cement edges and submerged, rusting-junk heart. She'd heard stories of boys skinny-dipping there, their limbs suddenly snagged by a bicycle frame, flailing uselessly against fate. She'd heard the stories from a friend of a friend, all her friends had. There was nothing there now, but silt and the pockmarks left on the water's impassive face by the rain.

They were at the first real crest of the hill. Her father gazed in a measured, distant way at the countryside below them; miles away lay the suburbs they called home, which slid slowly towards the city, coming to a halt where she imagined its walls might once have stood. Did American cities ever have walls, she wondered? Like Jericho laid low by the shrill call to arms of an army's horns or the foreign walled cities she'd read about, London, York, Rhodes, as she sat quiet and still like a cat in her room while her father roamed the house, chasing the loneliness from the shadows like hounds flushing grouse. She had found him once standing at the foot of their stairs clutching the banister until the colour had almost completely left his hand. He was looking upward to a point she knew she'd never see no matter how hard she stared. They stood there in mute disappointment, the light going out down the hall where the sun was setting through the kitchen window.

'Your mother,' he said finally, 'used to come down those stairs and she'd be singing and the song would carry in through the rooms and into my study and to my desk and the house would fill with her voice. It was like she was calling to me.' Then his features fell inwards, his eyes tightly shut as if that might stem the tears, and she didn't know if she had ever seen him look so old.

'Rose,' he handed her the gun and she was surprised by how cumbersome it felt. The rain had become a thin wave of drizzle here and settled on her face, making her lashes dewy and her cheeks cold. She tried to hide her struggle with the gun from him; she imagined sinewy arms, arms she felt were rightly hers, her birthright, when she dunked a ball or rifled a football; she wanted them to feel taut and full of leverage. With enough power there to swing the gun up into place and let off a round, cracking a clay pigeon and watching the red disc splinter to make a jagged splash of colour in the sky before falling away to the damp earth below. In reality, she felt held by the gun, not it by her. Her father helped her with it, placing it against her shoulder and holding his hand beneath the stock so that the barrel was still, the distant hills rendered fuzzy and out of focus against the defining point of the gun's sight. She squeezed the trigger, she could hear her father somewhere off in the distance telling her how to do it, not to jerk the trigger, to be gentle. The sharp whip and crack almost made her drop the gun to the ground, but her father's reassuring fist held it solemnly still before her. The recoil hadn't been the terrifying seizure she'd imagined, the untraceable arc the pellet made after its innocuous exit was a huge disappointment. She imagined that each shot fired would be an invitation, an opening to something unrealised; in her mind's eye she saw the sky splinter and crash, falling away like a great pane of glass as the bullet impacted, revealing the real world beyond as some sort of sanctity past the shimmering façade.

The rain was clear and solid as it fell; her father snapped the barrel back into place, making the gun look whole again. He turned swiftly, raising it to his cheek, and fired and a small bird fell from a branch: a sparrow, brown with a smear of yellow along its beak. He had it in the palm of his hand now, the body cooling, the life drifting away on the currents of air. Her face was hot and the tears came quickly as disgust and anger drew lines in her father's features. From a distance you can see the father offer Rose the bird and the furious shaking of the young girl's head and then he offers her the gun and she turns, her coat pulled up tight to her throat, her hair slicked down, thick with rain. It's silent, but he's saying something, the words are abrupt and rattle like gravel thrown up by a passing car. Then they're both still until her father slides the gun back uselessly into its case.

When Rose thinks back to that afternoon now she can see them both at a distance, her blue parka coat done up to the throat, her father's hair swept back, black and inky and looking as though the colour might run down his face in the drizzle. In the fuzzy tableau she's crying, her father looks enraged and ashamed. Then it's quiet and her father thrusts the gun towards her and she shakes her head and turns and walks away down the hill, becoming a speck as her father looks on after her and gently bites his bottom lip. He places the gun back in its case, his gaze unwavering, but knowing that something in the ever-expanding space between them is now twisted and wrong, and though he sets off briskly after her he's merely making up the yards that separate them. He can do nothing to ever eliminate the distance between them.

Years later, in the hospital where Rose was born, her father died, and as life left him with a gasp her father reached for her, one hand outstretched as he said one final, softly spoken thank-you. The nurse who has just walked in to check on him heard only those final words and wondered what had passed between them. She stepped forward and gently helped Rose unclench her fingers from around the bed cover and check her father's vital signs where there were now none. The nurse was always surprised to touch the neck and embrace the thin wrists and sallow skin and find nothing there, as if life was hiding from her like guests crouched in the darkness at a surprise party. Sometimes the nurse would hold on a second too long, expecting the beat to return, only to become aware of the curious eyes of a family member or friend already clinging to a shard of hope who mistook her lingering grip as a sign that their loved one was coming back, that life would suddenly flood through their veins and they'd sit up with a smile, full of longing and ready for the embrace.

# January 1980

In Washington Square there was a man who preached to the indifferent New Yorkers that passed him by. He stood on a piece of turf just where two paths intersected and sometimes he'd throw back his head and call to his God; other times he sounded humbled, his voice low, and he'd speak of the sins once clogging his arteries and heart; he made sinning sound like a burger, like he'd once gorged on evil and mankind would too, but then, Rose did concede, gluttony was one of the seven sins. He spoke of fires rising up and consuming the city, making everything clean. At his loudest and most pronounced he put her in mind of her father, though her father's voice had diminished as the years wore on and even though he insisted – usually at dinner as he waved his knife and fork and impaled food around – that the evils of the world still scratched at their window, he'd lost his lustre and volume when it came to condemning the wrongdoers that he insisted still sat mere feet from their front step.

Rose would sometimes take her lunch to the park, sweeping crumbs from her lap as she studied the towers of New York through the sparse boughs of the park's spindly trees. She'd tried to embrace the city, but its indifference was robust and some days she dreamt about travelling home and fixing up her father's old house in the shadow of those troubled hills. But that home had been sold long ago, and she'd bundled up the bad memories with the pale bedding and the curtains and burnt them in the back yard and wished the pain away with the dwindling smoke.

One evening, much to her surprise, Rose found herself in a brown and yellow church basement, partitioned off by a white folding wall that ran on castors and squeaked each time it closed in on itself to reveal another room beyond. The preacher in the park, as she'd begun to think of him, had sat down next to her one day while she ate her lunch and almost without her knowing had laid his hand gently on her wrist. She remembered a blackbird on the branch overhead turn his head and regard her with a rolling eye and then fly off with an abrupt snapping of his wings. The preacher spoke softly in a voice she

7

wished she'd heard more of in her life. His silver cross hung on a long chain and swung towards her as he sat forward, her eyes drawn to it as she took his voice in. She blushed, suddenly pink with longing and if not for this man then for something long missing in her life, her loneliness prompting memories of calamitous dates and odious men who she thought of as the personification of New York's crumbling streets, like something the city might have made.

One was called Reese, he had eyebrows that knitted together to form a line of dismay across his forehead; he was already drunk when she arrived at the restaurant, and was waving a piece of asparagus around. With mounting dread she realised that he'd taken it from an abandoned plate on the table next to theirs. He'd referred to the waitress as another cheap slut before they'd even emptied the bread basket and had broken off their conversation mid-sentence to head to the restroom, glancing back over his shoulder to inform her and a startled woman at the salad bar that the asparagus was sure to make his piss stink. She'd grabbed her bag and was up and away from the table before the bathroom door had stopped swinging. Rose made a blind left out of the restaurant and walked purposefully away, her heels a quickening clatter on the street, and wondered when the promise of another life that had once filled her as she pulled into the city had gone. She felt colourless and found an empty bench on which she sat and thought about Jack Lemmon ousted from his home by amorous workmates in the movie *The Apartment*, shivering in the cold, defences down.

That wooden bench, the one in Washington Square, and now these old rows of seats in a church basement in SoHo: here Rose was again, feeling that she was watching the world from outside in. There was a man, the Reverend James Bulley, standing up in front of a group of thirty or so people, some holding hands, others with heads bowed and eyes closed, and he was asking them to testify, to reach out and open up. It all sounded like instructions, but she wanted to be led, she was still in her twenties and she'd already had enough of fumbling her way through life. Rose missed her father's commands, the domineering tone of his voice; she'd forgiven him his lack of love a long time ago and settled into a kind of compliance that she found comfort in. She hadn't been the son he longed for and his wife had been dragged almost in two halves into the sky: her father had endured his share of pain and loss, no wonder he railed against the world. At least, she thought, he felt strongly about something.

The SoHo basement became her refuge three, sometimes four times a week. She met recovering alcoholics, drug addicts, the lost, the hopeless, others like her crushed by a city that lived remotely behind closed doors and sealed windows. Rose talked to her God and he listened. The room in her minute apartment slowly filled with crucifixes and iconography and she learned to love each tiny Jesus, the welcoming, open arms and the soft curve of her saviour's nose. She lit candles and enjoyed the glow of his beatific face. Rose slept beneath a picture of him that she'd found downtown; she kept a small figure pressed against her chest, her fingers in a tight embrace around her saviour. She tripped to work, and grinning in her cubicle she found herself gently fingering the small cross around her neck. Someone told her she looked like she was blooming and she did feel like a flower craning towards the sun, feeling the warmth and being filled up with life. His love was all-encompassing; it made her complete.

'They'll tell you this is unconstitutional,' said the Reverend James Bulley with the gentle hands and a rod in his voice. 'Tell you that it's wrong, tell you that it can't be taught in our schools.' His voice was low and invited the listener in. The basement was busier than usual tonight; she stood near the back and poured hot water from an urn onto the granules of coffee bunched up at the bottom of her plastic cup. She felt the heat fill the cup and ran her fingers over its side as if she were practising piano scales. The murmur of approving voices brought her head around. Then the preacher was speaking to her, to the thickening air around her. The thought pierced her heart – that not all men embraced the Lord like she did, that some even doubted his veracity. Satan sat in the towers and alleyways of this city, that much she knew; her father had always said as much, had warned her to stay away. She knew that his horned shadow sat across her heart some nights as she looked out of her window and so she pulled her coat close and trembled at the thought of the evil below, the dark stain of sin running in the streets. Sometimes she'd rush home, her short heels a rapid tattoo on the sidewalk as her pulse flared and the blood rushed through her veins and she felt him at her shoulder inviting her to stay, to slow and to succumb. She'd slam her apartment door behind her, the air caught at her throat, the sound of her heart filling her head and she'd say a silent prayer until the pulsing stopped and then she'd walk quickly to her room and fall into her saviour's loving arms until the panic ran from her. Some mornings she'd wake there, the beautiful features of her Lord smiling up at her like she once imagined a lover might.

She took to standing on street corners in the evening with the rest of her new friends from the basement, directed by Bulley; they took turns staring the Devil down. She could see him in the eyes of the passers-by, the scorn with which they surveyed her as she proffered a leaflet, implored them to open their hearts to God, to be saved on these streets, could they not see the bile rising around them, the tide readying to carry them away? She imagined Gomorrah before the city fell, before the sin was cut from its heart, her God and his angels falling from the sky as a rain of cleansing fire.

'You really believe this?' asked the man, though not unkindly. His question turned heads among her group who, until then, had been working their corner as assiduously and protectively as a drug dealer might theirs. The man was tall, his face set hard as if he always had somewhere to be, but it was difficult to tell what he might be thinking as he pored over the words on the leaflet she'd handed him; she could only stand and stare and didn't dare stop him to eulogise as it was the first flyer she'd passed out that day that hadn't been discarded moments later. He looked up and smiled at her and she saw the brief tenderness in his eyes before he glanced at his watch, nodded a brief goodbye and was gone. She wanted to tell him that yes, she really did believe all of this – to the outsider it might have looked like she lacked conviction, but with each flyer she gave out she felt a surge of pride and faith as if she were lit up from the inside like a lantern. She nodded emphatically to herself and stepped forward once again from their corner, the spirit of her father spurring her on; the conviction that she could help to make her flock multiply made her feel giddy.

Rose had been smitten before, had what felt like a schoolgirl crush. But that was before Jesus had entered her life and let her glimpse his eternal love. Apart from the occasional, fumbling nights spent as a jumble of limbs and a tangle of sheets with men who came and went leaving her feeling only rueful and incomplete, she only shared God's true love with one other thing: an abandoned warehouse set just outside the city, a hollow promise with cracked windows. Even writing about it in her diary had made Rose laugh, but it was a girlish laugh, a soft laugh; it made her blush to think of it. She'd first seen the building, looking abandoned and forlorn, set back from the concrete rise of the highway heading towards New Jersey, as she passed by in a friend's car, her jabbering companion failing to see the magic rising up from the bricks and tiles like glassy waves of undulating heat coming up from the surface of a freshly tarred road. She'd craned her neck until her companion had asked her who the hot guy she'd spotted in another car was, and then honked her horn with an emphatic finger.

'Did he see you staring, did he wave back?' her new workmate asked. And Rose found herself recalling the dark windows and wondered if she'd been seen, if its empty spaces were in some way reaching out to her. She passed her days on that idling commute to a temporary job and would feel her heart race a little as they came to the curve that led to the straight, speeding pass where the building would reveal itself to her. It had been empty for months as far as she could tell – a sign offering excellent rates and the first three months free looked tattered and abashed. Its corner curled down as if it couldn't or wouldn't meet her gaze. The building had already been painted three times in as many months, first a shimmering blue gloss that made it look like a giant wrapper for a discontinued chocolate bar. Then it was suddenly red, a lofty exclamation point that stood out against the horizon like a welt or a warning. Then it was dirty white again, an indifferent totem, still a bargain at half the price. In her dreams she stalked its rooms, never scared, always at home in its lofty space. Its wall were lit, there was a welcoming fire, the gentle murmur of a radio played the same country shows that her father liked to listen to in their kitchen. He'd stand staring out of the window and sing the

words he knew, hum the rest, his fingers tapping a restless yet happy
beat. Rose would wake in her apartment to low light and the sound
of the street, her alarm insistent and harsh, and think back to the cool
solitude of the building and see herself looking out of its windows and
then spot herself in one of the cars gliding past on the busy highway
in the distance. She'd feel safe there, she thought, at a distance.

Rose had finally taken a cab down to the warehouse late one night,
hailing the car on a whim from a bar she'd just walked out of, the
driver asking her if she wanted him to wait, but she waved him away,
craving the solitude and her mood buoyed by a bottle of wine and
some beers a stranger had bought. The building stood impassively still
as the cab's lights retreated and she reapplied her lipstick and brushed
her hair among the shadows. She felt afraid but then reassured as she
laid both hands against the cold stone of the warehouse wall. The
giant door was ajar and she ran her finger against the frame as she
slipped inside; it was darker than she'd imagined, there was no fire,
no music playing, no radio, her footsteps echoed, in the distance the
road sang with stray cars rushing to find home. She wished she were
among them, suddenly longing for the steep stairs of her apartment
block. She found a grid of light switches and ran her hand against
it, elated and surprised to find that at least some of the neon bars
overhead came to life to form a broken grid of white across the high
ceiling as a glowing, fractured cross. She climbed the long, steep, steel
stairs set against one wall and pulled herself up to one of the high
windows, craning her head upwards as if her nose were trying to
break the surface of a swimming pool. She clung to the serrated bricks
with the side of her foot and looked out; the view to the road was just
as she imagined it might be, though no faces looked up to discover
hers and no matter how hard she stared she couldn't find herself out
there among the concrete pillars and painted white lines, cocooned
behind a car door and making up the miles.

The next time Rose returned to the warehouse, she borrowed her
friend's car and took Christmas lights and balloons and cushions and
made what she considered looked most like a nest. She tried to herd
the errant balloons, racing after them with a giggling gallop, as they
caught on an untraceable current and bobbed gently away into the

building's corners, drifting upwards and just out of reach. She knotted the lines of fairy lights and made them into a long, glimmering lasso and couldn't help but gasp when they softly glowed into life. Lying among the cushions she breathed in deeply and then exhaled just as hard, trying to make the building's air mingle in with hers. So its timber and brick, corners and joists would be on her breath and then in her lungs and ultimately inside of her. Rose lay there panting like a racehorse that finished third and watched the light die in the arches above her. Like stars blinking out in space, she thought. She spoke to the walls and believed that they listened, she talked of her father and her mother and the burgeoning faith kicking into life inside her and thought of the place as her sanctuary. She brought more cushions and lights the next time she came and then one night found herself startled by the morning as it stole through the high windows, her hair matted and her mouth dry, the irregular balls of light twinkling at the periphery of her vision. She imagined taking a lover there, dragging him down among the cushions, embracing him tightly as the darkness hemmed them in. There was no lover now though, no one she cared enough about to share her space with; she was here alone with only the sound of speeding cars for company.


They saw the smoke hanging in the air before they reached the familiar rise of the highway. The road was backed up as the traffic slowed and stilled to take in the spectacle blooming in black plumes somewhere past the next turn-off. By the time they rolled slowly past, the warehouse was host to spires of orange, yellow and red, defiantly spitting its last. The cheap rates sign hung down like an unknotted tie, pale wisps of smoke gathering at its corners, the vinyl beginning to curl. Fire trucks directed jets of water upwards that hissed and steamed on impact, their revolving lights playing dully against what was left of the building's frame. Her friend turned in her seat and was surprised to see Rose pressed up against the window, tears dashing her crumpled features, fingers bent up against the glass. This one thing that had given her hope and a sense of belonging when she had none was now drifting in dirty plumes and into the sky forever.

In retrospect, the gutted building felt like a schoolgirl crush, the three-month fling before the first love proper once she'd found her Lord and been saved. Rose still felt pangs when she passed that way (though her new and more permanent post had saved her the long commute out to the suburbs), or thought about the dreamless sleep she'd enjoyed among the cushions on that vacant concrete floor. It was improbable and never likely to last, but the memory left her feeling happily flushed. She'd tried to tell her new friends about it, but had been shushed into silence by those who thought her kind of low-key madness might spread like the fire that had once engulfed her building.

Weeks later, after her dreams had been filled again and again with the shattering glass of the burning warehouse's windows, flaming beams crashing to the floor where she had once slept, Rose found herself once again back at the warehouse; forever changed, she stood within the building's husk; she'd lost her Christmas lights and cushions to the fire, but still half-expected to see the remnants of her belongings among the black dust that littered the warehouse floor. Rose tried the useless light switches; their sharp edges seared to a blunt point, shrivelled memories forged in the heat. She kicked at the pieces of wood scattered around her and stared up at the suddenly fleeting clouds moving through the sparse rafters above her head. She touched the walls, but the life had gone out of the building; she shouted into the darkness, but her questions were swallowed up and unanswered; she pressed both palms against the brickwork, willing her life to pulse through the rotten wood and black glass and into the soulless edifice and make it live again like her Lord had once commanded Lazarus to rise from his bed. She imagined her fairy lights radiant, the sound of the radio, her father nearby and her mother alive as a silhouette in the hallway before their God had taken her away. A footfall broke her reverie.

'You're here,' was all she said as the figure made a shape in the blackness and stepped out of the shadows. She reached out a hand instinctively; feeling the panic rising, clinging to some normality – she'd read that cats cleaned themselves furiously when they felt fear – and needing some blind reassurance, she wished she had some of the literature her group had given her to hand so that she might, even here, spread the good news, to impart his message, to feel normal again, to feel safe. But Rose knew this face, she knew this man, she knew the sound that the clattering shutter of her destiny made as it came slamming down, and yet, briefly, she felt that out here among this debris, inside her false idol (as someone had referred to the warehouse when she'd blurted out her story one evening back in the basement) she could be born again with the one good deed. That the circle would be complete: even if the building couldn't be redeemed then she might save a soul, the one that was stalking towards her, that among these ashes there might be at least one patch of hallowed ground. Had her Lord sent her here, directed her along this path all this time just to do the right thing?

Rose felt thrilled as if she'd suddenly spotted a way out, singled out to do his bidding, until the piece of wood she'd so recently kicked skittering across the floor caught her across the temple. For a moment nothing happened, she felt lighter somehow and gently touched the side of her head and was pleased to find no wound there and then her fingers felt wet and her head pulsed like her heart sometimes did when she'd been running too fast. Her head spun around on impact and she saw the room she'd once loved go blurring by as she fell to the floor. She rolled onto her back and saw the skeletal fingers that were all that was left of the ceiling high above her. Her one eye was wet with blood, her hair felt heavy and though her throat was dry she cried out for her God, but the sky was silent and so she lay trapped under the lengthening shadow of her fate as the darkness sat heavily and acted witness as she bargained her life away while the heavens moved impassively, mutely and uselessly above.

# February 1980

One night, Detective Louis Green had seen the rain fall upwards and retreat into the sky. It was late and he was young, eleven maybe twelve, he decided, thinking back on it as he often did. At first, the rain was an indifferent sheet coming out of the California sky, the light dwindling so that the rain came out of the farthest reaches of the inky black and became beams of thin light, vibrating ribbons tethered at once to both the heavens and the earth. Then they stilled, as spectacular pencils of steel and glass, and as the night advanced it somehow called the rain back. He saw the stillness, heard the quiet envelope where there had once been noise, the thrum of falling water held and then it withdrew. He saw the deluge reverse in on itself and pull back from the gutters and sloping roofs of his neighbours' houses, revealing itself in the bent arc of the streetlights but backwards, going up instead of down. It gathered itself in, sucked hard and inhaled, the moisture going out of the air; the damp signature impressed on the sky was gone. His forehead was pressed against the glass of his bedroom window, the circle of his breath a surprised oval in the smear of his own reflection.

Green craned his neck and looked up and attempted to follow the rain to its source, to find its destination in the dark hollow above. There was still water on his street, black and impassive as if it had never known life or fallen hundreds of feet to dash itself against the blades of grass in his garden, or the impassive paving stones and tarmac, but the sheets of rain had vanished, diminished and recoiled, he'd never forgotten it, and now on days like this one when the rain fell on him and pooled in the roads he always half-expected this most impactful of weather to turn tail and flee into the sky. Not least so he could marvel at it again and share the thrill with someone else. He'd long given up on people believing him, he could hear the absurdity in his voice as he recounted it – pre-pubescent boys weren't grounded, their imaginations weren't yet pinned to the earth, they took flights of fancy, glided over planets where the rain fell upwards, animals and toys talked back, their lives were rich, the fantastic kingdoms rendered far below were still theirs. Reality hadn't yet impeded on their thinking; first pets and parents still lived, marriages remained intact, love wasn't yet ash in their hands; the future was blinding, bright with hope. But his suburban window had overlooked a magical event that night and somehow the rain had fallen back into the sky, he knew.


Green wondered at Rose's dreams as she lay there; he opened his notebook, all business, little knowing that her hopes too had once been entwined with the heavens. There was blood across one side of her face, from a wound at her temple, a different shade of red to the one that spread out in a fan from the vivid hair on her head, but she looked impassive and peaceful, one arm caught behind her, the other spread out at her side, like a bird with a broken wing. Someone had called it in, a stranger's voice reporting her cooling body under the detached rafters of the burnt-out building, the damp concrete and stone holding her forever in place.

'Rose Henley,' Green said aloud, her driving licence between his fingers, her face looking taut in her photograph, her pulled-back hair making her features look flat and bleached out, the outline of her nose disappearing into the rest of her face. Here, the warehouse was darkest at its corners, as if light might never reach there. Green's flashlight beam felt blunt against the blackness. One of his officers accidentally kicked at a piece of timber and it bounced hard along the floor and came to rest up against his leg.

'Sir, sorry,' said the officer, but Green waved it away and looked at the other pieces of wood scattered around him. He knew that any of them could have caused the damage done to the girl's skull, but none were flecked with blood; besides, he thought, wood burns; it wouldn't take much to destroy a makeshift club that you'd just used to cave someone's skull in with.

Green's father had been a priest who wrestled, almost daily it seemed, with the hatred and sin his God had placed in the world. Though his faith remained intact, he was often defeated by the vagaries of hatred and the callousness of man: a man born in God's image. Nicholas Gillett Green had been a teacher, a good one, before he'd found God, or, as he sometimes said, God found him. He was often to be seen at the head of his class telling his boys the same thing that he'd told Green growing up: 'Louis, evil lives in the most innocuous places in the world – wood sheds, under bridges, in the dark in the hulls of boats, in the hearts of men.' It was as if he couldn't countenance or come to terms with the sheer banality of evil, the unflinching hammer blows of hatred often visited on the earth. Louis loved his father and his undiluted take on things; his old man's belief in real goodness and innocence was very much part of why Green had become a police officer in the first place. He truly did want to serve and protect, though he too had seen that almost dormant evil come to life in the stilled faces caught stark against bloody circumstance. Faces and bodies bent double by the long shadows his father had talked about at home and in his pulpit or to the upturned faces of his pupils; the impeachable storm at the shoulder of the next hill, a ceaseless force that kept coming. Green really had once found a young man's crumpled body under a bridge, his life sharply receding, and felt his father's form at his shoulder, a resigned sigh; a slow shake of the head at the monotony of fate, at the evil that men inevitably do.

Detective Green straightened up and told his men to fan out and take another pass at the long oblong of the warehouse floor, sifting through the detritus for a potential weapon as they went. Rose was in a black plastic body bag, a zipper dividing its front and then sealing its contents; the slamming of the ambulance door would be her last note on earth as she was carried away on what she must have once dreamt would be a long and glorious journey to meet her maker. The ambulance pulled away from the warehouse and onto the on-ramp and got quickly stuck in traffic on the parkway – a drunk driver had swerved up onto the verge and caused a tailback of slowly groaning traffic; a living, breathing beast of blinking lights and muted horns slowly shuffling their way towards the city.

Her friends lit scented candles for Rose in the squat basement in the city where she had once gone to worship. The curls of smoke not having to travel far until they unfurled along the low ceiling, someone had the foresight to take the batteries from the smoke alarm before they burst into ear-shattering life. Rose had been killed on Monday night, by Tuesday they were holding a vigil, handing out flyers with her face pasted across them – she looked surprised by the camera lens, a blur of pigeons taking flight behind her – they made an unwilling martyr of her memory, when all she wanted was to belong. Her friends stood in a tight group on the street, a rectangle of candlelight and scowling faces trained on the indifference of the passers-by. Their leader, Reverend Bulley, spoke about the sins of the city, he called their God down to cleanse the streets and bring damnation down on Rose's killer. To snuff out the one who had taken her from them, an eye for an eye.

Detective Louis Green watched them from across the street and felt their anger snaking into the air and wondered what his father would have made of them and their God constructed from fear and the promise of hell if his followers didn't bend to his omnipotent will. They reminded him of the bullies he'd spent time with at school, the smaller boys who had bigger friends who loomed behind them like trained dogs on taut leashes, snarling and ready to strike. The threat of them was enough for people to fall in line. Years later he wished he'd stood up to those people more. More latterly, he'd spent his time making up on those earlier misjudgements – wasn't being a cop just staring the bullies down sometime? He knew Rose had no family, but her diary had led him to these people; her apartment looked like a self-imposed sanctuary, heavy with iconic imagery, a still, beseeching wooden Jesus face down across her bed. He tried to imagine what the Lord's eyes needed to be shielded from that she'd placed him face down against her pillow. Green stood there among her things and wondered at the girl who slept under Christ's steady gaze; by her bed was a photo of her squinting into the camera – she looked, he guessed, about eleven years old, about his age when he'd seen the rain invert. She was dressed in a checked shirt and jeans hiked up high that were thrust into a pair of Wellington boots. Her hair was short and slicked down on one side; behind her fields and a knotted splay of bare trees, low drifting cloud visible between the spread of branches.

She was smiling with a lack of self-awareness that the young have in photographs, no pose, though one hand was in her back pocket – it was just her there, the fall sunshine picked out her features and her father called out for her to smile.

The Reverend James Bulley spoke as if he were giving a sermon. Detective Green wondered if he thought he was. Bulley told Green about how he'd saved Rose from the streets, offered her salvation in Washington Square that day and raised her up so she could better see her Lord. How this basement room had become her sanctuary. His fist punching his palm for emphasis, his thumb crooked and long, as if he'd used it over and over to yank sin back and put it firmly in its place like an obstinate child. The Reverend felt very hands-on. He was still talking as Green was beginning not to listen; this place was somewhere she could escape the evil bubbling in the streets. Green wondered at the still city above their heads and the silent lives being lived out with no idea of the imagined brimstone and fire that ran quickening and molten beneath their feet.

'So,' Green asked, already tired of Bulley's explosive rhetoric, 'do you know what she might have been doing alone in a burnt-out building? That's where we found her.' In spite of himself, he enjoyed the flash of confusion on Bulley's round face. His forehead furrowed like a freshly ploughed field and then flattened out as the surprise composed his features. His eyes were very big behind his glasses, his mouth a small circle.

'A burnt-out building?' Bulley's face was slack and led into his neck, as if the image of Rose alone among the broken wood and scorched bricks was pulling the skin down. Bulley's flock – as he referred to them – were staring unhappily at them from across the room as if they could sense the stress rising up from their leader like the first thin wisps of smoke from a man who's yet to realise that he's on fire.

Through its grand gates the thirteen-year-old Louis Green saw old Hollywood disappearing in the shape of the abandoned baroque house being pulled down. He and his friends used to play in there before the demolition men came, climbing through the hedges and past the signs warning them to keep out. Inside, red drapes caked with dust and long webs, their centres weighed down with fat spiders, waited for them, only adding to the drama of the dense shadows. Green and his friends were chased down by an imagined Dracula who was all fangs and bloody fingernails, there were monsters suddenly looming in and out of the light, their cries and cackles trailed upwards through the banisters and the contemplative silence of the stairwell, long empty rooms suddenly brimming with bursts of furious life, the thrum of youth in footfalls, pushing and jostling. You could almost hear the rooms sighing with sadness once they were vacant again, the boys long past then, rushing other parts of the house.

The roof came away with a wrench, the timber and slate giving in as Green's father's car was pulling out for the airport. The windows buckled inwards as if they'd been winded. Louis was barely two years old when his father had decided to give his life to his Lord. And now he was swapping his short-lived stint at his West Coast diocese for something he said he thought would be more real, something to test himself against out on the East Coast. The teenage Green was crushed, his friends were here; he liked the way the air tasted down near the water when they drove along the coastal roads. He liked the salt matting in his hair, the way his summer skin came off in thin, almost clear, mud-coloured pieces, curling at the edges like wet paper drying. He liked the endless silver-blue sky; he wanted to see the magic of the rain reversed once more before he left. He couldn't picture the heavens above Brooklyn reclaiming the weather; in fact, he couldn't picture a Brooklyn sky at all. He saw shades of grey brick, Batman as a caped silhouette among the towers; the imagined night was forever.

Nicholas Gillett Green came to God late. Louis was one when his mother left them both for another woman. His father's salvation came quickly in the shape of the church. He'd been a devoted follower and now, thanks to the kindness they'd shown him when he'd been at his most vulnerable, he wanted to lead. He passed through seminary quickly under his ex-wife's admonishing eye as Louis grew up in the sunshine, living between their houses; their indelible hatred and anger for the other pressed down hard on the boy and he wore their pain as clearly as he might a bad haircut. He saw them both sin as he slowly adjusted to living his life between them, yet never truly at home with either. He watched his father taking pride at his own reflection in his priestly garb – to Green he looked like God's assassin: sleek, trim and bible-black, his hair swept carefully back. He half-expected a handgun concealed in the pages of his father's Bible, rosary beads hiding a wire loop that quickly became a killer's tool. Meanwhile, he heard his mother's voice through the walls, her sighs mingling with another woman's (her first girlfriend had long since left); in those moments she called on her God as much as his father did his. He wondered whose God it was, if either of them had made the right choice. If God came back then, would he be a vengeful force like the books said, and would he frown upon his father's tight self-satisfied smile at himself in the mirror or his mother slumped happily among her sheets? Would he forgive them their sins or leave them as burnt outlines, black shadows casting an approximation of the things they once were? Louis would grow weary of any kind of God by the time he was in his twenties, but until then, the Lord was as real at his father's home as if he were waiting in the kitchen or reading a newspaper out on the back step. A presence that was always close, but just out of sight.

One of the first cases Green had been assigned to when he reached detective was to apprehend a man who posed as a priest in order to gain access to people's homes, earn their trust and then rob them. It was a familiar con, but no less devastating to the victim because of that. He thought of Robert Mitchum in *The Night of the Hunter*, love and hate tattooed across both hands, the supposed saviour who fell as heavily as a winter night, death trailing behind him in heavy chains of sin. Green's so-called priest had escalated from conning bewildered mothers out of their savings to beating a sixty-eight-year-old widower called Alexandar Zivojinovich to death and cleaning out the contents of his apartment. Now Green stood in the bright living room of Alex's home among the contents of an upturned cabinet, a worn copy of William Blake's poetry at his feet. He looked at the horned demon sat inexpressively on its cover, giant and hugely strong, waiting to unsteady the Lord and tip the heavens out of the sky. He saw angels fall; felt their torment as their skins burned and their wings fell away, giant white plumes floating slowly to earth. Green spoke to his father about it, about the conman turned killer, the convenience of the easily identifiable cloth that stood out and let him in, but could easily be lost as part of a milling crowd.

'I hope you're not blaming the uniform,' said Green's father; he wore a half-smile as he said it, but his tone wasn't unkind. He was quietly appalled by the turn this latest crime had taken, but he kept his pain hidden. He'd first been shocked by this new city when he and Louis had moved here. He was worried that neither of them would fit in. The people here spoke with their bodies, they were like weapons, coming in close with a whispered confidence, but their shoulders squared as if for a fight. He imagined them leaning into a strong headwind, ready for anything. As if this borough was a craft being carried in choppy waters that might dip and tilt at any moment. Green's father learned to carry himself with the same demeanour to gain their respect, earned his metaphorical sea legs so he might fit in, but he tried to soften his impact with each step; his fight was with Satan, not these people.

Nicholas Green poured his son a drink, and tried to see beyond his boy's evasive eyes. Green's new role as a detective made him look tired, he was weathered, he looked very unlike the little boy who had once run along beaches, sand spilled with each hurried step. Nicholas often wondered what that boy would have turned out like had he raised him in California. In old photos, Louis had blond streaks, his matted hair stuck out at angles like TV antennae: here he had become darker, both his colouring and his manner. He was starting to not only see death, but to rummage through the remains; he was literally getting his hands dirty. He was bigger than his father had ever been, he was wide, abrupt, a stop sign, his body was right angles, his hands were wide and thick, his fingers long and robust like tree roots breaking earth, but his lips were thin like his mother's, he had her eyes too, hazy blue and as questioning as he had become. He shared her doggedness, her persistence; his father would sometimes recoil as they argued, seeing his ex-wife's insistence on being right reaching out at him from his son like some spectre rising from a haunted mirror. He had been proud to see Louis thrive though; at first the young man hated his father and the place he'd been brought to. He resisted physically and mentally, they'd literally fall to the floor wrestling as Louis refused to set foot inside their new home, he'd become star-shaped, his legs and arms sudden spokes of resistance. But time and environment chipped away at him. He ditched the beach clothes, the bright colours, but slept in his favourite red T-shirt. Louis dreamt that he was still in the sunshine sometimes, the cooling breeze belying his burning skin. New York summers sucked the oxygen out of the air and made your scalp sweat and your clothes damp; it was hard to believe that the glassy white light here could come from the same sun that shone down on California.

They finally caught the would-be preacher when someone heard the disturbance in a neighbour's apartment. By the time the patrolmen burst through the door he was standing over his latest victim – Lucy Railing, eighty-three years old, suffering from emphysema, four grandchildren of whom she loved the eldest, Karl, the least – the leg of a broken chair raised above his head. The patrolmen rushed him before another blow could fall and got in a few of their own as he collapsed beneath them; they became a writhing, scrapping ball that Lucy would vaguely remember weeks later after the scar tissue had begun to heal and the black welt underneath one eye had finally started to become the colour of a raincloud.

The killer held Green's gaze across the table and told him how he'd stolen the priest's effects from a fancy dress store. Up until then, Green imagined the man had taken the things from a church somehow, got among the priest's things and spirited them away while their owner wasn't looking. He felt vaguely disappointed to find that the most obvious route was the one this man had chosen. His path from conman to brutal killer was sadly mundane too. He'd been found out by Alexandar, the old man he'd killed, who'd started questioning him closely on the scriptures and then wanted his worldview on the Church's approach to everything from abortion to homosexuality. Alexandar had struck him across the face with his copy of Blake's

*Songs of Innocence and of Experience* as he was reading to him from it and, as the killer told it, had made for the door. He brought Alexandar down with a crash and his head lolled cruelly sideways as it bounced off the unforgiving corner of his TV; he looked dead and so the killer made sure of it. This would-be-priest-cum-thief had worked long summers through school cleaning out battery hens, sorting through the dead bodies and the clucking drone as the eyes of the immobile yet still living chickens regarded his presence among them. Sometimes the hens would be halfway between heaven and earth, caught on the cusp of life, and with one sharp twist of their head he'd send them over into the endless abyss. That's how he saw Alexandar, he said, waiting to fall into the infinite empty, and so he tipped his hand, gave him a little push. After that, it had been easy, he was already weary of playing the part of the preacher, but it got him through the door, and now he didn't have to listen to their stories of how the Church had helped them, or of long-ago weddings and christenings and births and deaths, how their families had quietly abandoned them. These were lives now lived in the shadow of the Church; it had become a guiding hand helping them grope through the daily darkness. But he wasn't their salvation; he was the end of days. There were times like these, sitting across from a man impassively detailing his litany of gruesome deeds, when Green felt like death was everywhere. He was marked and weary, like Macbeth halfway across his lake of blood, but like the doomed king, he pushed only onwards until death and loss and love became his salvation and helped him see how he could help, how he too could become someone's saviour.

But even in the darkest reaches there were glimmers of light. Green often thought about Rudy Porter. It had been under a year into his career as a detective and Green had reached into the black and somehow brought Rudy Porter kicking back to life.

Rudy had been with his wife, Sarah Faust Porter, for as long as he could remember. They'd been teenagers and then lovers and then married by the time he was nineteen against the wishes of both their parents. Neither of them went to college, they were parents too by the time they reached their twenties. They had two sons, Stanley (who became known as Stan to everyone almost as soon as he could speak) and Mikey, both had graduated college, they'd been his children and he'd loved them, he still loved them. Stan lived in Boston and Mikey had moved south to Florida; Rudy still felt like the centre of their lives if only sometimes as a point on the map. The problem was Sarah. She'd fallen heavily in the kitchen four days before and hadn't moved since. Rudy had placed her in her favourite chair, it had the best view of the TV, and waited for her to wake. He put cups of tea at her side and emptied and refreshed them as they cooled. He held her hand; the colour was running into the fingertips and making them red and purple. Her face was grey, her skull heavier than he could ever remember. He tipped it back against the chair and she sat there as if she were regarding a newly found stain on the ceiling. Rudy missed her more than he could have ever imagined; how could one fall have so irrevocably changed their lives forever? He sat with her at nights and talked about when they were young and what they both might have wanted from the world. He talked about the time she left him over his teenage jealousies and how he'd discovered a new hollowness inside of himself, that first very real feeling of his heart breaking. His breath stuttered in sharp jolts like a sudden asthma attack in once healthy lungs. The numbness of his loneliness spread through his body: ice-cold fingers splayed across his chest and then burrowing into the small of his back, down his thighs, creeping along his toes. He woke daily to the first, sharp realisation of pain. And then one day she suddenly came back with a warning for him to cool down, to trust her, and so he did. She took his hand and they walked through their city. The boys grew and left and they both cried and clung to each other, their lives moving forward in increments. He thought of her in the hat that she wore to Mikey's wedding, pale blue: the wide brim casting half her face in shadow. He had never seen her look more beautiful and now he was crying as she sat in another shadow altogether, the life ushered out of her, her unseeing gaze staring only upwards as if that was where she was meant to go.

Green had no idea why he was the one they called to the apartment. Later, he would think it was because of his father's calling as a priest, that if his old man could listen and ease the minds of men then perhaps the son might have a similar aptitude, a gift, but he was never completely sure why he got the job. Patrolmen had been called to Rudy Porter's apartment when his son Stan had started to worry about where his father and mother might be. Their phone rang uselessly; Stan imagined it sat there in their apartment trilling with life as they lay asphyxiated yards away, slumped and just out of reach. The patrolman talked to Rudy through the door, but didn't think crashing through it would help the situation. Rudy's nervous reassurances sounded much more weary than they were manic or dangerous. Neither son could make it into town until later that night and there was a stench starting to settle around the doorway and across the building's landing. Something was waiting on the other side of that door and the patrolman didn't want to meet its unwavering eye.

Green sat across from Sarah, who was now bloated and cartoon-like; her arms stuck out and her engorged calves were set wide apart. He was momentarily worried that her dress was going to rise up. Her head was tilted forward and he waited nervously for her eyes to blink open and for her to come screeching into life. He felt like the butt of an ugly joke. The chair beneath her looked sodden. She was putrefying; the smell made his throat pinch and his eyes redden with tears. Though it was Rudy who was crying. He sat across from them both, hunched over, the tears making his body convulse. Green had never heard a human being make a noise like that, he wondered if that was the sound that grief made, that one day they would all wail like a lost or abandoned animal when it came to facing down their greatest fear. The primal ghosts of all their ancestors brought to bear when they finally sensed extinction. Death, he thought stupidly, really is the end.

'Sarah,' said Rudy. He was looking at him now, eyes streaming, his cheeks were white; he looked wild. 'She used to enjoy wildlife programmes, the Discovery Channel. Do you ever?'

He nodded, it was true too; he found some strange comfort in nature's abstract approach; life really was out of your hands. It was said that it wasn't so much that the Victorians couldn't stomach Charles Darwin's research that turned their world and its inherent beliefs on its head, but that they couldn't bear how indifferent and cruel nature could really be. There was no glorious path or journey; each man's fate wasn't aligned to the stars. Death could be waiting at the corner as easily and absurdly as it could at a zebra's watering hole.

'You know the polar bears?' Rudy was staring at him, Green nodded; sure he did. He felt as if Sarah were staring at him through her eyelids, checking that he really did too.

'They go out on the ice and they make a hole, you know,' said Rudy, but he wasn't talking to Green anymore, his eyes were trained on the window, he was looking hard at the polar bear sitting alone among all that white.

'And they wait, for days sometimes. And these beluga whales they come to the surface, they need the air, they're white like ghosts, they look like Casper, have you seen them?'

Green nodded; he wasn't sure that he wanted to hear about a polar bear crushing and killing and then eating a beluga whale as Sarah Porter sat just feet away, her insides rotting to an indiscriminate mush; it seemed to make the scenario they found themselves in even more surreal and rank. But he had nowhere to go, he needed to leave with the assurance that Rudy would let his wife go with him, that Rudy might finally loosen his grip and let himself be free. He looked at Sarah and wondered at the woman, not this ghoulish approximation of a once living thing.

'They come up through the ice, the whale, and they do this sort of half loop, the icy water coming off them in a sheet, it's an incredible thing to see,' said Rudy; he was close enough then to feel the spray of the freezing cold water.

'And the bear reaches out to embrace them, to get a hold of them, its claws out. And he gets a hold of the whale for a moment, but I don't know if it's the momentum of the whale or the water or the impact, but the whale keeps going, these long cuts down its side, these claw marks, and it just keeps on going. It hits the water and is gone and the bear sits back and it looks, I don't know, dumbfounded. Sarah used to say, I think she was teasing me, that polar bears get lonely out there on the ice and all they want when they reach out for the fish, they just want something to hold on to, that they love those whales, that it's the only thing they've seen for days and the loneliness is just killing them.'

He was crying now, hard.

'And I said to her, but when those bears catch the fish they kill them, they crush the life out of them, you know. And Sarah said ...'

And he allowed himself to look up at his once beautiful wife, her cheeks bloated, her hands fat, as if you might prick her and she'd deflate like a day-old party balloon. He saw his wife completely then and then he let her go, let the air out of him and the next part of his life in.

'And she said that the bears loved the whale so much that they couldn't help but hug them too hard and that their feelings were so strong that they ended up killing the thing they loved. Just from the holding on ...'

And then Green was across the room and he held Rudy Porter in his arms as he cried and cried and he was careful to turn the man's head away from the sight of his dead wife, so that he might see her as he once saw her. And he held him firmly but gently, so as not to crush the life from him, but to ensure that Rudy Porter might yet go on living.

# March 1980

Detective Green hated Henry Willow already. He'd been here for over an hour and he hadn't stopped talking yet. He lived his life out loud, his words so emphatic and bulging with self-belief and zeal that Green imagined he talked in italics. He could see the words gathering around him like a hazy cloud of cartoon bees.

'You've met the type, right?' he asked, wagging a finger at Green, who did all he could not to grab and bend it until it made a snapping sound and the man went down gasping, his eyes as bulging and confused as a fish finding itself out of water. For reasons that Green couldn't even begin to fathom, this man had once dated Rose Henley. He was still talking; Green imagined the air conditioning clogged with consonants, the plughole of the sink set at the far wall filling with the letters z and y like dead flies. The words tumbled slowly down from the ceiling like small pieces of rust and gathered in crumbling piles on the floor.

'You know, professional, solvent, successful,' said Henry. 'But they can't pin a man down, so they keep making the same mistake over and over again every Friday night.' He paused almost triumphantly. 'I am that mistake.'

'I've been the other man a few times, you know, even once in my own marriage for a while.' That was it, one solitary note of regret that appeared and disappeared in his bullish eulogy as quickly as debris in a flash flood.

'My first wife, my only wife, she was running around on me back there. I was no saint, you know how it is, a night here, a little romance there, some shit at the office, but she fell in love with this guy and I was gone, out of the picture.' He slumped a little; it looked as though it was taking everything he had not to pitch forward or push the table away. But then he recovered his composure and sat up straight and held on to the knot on his tie as if for reassurance, like it might centre him; he was full of bravura, but his eyes kept darting around and giving him away; he looked like a man struggling to keep a noose off his neck. Green leaned in.

'Henry, Hank, let me call you Hank, tell me, how did you meet Rose?' Willow gave him an abrupt look; a fleshy line appeared above his eyes, he looked quizzical.

'You mean Red – Rose was her real name?' asked Henry. 'She told me that everyone called her Red. I asked her a few times what her real name was and she wouldn't say, she just said it was what her dad called her and that I should too, which I found pretty weird to begin with. I remember asking her once what her mother called her, trying to catch her out, you know? And she said she didn't want to talk about her mother. She shut down like that a lot, like women do. You get that?'

He looked up at Green as if they'd just met at a bar, one guy to another. He saw him sitting there in the half-light, perched on a stool, talking sports, telling off-colour jokes a little too loudly, trying to befriend the barmaid, letting his hand linger on hers as she took his order. Is that where he'd met Red, at a bar?

'No, she wasn't a big drinker,' said Willow. 'She wasn't big on anything really, except the good Lord.'

Henry looked incredulous, a complete non-believer.

'Did you go up and see her apartment, all those crucifixes and Jesus staring down at you every which way? It gave me the creeps.'

Green felt his stomach lurch at the mention of Willow being in Red's apartment; his reaction surprised and unsettled him.

'There was one Jesus, big fucking thing, sort of propped up on her pillow, I got the feeling she slept with it, she moved it pretty quickly when I went in there, she looked embarrassed. I came to in the night one time and there was Jesus staring across at me and another one above me pinned to his cross leaning out from the wall as if he was trying to pull away or his weight was too much for the nails in his hands and he was falling forward. I thought he was going to hit me in the face.'

Henry stopped as if the plastic icon was looming over him once more, impassive features set in violent relief.

'It made romance pretty hard, you know. I shouldn't have been surprised given the way I met her in Washington Square, on one of the benches there. She came and sat next to me, I thought she was an office girl on the make, which I suppose she was, but she handed me this flyer and told me she could save me. I just started laughing, I thought it was one of the greatest pick-up lines I'd ever heard, I thought about filing it away and using it later, but she meant it, her eyes, she had these amazing pale green eyes, just opened up, filled with this disbelief when I cracked up, this really puzzled and hurt look came across her face, I thought she was going to start crying.'

Green could see her there in the park, nervously picking out the soul she should save next. Waiting for a signal from her Lord as she set down lightly next to Willow, and he'd laughed and told her what a great line it was, but had been quick enough to take in the blaze of red hair and the unblinking green eyes, her mother's pretty oval face, her father's resolute features, it made Green think of a figurehead at the prow of an old ship, pushing determinedly forward, clear-eyed and tenacious, a thing of quiet beauty finding new places to land. Henry brought him quickly back to earth.

'So I waved her off, you know, another nut. City's filled with them. I took the flyer though and she looked back at me as I was reading it, just checking I hadn't tossed it, I guess. And I kept it, I put it in my pocket, it was just this thing about attending one of their church meetings, but it wasn't really a church, was it? More a group thing, it sounded screwy to me, like a cult or something, but she was a picture, though I figured she must be some kind of honey trap, to pull guys like me in. You know, let me save you and then you get there and they want twenty bucks for a donation or something and then they get to assert their will upon you, like a strip joint without the happy ending.' He laughed until the air went out of him.

Green watched his face happily spasm and wondered what Red might have found there, that she wanted to make space among her things for him.

'And then the damndest fucking thing,' said Henry. 'That guy goes and nearly kills me and I got to thinking about my own mortality and the frailty of life, the exact same stuff she's been talking about, it was like she was warning me, trying to guide my steps, you know, someone really had sent me down an angel.'

Henry Willow looked disgusted at the thought; he looked disgusted with himself.

'I must have been out of my mind.'

'Someone tried to kill you, Hank?' asked Green, mentally thumbing through records for some kind of near-atrocity that might feature Henry Willow's bemused features crinkled with horror and relief as a bullet or blade came within inches of confounding his fate forever.

'Not me, the only person he was trying to off was himself and he managed that, boy, did he manage that.'

Green gave a very audible sigh that sounded like the slow leak of an old tyre. All these words and the question was only becoming more confused. Willow was leaning back in his chair; he was expounding on the subject, the words leaving him in a stream and heading towards the ceiling like moths racing for the source of the light.


They called it The Beast and it haunted his dreams. It promised to transport them from their homes across the border and into the New World, but took payment in dangling arms and legs, trailing limbs becoming detritus on the tracks; a blood toll, some called it. Alejandro's father and uncles told him stories of friends who'd tried to climb the train, latch on to its curved roof, and had held on unsteadily until The Beast moaned and bucked, throwing them up in the air and catching them between its carriages and cars, swallowing them up in the shadows and thin slices of light, their screams drowned by the endless turning of wheels and the catch of the heavy chains that pulled and pushed The Beast along. When it came to his turn, Alejandro had held on, but one of his friends, Guilhermo, slid along the roof of the train and went clattering backwards and was swallowed up by the blackness. Guilhermo imagined a sea monster from his childhood snatching him and dragging him down into the swirling depths, his screams lost among the greens and blues as he slid backwards and down. But, much to his surprise, there he sat quite alive on the steel tracks in a cloud of dust, all the colour completely gone from his face, two surprised eyes in a near-translucent face. He was trying to give a dazed wave to the departing train, but half of his hand was gone.

Even if you survived the fall from The Beast, as Guilhermo had, you were left there doomed and broken between the tracks trying to sit up as the train pulled away, your friends desperate to come back and help you, but more determined yet to reach America. The fingers from your right hand – spread out along the ground around you – were now paying to carry those same friends for the next few miles or more, the heat from the turning wheels searing the wound, your hand now a half, completely fingerless, but sealed, one estranged thumb all that was left, and the one thought still resonating in your head: how will I get back up on The Beast now?

Alejandro left the California he'd fought so hard to enter illegally the day immigration officers raided the restaurant he'd been working in and took his father and uncle away. They hustled them out, his father half-heartedly waving a filleting knife around that had been lying on the worktop until the police the officers had brought with them threatened to fill the kitchen with tear gas. Alejandro still had his other job, cleaning an elementary school at dawn each day; he liked the vacant parking lot, the school's wide, empty corridors and the way the gentle morning light flooded softly through them, the squeak of his shoes in the gym, but Los Angeles frightened him, it felt impervious to his being, as if the very streets and walls could tell he didn't belong there. The streets hissed his name. People either thought he was a gang member or an illegal immigrant, or both, so he walked cowed, as if in chains, tied somehow to the earth. Feeling utterly removed, like the alien he was.

Alejandro thought about Guilhermo and wondered where his friend who had fallen from the train was now; he'd call home when he could and speak to his sister or her husband, but no one knew where Guilhermo had gone, he'd disappeared once he'd slid from the train as if once he'd fallen out of The Beast's sight then he suddenly ceased to exist. Alejandro saw his friend lift his fingerless hand to wave goodbye that day and imagined the space where his fingers had once been spreading along his hand and down his arm, eating away at the limb, leaving only air. Guilhermo's panic and dismay as his elbow was rubbed out like a child retracing his mistakes with an eraser. In Alejandro's mind, his friend's jaw hung open, his mouth a spreading, startled O, but there was no blood or pain, only confusion as his teeth came into view and then his nose was gone and Alejandro could see the sky behind his friend's face and then the shoulders slumped as though they had no purpose with no head to support and then it was quiet, the body was gone before it had time to fall, eaten up by nothingness, out of mind and sight. In the distance, The Beast sounded its horn and turned a long corner and pulled slowly away, indifferent carriages shunting their way towards an uncertain future.

Alejandro had read in a magazine that Robert Mitchum had once ridden the rails west to Hollywood and infamy, but Alejandro was now going the other way. He knew of friends who had come over the border and had been picked up in Texas and in California; the closer you clung to the land you came from, the more quickly you could be suddenly snatched back as if someone were monitoring your movements, waiting to pounce. He imagined crocodiles and wildebeest suddenly alive and then dead at watering holes, death coming in an explosion of water and the rutting struggle for life; he saw Guilhermo literally fall through the spaces between.

The first time Alejandro had attempted to board a moving train, he counted his breaths to slow them down, to settle himself the way his father had showed him; the clanking of the yard terrified him, the churning of the wheels, the very real sound that metal on metal made. He felt small, as if he were being watched from the sky, a warm life form set as a spot of red among the cold, hulking green of the lifeless rolling stock that surrounded him. He felt hemmed in even though he knew he could weave through the cars and get safely back to the fence he'd just clambered over. His uncles had taught him how to hoist himself up on a moving train – they likened it to snaring a bolting calf, the dip and feint and then thrusting your arm out, avoiding the rail, doing anything to dodge that feeling of hopelessness in your stomach as you mistimed your step and were pulled under the clanging monster, your leg lost to the unforgiving wheels. He saw himself as a young matador, pinned into a gleaming suit of lights, his cape a defiant block of red as the train charged him down, roaring forward, the thunder of imaginary hooves. He sat in the corner of the truck, legs folded up in on himself, feeling frightened; light came in at intervals, a bell rang clearly somewhere across the yards, tolling for someone, he thought, but not for him, he was already gone.

In his dreams Alejandro was following the river down, floating along, in the reeds of the bank, his fingers tracing the water's surface; the sun shone in his eyes, his father stood nearby, a silhouette calling out to him: 'Alejandro, where are you going?' 'I don't know, Papa,' he said; he was lost to the current, the rapids were a distant murmur, a quiet threat, foreboding pools and rocks, something was swimming close by and just beneath the surface. He came rushing to life as the crocodile broke the channel, its elongated jaw endless and gleaming, wet with hunger and opportunity.

Red had found Alejandro in Washington Square. Lost, eyes like a frightened animal in the long grass trying to evade the hunter. He flinched when she sat next to him and she instinctively placed a hand on his arm to settle him. She thought about how she'd been lost when she'd first come to the city, how dark and improbable it had all seemed. She'd travel across to Brooklyn at night just to stare back at Manhattan and marvel at its geometry of lights and try to figure a way in, find a way to fit. Alejandro, she learned, was sleeping on the floor of a family friend's studio apartment way uptown, working three illegal, poorly paid cleaning jobs as well as some shifts in an all-night grocery store that was prone to ransacking and hit-and-run thefts where the produce set out on the sidewalk would be spirited away in a flurry of grabbing hands and the all-too-familiar fading thunder of feet. He'd given chase once, before he knew better, but stopped when the assailants did, turning around to coolly observe their would-be pursuer.

'Don't be a fucking hero, idiot. Walk on,' one of them said, raising his chin slowly. The three of them stared hard at him, unwavering glances filled with indolence and quiet rage; he guessed they were all younger than he was. He'd travelled this far to be undone by teenagers. He trudged back to the store, picking up discarded fruit and vegetables, his hands full of now useless food. As he dropped the pieces in the bin he wondered why he'd come here to this unflinching city that shrugged souls off, to sleep on a friend of a friend's floor and be quite alone. In Los Angeles, he was afraid of being seen; here he was a ghost, another shadow, he wasn't even a number; he didn't even count.

Red took him down to the basement and introduced him around; he clutched the cup of coffee she'd given him the way a child clings to a favourite blanket. He couldn't understand or believe the warmth of these people, the unblinking welcome of strangers; their enthusiasm pressed down on him. He sat and listened to their leader, the Reverend James Bulley, he was a red face on a fat body in a flowing robe that danced around him as he paced around in front of them, his fist repeatedly slamming into a pudgy hand. Alejandro couldn't make out all the words, Bulley's voice rose and fell in sudden peaks, emphasis came in a fierce whisper as he ducked out of sight, and then rose again to hammer his point home. Forgiveness was set at gale force, revenge almost muted, underhand, Bulley's world was aflame; the city and all its sinners were on fire. Alejandro looked to Red for some comprehension, but she was transfixed, eyes and mouth wide; she turned to glance at Alejandro and grabbed his hand excitedly, her smile was wide, excited and open, she looked like an awed child who had just spotted a hot air balloon overhead, he was surprised that she hadn't raised an arm to point it out.

It was then that Alejandro finally tuned into Bulley's relentless rhetoric; he was talking about Tomas de Torquemada, the Grand Inquisitor who masterminded the Spanish Inquisition with his relentless pursuit to bend people to his Catholic will. He tortured and terrified a country under the auspices of the Catholic Church, flushing Jews out of their hiding places like pheasants startled and forced to take to a sky filled with shot. Alejandro knew he was some kind of monster, a bogeyman, but Alejandro had been raised a Catholic, Torquemada's sins were allowed to wash over him; his evil was shrouded and hidden in the Church's long shadows.

Alejandro lay inverted, tied to the ladder. Iron prongs held his jaws apart, something filled both nostrils and a piece of linen was draped loosely over his mouth; eight-litre-deep jugs of water sat on a shelf on the far wall, the candlelight casting grotesque shadows. Torquemada sat off to one side, the torturer and a doctor set between him and Alejandro. A clerk sat to his left, poised to record events as they unfolded. The Grand Inquisitor was talking to him, telling him how he could be saved if only he would repent, if he would open up to them, become a convert to Catholicism. Alejandro tried to explain his faith, how he'd been raised a Catholic, but the linen fell into his mouth, clogging his throat and snatching the words away. He was a Jew, said Torquemada, pretending to be a Catholic, his eyes burned red, he was secretly subverting the Catholic faith; he signalled the torturer forward, a sloshing jug filled with water held in both hands. As the water was poured into Alejandro's mouth, the linen washed into the opening of his throat, meaning he couldn't spit the water out, so he drank and drank, feeling as if he were being pulled under, the sensation of drowning overwhelming him. He strained and pulled, his back arched and yet the water kept on coming, Torquemada loomed into view, his leering face was suddenly the whole world, the only thing that Alejandro could see or hear, he would find his God, he would recant, he must recant.

It was that final word that pulled him from his reverie. The room around him righted as the voices united as one. They were repeating Bulley's call to recant, saying the word over and over like football fans calling for defence as they found their team on the back foot. It suddenly occurred to Alejandro that Bulley had come to praise Torquemada, not bury or denounce him. The Grand Inquisitor, Bulley was insisting, had, ultimately, more faith than his fellow man, he was willing to fight for his God; he would kill for what he believed in. Bulley's hands were in the air; he was calling his God down the way a soldier signals the target for a payload, as death from above.

'Isn't he amazing?' Red's cheeks were flushed with excitement. She and Alejandro were standing on the street, the rest of the beaming congregation moving around them, points of light heading towards darkness. She grabbed his hand and pulled him along; he really had nowhere to go and so he followed, swept along in the rising tide of her enthusiasm. She bought him a coffee and while he sat there as a smeared reflection in a tall window, cut in half by the company's logo that ran around the building like a ribbon on a gift, she told him about her mother's death and how her father had dressed her as a boy and how Rose had become Red and about the painting of Joan of Arc she so revered that it was one of the few things that she'd brought to the city with her and how, when she felt her faith wavering, she looked to Joan for guidance, to feel her spirit rising through the flames.

'Joan fought for the voices she heard too?' he asked, though not unkindly, not that Red caught the tic of anger or disbelief in his voice.

'Exactly.' She sat forward in her seat, her unwavering green eyes looking right into him; she looked beautiful, but so far away, unobtainable, he thought, like a normal life in this new world.

Alejandro's sister's voice broke before she could finish the sentence. Alejandro stood in the phone booth on the corner directly opposite the grocery store, gingerly holding the receiver a few inches from his mouth, afraid of what might lie there. Traffic idled south as the light ran out of the sky somewhere downtown and his sister told him that they'd finally found Guilhermo's body a mere half mile from the train tracks where he'd fallen from the train that day. He'd gone into shock after he'd stumbled clear of the tracks, wandered into the fields in a daze and collapsed in the tall grass and died there alone.

'So he really had been swallowed up?' he asked his sister, imagining his friend falling from view, disappearing out of sight and suddenly invisible. His was a lonely death in an empty field so many miles from home. Alejandro felt petrified, rooted to the spot seeing Guilhermo lying there among the stalks of the grass reaching ever upward towards the sky and then carried away. The Beast had been sated, little wonder that he'd made it across the border and into this country; Guilhermo's death had eased their passage. It had taken from his friend and given Alejandro his freedom and for what?

The next time he'd returned to the basement he found himself quickly surrounded by the other members of the congregation; they silently encircled him and linked hands and his eyes widened with surprise until Red smiled at him.

'I told them what happened to your friend, they wanted to pray for you, they wanted you to know you were loved.'

He looked at the faces around him; the same faces he'd seen swept along by the bloody fervour of Bulley's rhetoric, and felt confusion instead of revulsion. He'd only kept coming back here to see Red and now he felt a sense of uneasy belonging, as if he'd surreptitiously found a way in. He suddenly understood how Red had unlocked the city; she'd become a part of something bigger than herself. Immersed herself in an alien culture and made it her own. Isn't that what he needed to do?

He'd sit at night with Red and try to let Bulley's sermons wash over him, cleanse his sins and baptise him in one surging tide of words, but all he could hear was the hate and the sneering, the polemic rage of us and them. The revenge Bulley wanted upon mankind, on those who didn't feel or see things the way he saw them. It seemed a high price to pay for that feeling of unanimity, to be disenfranchised universally in the hope of finding a feeling of harmony that was at odds with the world; it made no sense as far as he could see and for Alejandro it never would.

When Alejandro was younger, he and Guilhermo would borrow his older brother's truck and drive out to the hills and climb into a low range of mountains, huddle in their sleeping bags to watch light splinter the sky and feel the darkness reach out above them and talk about the inevitable move they'd one day make to America, the cities they'd see, the girls they'd meet, the adventures they'd have. They saw themselves as returning heroes one day, a lifetime of stories written in the short years they'd spent across the border. As the sun came up, Guilhermo would climb to the highest point he could find and teeter on a cliff edge and call his friend up to join him, but Alejandro would always resist and hang back, too afraid to stand at the very place where the earth gave in to the sky.

'The higher you go,' said Guilhermo, leaning dangerously forward into space in a way that made Alejandro's stomach flip over, 'the more you can see. If you want to know the answers then you have to climb and we, Alejandro, we'll climb.'

It was something his friend always said when they were alone out in the countryside and he thought about him now as he stood on the roof of his building. Dusk was a thick, horizontal stripe of orange, blue and black and New York winked into life below it. He leaned forward, ignoring the moving street below; he was above it all; he positioned his body the way his friend had, searching for the answers, climbing ever higher.

He thought back to the basement and to Red and to Bulley's outrage, his anger caught in traces of spit at the corners of his mouth. He had heard the stories of Torquemada that Bulley never told, how he would take his victims up to a scaffold, their wrists tied with rope. He'd ask for their confession, ask that they recant, and when they would not, he'd push them over the edge almost wrenching their arms from their sockets, they'd dangle there, so very alone, their arms pulled uselessly above their heads, the pain making them cry out, their breath coming in short, hard spurts trying to find the words to sate the insane Grand Inquisitor who stood above them, so wrapped up in his God that he couldn't see the cloak of other people's skin that he wore, or the blood of the innocent covering his hands and face; he was blind to their pain and anguish while groping uselessly for the path to purity.

Alejandro resisted his grip and was suddenly free to find the answers his friend had promised him. In the distance he saw and heard The Beast – the train that had once promised to carry them into America and a new world of possibilities – come firing into life, wheels turning on an endless track, the sparks jumping; he felt the heat as it passed, the shouts of the people trying to board, attaching themselves to the streaking engine. He saw Guilhermo fall and as his friend fell then he was falling with him, the pair of them shuttered, stuttering shadows caught in the daylight between the carriages. The Beast left them lying there on the tracks, caught up in clouds of dust and the sound of their surprised laughter, together again for one last time.

Those were the things that Alejandro thought as he dropped down through the night air, the stars rising up around him; he looked up one last time like a diver trying to locate the bow of the boat in the choppy waters above him. Twelve storeys below, Henry Willow saw the body of Alejandro falling towards him as if it were rushing to get to the street. That was how Henry would always remember Alejandro, coming into sharp relief, like an image on videotape set on fast forward. Alejandro blotted out the sky above but made no sound. Willow drunkenly staggered backwards as Alejandro hit the sidewalk; he made a dull, wet sound on impact, completely broken. Something rose up and hit Willow in the face, but he was afraid to reach up and touch it and so he stood there with a whimper building in his throat and blood on his face in a smear that made it look like he was wearing a mask across his eyes. He screamed and sat down. A car skidded to a halt, doors slammed and someone came running and Willow could only point mutely at the man now shaped like a star that had somehow exploded out of the sky.

'And I got on the phone pretty soon after that, you know?' said Henry Willow.

'I was pretty shaken up and I called Red and she calmed me right down, I took it as a sign that she and I might mean something, I'm a fucking idiot, sorry. But she was right with me on it, said that I'd been sent a clear signal, a sign from above. A sign from above, she wasn't even fucking joking when she said that, can you believe that?'

Willow looked as rumpled as the clothes he was wearing, as if he were back there among the debris of Alejandro, his voice caught deep in his throat, wearing pieces of another man on his skin and suit.

'Where was this exactly, where the guy fell?' Green asked; he had no idea why, but he needed to know the name of the jumper, the hopeless case who had driven Willow back to Red and her church; he thought there might still be some answers lying there.

Willow scribbled the street address down.

'Can I go now?' Willow asked; he was like a shaken bottle of beer that had emptied out; all that fizz gone, thought Green.

'Sure, one thing,' said Green. 'What happened to you two, Hank, why did you stop seeing her?'

'That crazy church, she was obsessed with the place and those people. You never felt more outside.' Willow's colour was coming back to his cheeks, his ire roused, his emotions slopping around.

'And that guy, Bulley, did you ever listen to the stuff he was spewing out? It was just hate-mongering and Red would look at him like he mattered so much, she told me he spoke the truth. You ask me, his idea of truth would have been to take guns into the street and offing anyone who didn't agree with his way of thinking. He gave me the creeps, they both did eventually, she told me once that she'd die for him.'

Maybe she did, thought Green, but he kept that thought to himself as he showed Henry Willow the way out.

# April 1980

Detective Green looked at the letter he'd written himself on the day that he'd finally stopped drinking.

*The centre will not hold,* it concluded. *Look for me at the end of the bar and I won't be there.*

He smiled inwardly, what a cliché, a broken-down, drunk cop with a string of failed relationships, an ex-wife (Nancy Young Green, who'd only agreed to share his name while keeping hers), a child in the ground, and now he had a new twist to add to the downward spiral of his life: he was falling for a dead girl, or the idea of her at least. One who had been brutally beaten to death with a blunt instrument that they couldn't find. He couldn't even offer her redemption or release by capturing the person who had done this; there was nothing he could give her.

Though it was hard to feel down on a morning like this; the sun reflected in a thin shaft off the kitchen worktop, the air was clear glass cut through with a smear of faint blue. The city was neither too claustrophobically hot nor bitingly cold, it was just right.

'Like Goldilock's porridge,' he muttered, surprised by the lightness of his mood. Days when the city shone almost always cheered him, they reminded him of California and his father, poker thin, always in black, an inverted exclamation mark, a dark shadow the sun couldn't obliterate. He wished he'd carried his father's understanding: sometimes he could be like a blunt weapon in comparison. He remembered his father's bravery after his marriage had crumbled and he saw his mother bloom. She would come to their house and drift in through the door, her lift idling momentarily outside and then pulling sharply away, the sudden snap of its engine foreshadowing the impact she was about to make on both of them. It was like a plane hitting the house, he thought, the tornado from Oz spiralling their home skywards to its doom.

Louis stood outside his father's study one afternoon, and heard his mother in there, her voice rising and falling, quivering with a quiet anger; he couldn't begin to imagine where it came from. He caught glimpses through an inch or two of doorway, quick flashes of determination and hate.

'You know that moment,' she said, her face close enough to his father's that she could have leant forward and bitten through his cheek, there were times Green thought she might, 'when you realise that you can't be with the person next to you for the next ten minutes, let alone the next ten years?' She hovered there like a mosquito waiting to draw blood. 'I can't even remember how long ago that was now.'

Each time his mother came back it was if she were trying to tip all the furniture in their home over before she left again; she wanted carnage, she wanted to be free, but not forgotten once she'd gone, she wanted to leave a mark. Green didn't understand it then and he found it hard to fathom now. Those moments would come back to him when he'd investigate break-ins where the perpetrators would take what they wanted and then streak the walls with piss and shit, kill the family pet, scrawl obscenities on the wall; he'd stand there among the wreckage, the muted sobs of the owners ankle deep in remnants and memories they couldn't possibly piece together again. The thieves' anger and anarchy (not to mention the noise they made) escalated the chances of them being caught, but he guessed they were beyond the nuances of carefully calculated crime; they wanted revenge on something they couldn't quite place, they railed against their world by smashing someone else's into tiny pieces. When he thought of his mother, he thought of them, defiant and unrepentant, standing among the detritus of lives they'd chosen to stand upon, screaming into the black.

Green was standing on the spot where Alejandro had fallen from the sky and landed a broken man; he looked up, but the cross of blue between the buildings above him was giving nothing away. He half-expected a black silhouette to fall suddenly towards him and dash out the light, but it was only a crow that flew across his eyeline to startle him. Green had found something in Rose's unexplained death he hadn't been expecting and now here he was on the ground trying to reach up and find the answers that lay somewhere between heaven and earth. He imagined night falling and Alejandro pitching out of the darkness; Henry Willow couldn't remember if Alejandro had cried out as he flailed against gravity and thundered downwards, it could have been the shock that had silenced him, surmised Green: no one expects to be thrown off their own apartment building, cast out and caught in the moment, before taking the inevitable long journey down.

Green took the stairs quickly, pushed through the door and past the water tower and stood where Alejandro had stood and studied the low wall that was the beginning and end of the roof. It was high enough to stop someone that might have stumbled into it going up and over to their doom, but low enough that it wouldn't be so hard to kick someone into oblivion if they'd been standing there wondering at their place in the world. The police report had surprised him; as far as they could tell, Alejandro had been kicked in the back – he'd never jumped from the building; someone had forced his hand. There was something that looked like a boot-shaped bruise imprinted on his back: whoever had elected to harry Alejandro on from this life to the next had been emphatic about it. He imagined they hoped his injuries would hide their handiwork, but Alejandro had flopped forward like a poor diver hitting the water hard, he'd never turned in the air; his features might have been mulch, his bones fragmenting inside him, but his back still yielded up the outline of a heel, the sole of someone's shoe; it was as if they'd stamped or stood on the hapless Alejandro before throwing him away.

Green spoke to the officers who had looked into his death, the case was still open, but tracing the source of an illegal immigrant who no one would admit to sheltering let alone employing meant that they were only chasing another ghost in a city that was filled with them. Green read the notes and began to treat it like he would any other case: he went back to talk to those who knew the victim and check for himself; Bulley thought he'd simply lost one more soul to the darkness that haunted every shadowy corner of his world. His old boss at the grocery store – who wouldn't admit to knowing Alejandro until Green could convince him that he wasn't there to bust him for hiring illegals – had surmised that he'd just stopped showing up, that a better offer had come up or he'd just been sent back home like so many before him. The people at his apartment were part of the shifting, floating workforce that underpinned the city, working illegal and long hours – the last people they wanted to talk to were the cops. He saw only mistrust and fear in their faces: it could have been any of them up on that roof and then dashed on the sidewalk below; they knew as much about Alejandro as he knew about them, and it was hard to look or care for someone who wasn't there. You couldn't blame these people for never trying to moor themselves to something solid when the version of the city they lived in was always at sea and they were constantly adrift; it was enough to keep their heads above water let alone look out for others and stop them from going under too.

'I thought Red knew Alejandro, that they were friends, that she was the one who brought him here?' Green asked Bulley, but Bulley, his eyes like a surprised owl through his glasses, gave a deft shake of his head.

'She welcomed everyone in,' said Bulley. 'She stood at our doorway, she favoured no one person over the other, she watched over everyone, she saw to their comings and goings.'

'They had coffee a few times,' said Green, but he could feel himself grappling with the unknown, he couldn't hold on to anything, no foothold so he might begin to climb. If there was a trail of hopelessness and despair leading from this basement to that roof he couldn't yet see it, it had been lost in the commotion of the streets leading away from here.

'No man can achieve such glories or power without either breaking the law or his own moral code.' Robert Walker's father had said those words on the boy's twelfth birthday. Whether he was talking to himself or his son remained a mystery, one thing Robert Walker wished he'd asked his father when he still had the chance. He had stood in his father's office overlooking Manhattan while his father pored over sheaves of paper on his desk, a great oblong of carved wood almost as deep as it was wide, obscured by notebooks and reports, pieces of neatly typed A4 marred by his father's squirrely signature, a scribbled line of black ink that ran from a fat flourish to an inconspicuous scrawl to nothing. Like a python digesting a boar, Walker would think later, or the trajectory of my father's miserable life.

'"Power tends to corrupt", he liked that one too,' said Walker to himself, lighting a cigarette, now seated in his own office years later, another rectangle of glass and light sealed into place high above Manhattan. '"Absolute power corrupts absolutely."' He mused, 'So then, does that mean that great men are almost always bad men? Does that mean, given the company he kept and the precedent that history or Shakespeare set, that my father wasn't such a bad guy after all?' Walker sighed. The notion of power corrupting his ideology the way cancer went after certain cells troubled his father, especially later in life as he weakened and fell ill. Walker Senior had begun to imagine that his inevitable demise was a manifestation of his own deeds; karma had never bothered him until he was unwell and then he began to carefully measure the metaphorical scales set before him. 'Karma, he believes in fucking karma now?' Robert Walker had asked sneeringly of a doctor who had conveyed his father's words to him. Walker thought back to the old man there among the tubes, the dull beep signalling life intermittently: the too-bright lights. Karma and fairness didn't bother Robert Walker one bit, not anymore.

It was late, most of the city's workers had gone home for the night and, from the distance, Walker's office looked like it was suspended hundreds of feet in the air, hovering as a point of light that might rise suddenly, tilt and sweep towards the horizon, Walker caught as a thin blade of black against the ever-receding oblong of neon. It hadn't always been this way, thought Walker, a momentary face at the window, a satellite above the city, his father had only started to wonder at what he might leave behind, at the shape of his legacy, once he'd survived his first serious illness and seen friends and associates wither and die. Walker had watched the old man weighing up the odds, checking to see what bargaining power he might have with his God when they did finally meet. 'There aren't enough chips in the world, or enough rolls of the dice to win this one, dear Father,' he said half-mockingly as the old man sat there scowling at reports and spreadsheets, tallying up and counting the cost of his actions, the things he'd wrought.

Robert Walker's father was a collector. Men had collected things for centuries; this was nothing new – cars, wives, companies, houses; the small stuff, as his father put it. For him, it was the collection of ideas, thoughts, words and phrases, the essence of things, which was how he often referred to it when he was asked what it was that he did exactly. In truth, his father filled the air with notions; he populated conversations and speeches with everyday parlance, jargon; words. It was as if he pinned letters on currents of air, black typeface against blue sky, so that the entire world might read them, say them aloud and bring them to life. It was something his father had done before him, his father before him too, and his before that. The grand patriarch of the family had been a speechwriter, a pamphleteer who had risen through the ranks of industries and then, almost inevitably, into the government of the day. He'd created and nurtured phrases that haunted boardrooms and meetings, literally echoed through the ages and down to the modern day.

Walker's father had finessed the whole process, when he told the story, as he often did; the phrase 'going forward', he said that was one of his, while 'paradigm shift' was something he'd conjured up late one night while trying to unlock the way power was moving out from under one of his bosses' feet as if it had suddenly been granted free will. The use of it the next day had made shareholders quizzical, but a journalist had scribbled it down and then called it in with his report and had set it free. It floated into the ether and then down into the subconscious before materialising on the tongues of others, a small yet important part that helped make up the jigsaw of modern language. Another tiny piece of the arsenal utilised by the business world to put their point across, to explain things to the layman, to make themselves heard in the headlines. This is how he worked; it was intangible, but such a powerful tool, and one that some men were willing to pay a high price for. Walker's father was the first to suggest that information be 'cascaded', he drew 'the bottom line', he 'sweated assets' and 'boiled the ocean' (which never came to life the way he'd once hoped), but 'touch base' did, and from his day to this, people still 'brainstormed' – no one thought collectively once he'd come up with that – he imagined hemispheres moving at a glacial pace, lightning bolts flashing forth to impale the earth; it was his legacy, anyone could see that, it was hardly rocket science ...

Once Walker's forefather had made the move from big business to government high office, his political speeches were triumphant, polishing edicts to the nation until they vibrated and shone, the power of his words causing a frisson through adoring crowds. He made leaders legendary; their oratory skills confounded the opposition and made fools of non-believers. His only son carried his enigmatic gene; he founded building blocks in the lexicon that felt as if they'd always been there, holding things in place. And so they became the Walker bloodline, the family who would forever be remembered for naming the names. Moving silently behind the words that shaped the day, sugaring the pill, helping the medicine go down.

The struggle for power, the gruesome spectacle of war: frenetic images of toil and bloodshed and the battle's cruel, shrieking maw; someone had to make sense of what people were seeing and feeling. Make it more palatable somehow. War had been with them forever, as had his family's words to mask the endless horrors. As generation upon generation sent their young men to die, the Walkers looked on and labelled the carnage as a chemist might some innocuous-looking glass jars filled with silent poisons. 'The Big Push' came from their jotters and notes, as did the almost inevitable 'The Big Show', which made people think of a friendly vaudevillian haranguing a crowd, not teenage soldiers racing to their deaths or the bloody carnage of dead horses, legs twisted upwards like blackened trees after a storm. Soldiers went racing into the trenches as the 'Black Hand Gang', they learned how to 'Bring Smoke'; as war moved into Vietnam and Korea, soldiers could be heard to 'Embrace the Suck', and as the nuclear age dawned in clouds the colour of dirty filings, the Walker family outdid themselves in an attempt to bring some grandeur to the kind of warfare that could disseminate toxins and horror in great belches of fear and noise. They talked of a 'Broken Arrow', a 'Faded Giant', the 'Dull Sword', an 'Empty Quiver'; never once did they mention the smears nuclear weapons made of people, distilling them down to ragged shadows. Everything was played out in the 'Theatre of War', a phrase so bold and grandstanding that all his forefathers attempted to lay claim to its creation. Robert Walker would sometimes tell people that it was one of his when he tried to explain to them what it was he did, but it only heightened their confusion. He was, as he never tired of telling people, literally making history.

When it came to Robert Walker's turn, he'd tried to resist his father's words, even if they had made his family infamous, built their grand houses and bought them acres of land. He imagined he could bend the Walkers' strangely attuned DNA to his own will. He would, he determined, bring life to new words and meanings that spoke only of love and happiness, things of joy and beauty; simply put, he'd let the light in. But, as it transpired, the world didn't want to listen to phrases conceived to celebrate life and the living, they didn't want to hear those words, it was as if they'd seen enough glory; they were, he realised, not afraid to stand in the sunshine alone, hear that they were loved, it was the dark spectre of incomprehensible, crushing power and the unassailable wreckage of conflict and war that they needed to be shielded from. They wanted something to save them from that, they didn't want to see the long, bloody shadow of the irresolvable at their window, they'd rather a safety curtain of ideas and a mask of kind and comforting words no matter what lay beyond and, he thought finally, who could blame them?

And in becoming the prism through which he let people see that light he somehow shaped himself; he was the conduit through which the evils of the world came, caught up in the bottleneck of his being, he was a filter that was slowly filling up with blood and a poisonous black that was harder to wash away with each passing year. No wonder his father had tried to cleanse himself; absolve himself of those collated sins. He and his father both carried the family taint; he thought of men who had once claimed to eat the sins of others and imagined someone gorging on the evil in his heart, the tar-like darkness that made up his being. Finally pushing their chair back with a sigh, complaining how they could eat no more, they were full, sated. How did you count the decades of lies he and his family had told? Did it matter that they had blunted war's brutalities, dressed wounds with ribbons, embellished the horror; placed a bauble where a limb had once been? Of course it did and he could either be finally damned by it as his father once had or embrace this strange gift the gods had given him.

On taking control of his father's company, he'd quickly changed its name to Snake Oil, and watched its share price buckle and fall sharply like a drunk trying to negotiate a flight of stairs. His advisors reacted badly, as did his investors; trade papers and the financial pages branded him an arrogant fool, but the ship steadied, as he knew it would, and he felt his company lurching forward into the new decade much as he had planned and hoped it would; insiders branded him a fool, but the public suddenly had an inkling of who he was, a maverick, a renaissance man; he was stepping out onto the stage and into the wider world in the hope that one day he might possess it.

# June 1961

James Bulley remembered the flames and the voices calling for help. His father pulling him along by his hand, past the smell of burning, their home literally turning to dust, the oxygen being sucked out of the air, the feeling that at any moment his hair might turn to tinder and ignite around his head, giving him a halo of orange and red. Then suddenly they were outside, the crack of falling wood behind them; something combusted and blew inward, a window fell in on itself, glass shattered and someone screamed his father's name and then the world exploded and inverted and he was suddenly twenty feet away from where he'd been standing with his leg caught up behind him. Something had happened to his thumb, it felt dislocated and useless, like it wasn't his thumb anymore; something in his eye was making him blink. He sat up and a high, singing alarm went off in his head. Behind him their house was now a dirty black cloud tethered to a series of jagged, wooden spikes that looked like spindly fingers pointing at the sky. And then James's father was standing over him, blood across his face and on one of his hands; he was screaming something, but the high-pitched keening in James's ears made it impossible to hear him. His father grabbed at the boy's wrist and then was suddenly jolted backwards and briefly out of sight; James watched confusedly as his father's legs shot up in the air and then there was Jakub standing triumphantly behind his father, his clothes were smoking and he looked as though he'd been smeared with oil, his jaw was set at an odd angle, some of his teeth were missing. The whites of his eyes magnified against the burnt black of his skin.

Years later, James would remember the smell, he could feel it in his nostrils, taste the suddenly decaying flesh on his tongue; the charcoal of a barbecue brought it flooding back, sulphur conjured up the ghost of Jakub's hair, a lick of flame at the crown that he hadn't seemed to have noticed yet; the scent was overwhelming, nauseating yet sweet, putrid, the thick smell of steak, he imagined leather being held over a flame until it curled and smoked. Then his father was standing next to Jakub, he pulled his revolver from inside his jacket and placed it at

Jakub's temple and fired. The sound broke through the white noise that was now making up the inside of James's skull, he imagined the bullet ricocheting inside Jakub's head, spinning around like a rider on the Wall of Death and then Jakub was gone, a spray of blood described a wobbling arc, and then James was up, his father grabbing at him and dragging him into their car. His father was screaming.

'I'll make landfill from their bones!' Blue's voice was reaching James like a radio signal that had travelled too far and was quickly waning. He watched his father strike the dashboard repeatedly with his open hand. His whole frame was shaking and he was driving like a man with a tornado filling the sky in his rear-view mirror. Until, quite suddenly, he pulled the car wildly over into a small side road and stilled. He turned in his seat and placed a hand gently on his son's shoulder, he looked undone, diminished somehow, he looked like a boy himself, wearing a grown-up's suit for a joke, his head shrunken, peeking out of the collar, the knot of the tie too wide. Not only had James's father lost his congregation and people, he had, as he would later admit, finally lost everything, even his way.

His father, Blue, was raised between a commune in the Connecticut countryside and his father's house in the suburbs of New Haven. He once said that he'd left the best part of himself on the road somewhere in between in the hope that neither his father or mother, in their battle to be the parent he'd come to rely on and, as they saw it, truly love, would snuff out the best of him if they got hold of it. At his father's house his mother was a slut who'd taken up with vagrants, undesirables and goddamn hippies. While at his mother's commune, his father was an uptight idiot who'd done nothing to make her ever want to stay at home; he was blinkered to what was really going on in the world, he was a fool.

It was all so much noise to the young Blue. He remembered the smells of the commune most clearly, the sweet odour of dope and the bitter rank of old sweat. One moment, he'd be standing with his father, who insisted on wearing a tie even at weekends, when he'd swap a regular shirt for a short-sleeved version so that he might relax, and then, literally hours later, Blue would be marooned in the half-light under a canvas awning, topless men and women milling around, touching his hair abstractedly, their pupils exploding in their heads, the bite of their sweat on his tongue. His mother had a new boyfriend, she'd introduce Blue to new people and then pull him close to tell him how she loved him, before, inevitably, telling him what was wrong with the world she'd chosen to leave behind. She used universal themes, talked of a wider world, but really she was talking about her husband, still standing there in their kitchen, looking nervously out of the window, wondering if his estranged wife was winning the battle for Blue's heart and mind.

'Is he happy, Blue?' she'd ask, her breath hot, soured by whiskey, but then her tone would lighten, become quizzical. 'How can he be happy there? Those people are dead inside.' And then she'd lean back with a stoned grin, mistaking her pronouncement for something profound. Blue stood there mutely among the swirling colours and the dull, thudding bass, while on the other side of the marquee someone was approximating Dylan's catalogue badly; Blue's jacket was still buttoned, his small suitcase held securely under his arm, his glasses were set on the bridge of his nose, but a loop of bootlace around his neck made sure they weren't lost if they ever came loose, and he'd wonder where he belonged in any of this. He fantasised about throwing himself from his father's car as they thundered through the swells of greens and browns towards his mother's new utopia; his father drove with a determination that bordered on the unhinged, he could see his dad working his jaw as he clutched the wheel, leaning forward in his seat like an athlete lunging for the finishing line. Blue imagined himself jimmying the door open and reaching for the air, gasping hard as he hit the floor and rolled, sunlight and tarmac, sunlight and tarmac, coming to a sliding halt like a baseball player reaching for home, a crumpled heap raising dust, with torn knees and scuffed skin, a disconsolate shoe sitting in the road behind him.

The young boy's solace was unexpected and came from both arms of his disenfranchised family; at one point Blue liked to think that it was a very deliberate salvation his God had handed down to him. His father instilled faith in him the way a sergeant major might impress a particularly knotty drill command on his platoon. Each Sunday he was at home, Blue and his dad would sit in the same spot at the far end of the final pew in the church where his parents had married and experience the parables and lessons of the Lord drifting ever upwards to the joists and eaves of the long, brightly lit hall and then fall slowly downwards like feathers on warm air and settle on their heads and shoulders so that they might carry them and their message out into the world. In Blue's alternate world too, among his mother's friends and suitors, in among the dope plants and the free love, God was there, reading groups were common as was Bible study; even those, he'd later realise, who'd chosen to step outside of society still wanted some connection to the old world they'd left behind, a foot in the past; faith was their trail of breadcrumbs through the dark woods of the unknown if they ever needed to find a way back.

Like his mother, Blue envisaged some kind of heaven on earth. A plot of land and homes and people who might share in his vision – love, he thought, is truly all. Years later his father had finally succumbed to a heart attack, they'd found him with his fists clenched, his body tense; even in death, thought his only son when he'd got the call, he couldn't leave go of his anger. It was as if his rage had throttled him inwardly; wound him so tight that there was barely room left for his heart to beat freely in his chest.

Blue's mother had packed up and finally left them years before that. He and his father had travelled to see her one weekend and where her maze of tents and trailers had once been was just squares and rectangles of bleached grass and trash drifting into small mounds. His father stood among the silence and began to shout at the remote horizon. Then he stood very still and bowed his head, Blue watched a fat fly traverse the length of his back and then perch on his father's shoulder as if too considering the now bare landscape that had swallowed up his mother and her friends. Blue's mother had truly embraced the freedom that she always spoke of and had finally cast herself free of her moorings. Briefly, Blue imagined him and his father holding long ropes leading up to the basket of a low-hanging hot air balloon, his mother waving down to them and then lifting the ropes and throwing them back towards the earth, the heavy coils landing at their feet with a thud and then the balloon rising ever higher until it was just a black sphere set against the sun. Blue couldn't see his mother anymore, but he kept on waving until his arm was tired and he lowered it slowly, feeling the blood coming back into the tips of his fingers; the gentle vibration tickled as he watched the colour creeping back into the palms of his hand.

He was still a relatively young man, but by now Blue had a congregation of his own; he'd travelled at first in order to spread the gospel and each time he moved on he discovered that he was taking people with him, entranced by his rhetoric; women were charmed by him, men wanted to befriend him, his benefactors were endless and for a while, buoyed by the generosity of others, he returned home and preached to some of the people he'd grown up around, but with his father's death he decided to sell the home he grew up in to build a house for others. Settling on a plot of land in the Tennessee countryside he set about creating a commune where each man and woman might live freely, where they might be allowed to revel in their God, not meet with him each Sunday, but spend their days at his side. So charismatic a preacher was he that some of his flock had followed him from his church in New Haven to start a new world in the fields and meadows of the South.

In Blue's dreams, his God came to him in golden robes and spoke of a future bathed in glory, of a destiny that would see him seated at his Lord's right hand, but first, he must fight the good fight. But the battle eluded him. Blue had imagined a higher ground, a spiritual quest, but as his congregation grew he spent his days mired among strangers who were also trying to find their path through life. His house became a refuge for drifters and the homeless, they looked to him for counsel, they wanted him to lead, but he was lost among them. The tents and trailers they brought with them became an ever-increasing dirty circle radiating out from the centre that was his home; as the sprawl continued so did the roaring in his head. He stood on his porch one morning and saw the irregular horizon that his view had become: broken tent poles, the scattering of TV aerials, a neon cross strapped to the front of a RV that blinked intermittently and haunted his peripheral vision at night like an elusive ghoul.

Blue walked to the very edge of his land with some of his men and began to erect a high wooden fence; he imagined the sins of the world washing up at his door and the tide being stemmed by his sturdy perimeter wall. What he didn't yet know was that he was locking the evil in. Incubating the germ of unhappiness and self-doubt, bringing something into being that would eat at the very roots of his faith. Though, as he stood there and watched his men work, he could only embrace the idea of a far-off future of self-examination and understanding: he would lead and others would follow. And, finally, he'd found love among his flock and they were expecting their first child; he pretended not to care about its sex, but alone at night he prayed to his God and asked for a boy as he knelt among the lengthening shadows and felt the spirit filling him up, commanding him to do his Lord's bidding. He filled his glass with whiskey and admired the new fence as it rose into the air, it seemed to touch the sky; he wondered how he could keep the world at bay while keeping his people by his side. He thought of John 3:35: *The Father loves the Son and has placed everything in his hands.* He considered his legacy; he wanted an empire he could pass on.

# May 1980

They found Henry Willow in a quiet corner of Black Star Park; his body hung from a Silver Maple tree like a broken kite tossed up there by the wind. His arms threaded through the branches, his wrists and ankles were tethered to the boughs with long curls of ribbon, his body buckled forward slightly, his head hung down, as if he was ashamed to have found himself there. A group of cops stood around looking up at him, a ladder steadied against the unmoving tree, the tableau now set behind an uneven square barrier of yellow tape, temporary steel poles set at right angles. Red and blue light swam slowly against the glistening bark of the tree as Green stood among the men, voices coming through their walkie-talkies like the drone of distant bees. Green squinted up at the broken man and conceded that while he had briefly thought about strangling him the last time they'd sat across from one another, he couldn't quite fathom who might want Henry Willow dead. Green thought about Henry cheating death by inches as Alejandro had come out of the sky that night and had almost pressed the life out of him the way the sole of a boot might extinguish a fly. The final thudding end that had snatched Alejandro away, reduced his features to indifference, and now, thought Green, it was like his sudden impact had somehow sent Willow up into the sky to snare him on this tree, like two acrobats at either end of a seesaw, one descending sharply with a thump, the other thrown into the air reaching for the dull gleam of the trapeze.

He stood back and let his men do their work, gingerly lowering Willow to the ground, his head stuck out a right angle once he reached the floor. Neck's broken, thought Green as they stood over him almost as if they expected him to stir. It wasn't the only thing: his nose lay hard against his face as if someone had leant against it until it gave in and his eyes were black and grey rings, one hand was a fist of broken fingers. 'They beat him down before they hung him up,' someone said in the quiet.

Green walked away from the shade and into the light, looking up at the tall buildings that made up the right angle of concrete and glass abutting the oblong of urban green that acted as the park's main playing field. The Blue Lakes apartment building looked down onto the park; he was surprised to see it there. He'd once spent a New Year's Eve in its upper reaches, invited there with a date whose name he now struggled to remember, and had ended up stepping in between some revellers whose mood had turned ugly. Drunks, he thought, God, how I hate them, how I hated myself when I was one.

From a distance the soft orange light made it look like a fire had raged earlier and was now dwindling in the burnt-out rooms and lighting up the Blue Lakes' top floor. The shadow of a man set in its tall window was drunk and swayed slightly as he sang: 'Should old acquaintance be forgot for the sake of old man's eyes.

'That's what my sister used to sing,' he grinned to no one in particular, but he was winking at Green. 'Old man's eyes,' he hissed by way of explanation, just in case Green or anyone else might have missed it.

As one year ended and another began, the promise in the air was almost stifling, as thick as the reams of streamers caught around the legs of the chairs. They snaked like coloured cables across the floor and over the tables that had been pulled back as midnight had struck and people had reached out for each other across the thin divide between the disappointment of the last twelve listless months and the promise of the next three hundred and sixty-five days.

Green wasn't thinking about the future: captivated by the reams of coloured paper at his feet, he was reliving a war movie from his youth where they had to cut the right wire to defuse the bomb and save the garrison. Which one was live and which was one was earth, he thought, as the streamers bunched up thickly, jettisoned endlessly in smoky plumes from tiny plastic cups, the popping accompanied by a softly unfurling curl of paper and a sudden tiny spark. The balloons ended his reverie as they bounced off the bridge of his nose just as the clock chimed midnight; moments later he could still feel it gently vibrating throughout the room. He watched the weaving drunk singing happily to himself as he tried to negotiate the party hat that kept slipping forward and covering his eyes. Then the city through the windows came alive with fireworks, the spray of light a fan suddenly framing its towers before falling silently towards the distant earth.

Before him, as Green's date let her hand drift from his wrist to place her hand in his, just before the singing started in earnest, other couples began to linger, some in an awkward, unrequited embrace, like two people learning to dance together for the first time, he thought, while others stepped quickly apart as the last chime struck, leaving a vacuum of one-sided longing to fill up the space between them. The affable drunk was now silent – mesmerised by the colourful display that had long since faded outside, he held on to the window frame as if the spray of orange, red and gold were permanently imprinted on his retina, the dark sky filled with fireworks each time he closed his eyes. Others were drifting like unsteady satellites around the room, their moorings and then equilibrium lost to an evening of champagne and vodka cocktails; broken glass was tramped down deep into the carpet, shards of starlight winking up at him.

He never saw the argument start, but he felt it, the ions in the air changed, his skin prickled, he'd felt it a hundred times before, he wasn't sure if it was intuition or an instinct to survive, but when it came to him it was as clear and distinct as a tolling bell. He had seen the group enter not long before midnight; they came into the room like sailors on shore leave looking for one last drink before final call. One of them had got into a spat at the temporary bar – it was set on wheels and went juddering sideways as the argument intensified and the pushing began – over some imagined slight and then suddenly they were all diving in, a collective howl of anger and hurt. One man fell back and Green stepped between him and the red-faced gang whose features were now pinched and drunk. Eyes half-open, but suddenly alert and baying for blood.

'I'm a cop,' Green snapped, focusing on the man closest to him, waiting for the inevitable blow to his face or neck and calculating in that briefest of moments whether he could get someone up here on New Year's Eve and process an assault. Or should he react quickly, pummel him until the man came to, suddenly sobered and bruised and set on one knee, one of New York's finest flailing away at him, determined to tramp him down, set him on his ass among all that broken glass? He saw the man's nostrils literally flare with anger as his friend quickly pulled him back, his fist coming within inches of Green's face. Even the drunk at the window, his eyes no longer filled with rainbows, was straining to see what the furore was. It was quiet by then though, just the gentle lull of Christmas carols, as if everyone was hushed and still waiting for the main event.

As one of Green's men had guessed, Henry Willow had been beaten down before he'd been hung up. As they peered more closely at his broken features, it became clear that there was something in his mouth. A pool ball, a red number three, sitting behind Willow's shattered teeth; Green could imagine leaning forward and making it spin, the revolving digit a blur as it turned over and over in his mouth. One of his men did lean forward as if to touch it, but Green stopped him, he knew it'd be stuck fast. He'd once worked a mob hit where the victim – a chronic gambler who had run out of luck and credit – had been found slumped in a chair in his own kitchen with an eight-ball locked in hard inside his mouth, his throat cut and his head slung almost casually back as if he'd found something to admire about the light fitting on the ceiling.

'You can get the ball in there, with a very firm nudge,' one of his men had said as they stood over the dead man, indicating the eight-ball behind the row of gleaming, broken and bloody teeth, like a novelty glass eye that had found itself a strange new setting. 'The teeth have some give going in, they lean back, but it's not coming back out unless your teeth come with it.' He looked at the exposed windpipe inside the bloody maw where the man's throat had once been. 'Though I'm guessing that was the least of his problems.'

Green thought of the ball being forced into the victim's mouth, a heavy hand pulling his hair back, another pushing the pool ball home as the teeth slowly gave in and the mouth yawned in agony; he could only imagine the horror of the man's head snapping upright, surprised to still find himself alive, and then the stinging realisation of the pool ball sitting squarely in the centre of his skull. Moving cumbersomely around behind his face, the panic for air; the terror of letting the ball roll too far back and closing off the oxygen to his throat.

The victim in the kitchen had his hands free, the marks on his body were consistent with his thrashing around, bouncing off the cabinets, running into the walls, trying desperately to shift the eight-ball from inside his head. They'd let him run around for a while in there if only to amuse themselves; it was hard to teach a lesson to a dying man. Green wondered how long they'd let him stumble around, pots and crockery crashing around him, clawing at his own features, their laughing finally stilled only to push him back into his chair, his head pulsing, his gums and teeth smeared with blood, his mouth thick with spit and panic and then his legs pumping and thrashing with fear as they brought the blade quickly across his throat and his very life shook from him in ever-receding palpitations, his body bucking and then tremulous and then still.

Green told his father as much as he could about Henry Willow and the pool ball when he called him that night. His father had moved upstate, nearer now to Boston than he was to New York. His last parish, as it would surely be, was sedate and small, a thank-you, Green thought, for all the joy and help he'd brought to this unflinching city. His father now moved among a small population of widows and retirees, people who golfed, who waited to see their grandchildren at the weekend, who sometimes wondered if their small town and lives might ever ignite again. Green counted on his father's counsel too.

It was Green's duty to collect the bodies and the broken bones and the deceit and the fury and the malice and the hatred and the lies from the last five days of work and then he'd sift through them with his father as they talked long distance at the weekend. Taking the bloody components that had made up his week, dismantling them one by one, breaking down the whole to help take away the power it held over Green, as if deconstructing the parts could help him resolve the unholy mess they made. Nicholas Green likened it to the giant jigsaws the pair of them would pore over together when Louis was a boy, expansive fields of corn, hills and valleys, Mount Rushmore, spaceships rocketing across the curve of the earth, Old Masters cut into hundreds of intricate, interlocking pieces. They'd spend days seated at their uneven dining table watching the sky reveal itself, the sun rising at the corner of the jigsaw so it might light the way to resolving the complete puzzle. These days he and his father would spend their time on the phone dismantling this sprawling imagined puzzle that looked like it might have been inspired by one of Bosch's hellish scenarios, and they'd go back and forth and pull it apart piece by complex piece, as meticulously as they'd completed those great vistas when they were both younger men, until nothing remained and Green could see clearly again, before he had to bear witness to yet another tragedy.

'That's what happens when you stop going to church on Sunday,' Green's father would say, but he was teasing his son, not testing him. 'You're left with all those unresolved thoughts and questions floating around your head – I daren't imagine your dreams.' A pause, as Green fought to scramble the things he was seeing and had seen as his father tried to will his boy's living nightmares away.

'You can come up here, you know,' Green's dad said. 'Ghosts rarely leave the city, they can't bear to be out in the suburbs, let alone in the wilds of the country.'

Louis answered his father as he always did: 'I'll think about it, Dad, I will.' He did too, though he knew that with every case left unresolved he was becoming more immersed in the city, part of its make-up. It was a question of making things balance. He felt that every death or act of violence left unanswered, that he couldn't solve, distorted his view of the city's streets somehow; a film of sin that muddied his original vision of the place he now called home. Smearing the view like a stain on a high window he couldn't shift. He looked to the sky some mornings and found himself extending an arm as if to wipe away something hanging there on the air, like a cobweb just beyond his reach. One day he imagined a place uncluttered by crime, absolved somehow, clear-eyed and filled with resolution, completely cleansed. It was his dream.


Robert Walker didn't dream, he inhabited a whole other world to Detective Green, he had ground bones to dust, worshipped false idols, lain with other men's wives. He took the commandments as some kind of challenge, a list to be ticked off; he wished he were Catholic sometimes, so that he could attend confession and talk and talk until he felt the priest gag through the thin curtain that divided them, hear him brim and overflow with Walker's sins, gorged and unwillingly sated, delirious with the crimes of mankind, sodden with life's riches, dank from his misdeeds. Walker made do, however, by feasting on the misery of others.

His father had sent him away when he was a young man; Walker had tied up their housekeeper at their Long Island home and spent the day putting in every window he could reach in their grand house with a selection of his father's golf clubs. At twelve years old, he couldn't quite reach the upper panes of glass and was having something far too much like fun to drag a ladder out of the garage to ensure the front of their home was a fully fractured mosaic of violence and rage. He'd tried hitting golf balls into the house at first, but his swing was indifferent and unpractised and the balls kept spinning away from him at obtuse angles and landing far off in the grass. He took a generous swig of his father's Famous Grouse and wrinkled his face in exaggerated distaste; it didn't matter, it was the fuel to his fire. He enjoyed the dreamlike state it was inducing, the soft outline of his thoughts intermingling with the sharp crack and jangle of the breaking glass. The wooden clubs took extra effort to make any real impact, so he finally settled on a Wilson five iron that he'd seen his father carry around as if it were the last line of defence between him and the rest of the world. As if Death might one day come creeping out of the trees as his father stood in the rough trying to secure a spot on the fairway and drag him noisily away to his fate, his dad trying to bash the ghoul's head in with his club as he bumped along the ground. Walker giggled at the idea and dropped the bottle from his hand, which splintered as soon as it hit the paving slabs on which he was standing. 'Fuck it,' he murmured, kicking the broken bottle among the other shards that surrounded him; the sun was shining and the pieces gleamed as he stood among them swinging his father's club around.

Later, when he was grown, when Walker's father had finally given in and ceded him control of his company, he'd try to put his father's windows in once again. Metaphorically this time, as his father had built his empire on the treacherous ground of business and battlefields, so he tried to make it live by nurturing it, using his family's extraordinary gift to spread love, make happiness a building block in people's lives. But it was never for the greater good of others, it wasn't something he was doing out of the goodness of his heart – in reality, if his father had made his fortune from doing positive deeds then Walker would have wanted his to be wholly negative; the complete opposite.

When it came to his dad he was contrary, he wanted to turn the old man's world upside down. Walker didn't care if he succeeded: for him success was his father realising that he'd raised a failure and others seeing his failings too. This was something his father might have guessed at as he pulled up and into the long driveway of their house and saw the light rising up from the grounds now filled with broken glass and thought his house on fire and his son stood among the gentle lick of flames, spinning around and around, his expression exultant. And no one was more surprised than he when his son came rushing towards his car with his five iron (he recognised it instantly, it was his favourite) high in the air, screaming as if hell were opening up behind him, a tear in the earth bringing all his bad dreams to light, and then Walker struck the car's bonnet hard, one, two, three times, the sound glorious and unsettling all at once. The metal made a pinging sound and gave quickly in. Robert Walker looked squarely at his father through the windscreen and placed his favourite club carefully on the dashed paintwork, the head pointing straight at him, and then he took off running for the woods that surrounded the quiet lawns, he was vomiting up his father's Famous Grouse whisky before he'd even reached the perimeter.

The school his father sent Robert Walker to in the Tennessee countryside wasn't dissimilar to his dad's aspiring pile – cornices, faux turrets (he was surprised they hadn't fitted a portcullis and dug a moat and had done with it), endless lawns, and an unyielding wall of trees that felt like the edge of the world – but whereas his father's home was a procession of ghostly rooms mostly un-entered and unloved, the wide halls here were filled with bustle and noise. The clattering of idiots, Walker thought, as they filed past him, the regimented tattoo of feet punctuated with a bell that went right through him. His father insisted this place was for his own good, but he couldn't begin to fathom how. The days were long, the sunshine ceaseless, and the nights thrummed with the low hum of cicadas somewhere beyond the trees, the dull heat was stifling, he'd lie there in his room and kick the sheets off only to wake again with his midriff exposed and cold and cocoon himself in the sheets once more until he overheated and threw them to the floor. It became the template for those long nights. He was one of the few boys who didn't have to double up and share a room, his father having paid extra fees to keep him isolated. He had no desire, as he put it, 'to blunt the keenness of others or ruin some other young mind with your deathly, perishing presence'. His father's sense of humour was the thing he liked about him best. It might have been the only thing.

This occurred to Walker as he found himself deep in the woods alone and completely lost one night. He looked up to the sky as if the stars might somehow guide him, as if he were a captain at the helm of a tanker negotiating the channels of the sea below by the firmament above. Though the canopy above wasn't a dome of stars, it was a thicket of branches and impenetrable boughs, the sky was a mystery even if he could have read and understood its glittering codes. He blundered on – climbing from his window had seemed inspired, he'd left home that way many times before now, skittering across the steep angle of tiles that led to the flat roof above the kitchen and then lowering himself down before dropping with a soft thud onto the grass below. It wasn't so different here, even if he'd had to negotiate a particularly pronounced drainpipe and had to suddenly latch on to a ledge like a cat that's missed its footing. His heart was pumping hard by the time he reached the neatly cut lawns, the edge of the woods rising up before him like a warning as he slipped among them as deftly as an actor disappearing among a stage's wings.

Though no matter how forthright his intentions – to get away – his momentum could hardly carry him forward if he couldn't see the path in front of him. Panic crept up his legs and curled around his thighs, slithering into his crotch and then deep into his stomach. He looked back for the lights of the schoolhouse, but all he saw were blacks and blues and purples layered in diagonals of fallen trees and the triangles of dense night that held them in place. His skin was slick with the humidity, but he imagined he could see his breath as the uneven, branch-strewn ground below him crackled and snapped with each footfall. He stopped running entirely when he almost collided with an oak that was wider than his father's car; he looked up at it, but knew he had no idea of seeing where it might end. He sat dramatically down as if someone were watching; the forest floor was slick and he raised his hands to cover his head and began to cry. The tears came in hard, jagged spurts, his shoulders shaking with some imagined sorrow.

Walker hadn't cried since his mother had died giving birth to his stillborn brother (did that still count as giving birth, he wondered?). Her weakened heart giving out under the pressure of a traumatic protracted labour. His father and their doctor had tried to talk her out of trying for another child, but she insisted that she didn't want Robert to grow up alone, as she had done. Walker imagined tiled walls and voices edgy with concern, the monitor slowing to a standstill, nothing left to bring its electronic beep to life. His father waiting for the inevitable cry that sounded someone, his son, being brought into being, but hearing only the silence, the snap of latex gloves, the low murmur of the indifferent machines. They buried them together, his stillborn sibling safe in his mother's arms where Walker longed to be. It was the start of the divide between Walker and his father that would become a chasm. The son blamed the father for failing to talk her out of trying for a second child; in turn, the father blamed his son's inability to thrive alone and therefore, by his actions, coerce his mother into trying to extend their family before ultimately snuffing it out. The only thing that could unite them, albeit briefly, was a family therapist who they both considered a complete idiot. 'I should bang your heads together,' he said once in a misguided and desperate attempt at levity. The room felt like it was filled with shadows. Walker's father cleared his throat. 'Try that and I'll put you through the window,' he said. It was the first time Robert had smiled in months.

Robert Walker got to his feet, imagining his father telling him to get the hell up; his sudden surge of anger pushed him forward once more. His pants were wet; his shoes struggled to find purchase on the mud and greasy bark underfoot. He stepped forward, his hands reaching out for a branch or trunk, and almost fell forward as he suddenly found himself standing in a ploughed field, the soft dirt reaching up to his ankles. The darkness was so unyielding and impenetrable as to be enigmatic; he closed his eyes and then quickly opened them again, his hands out before him like a blind man whose cane has suddenly been kicked away. Open and then closed and then opened again. The countryside was nondescript in its darkness, the quiet held him in place; he felt he should march on like his father would have done, but to where?

He closed his eyes once again and felt the yielding earth beneath his feet; he toyed with the idea of heading back to school and climbing back into his bedroom, but felt the ghosts of the forests and knew he couldn't go back that way again. He imagined dread behind every tree, the forest floor squirming with sudden life, alive in the mud the way he'd once seen ocean floors come to life on film, the sand stirred and the haunting jaws of some unseen creature snapping to life with the certainty of death at its lips. He opened his eyes the way one forces oneself awake from the clutches of a bad dream. He felt the cold air on his neck, loneliness overwhelming him. Then he saw the light in the distance, a mere speck of hope, but something to aim for. He felt stupidly idealistic and hopeless and far too young to be consumed by his own thoughts, he felt feckless and weak, his pale legs and arms were nothing he could rely on, suddenly he didn't even trust himself to reach the light. He fought against the misgivings, sucked hard on the cold air and put his shoulders down and marched, a solitary figure quickly lost to the darkness; if someone had been watching from a distance they might have wondered where the little boy had gone.

James Bulley was sitting on the perimeter of his father's compound, high in one of the two towers that had been erected either side of the gate. The place reminded him of the toy fort he used to play with when he was much younger, the idea of which made him happy. He was wrapped in an old blanket and seated on a rocking chair that had once belonged to his grandmother. It was quiet; his father had long since retired to the main house with one of his new wives, a teenage girl called Karen, not much older than Bulley himself, they'd been friends briefly, playing among the tents and trucks and trailers that covered the compound like a living, breathing maze.

Then she'd caught Blue's attention and he wasn't allowed to play with her anymore, he called her Miss Gable now and when she caught his eye they were polite like strangers are polite and blushed like they were covered in a mutual shame, as if they shared a terrible secret that was a burden to them both and if they should speak too often or spend too much time in the other's company then the façade would shatter and their fine web of lies would unravel and the terrible truth would out like spilled guts. They weren't to be trusted; more so, they were made to believe that they couldn't trust themselves.

Bulley was thinking about this and Karen and the soft sounds she made when she was in his father's room, sounds he couldn't comprehend, but that made him uneasy, he could feel the tops of his ears burning in shame, his face aflame as if he'd been dipped headfirst in sin, into the lake of fire, but he struggled uselessly when he tried to imagine why something going on beyond his father's wall could make him itch so uncontrollably. He distracted himself by playing with his father's unwieldy binoculars, which he'd hung around his neck as proudly as a general might display his medals, directing them across the expanse of black before him. The perimeter lights barely broke the unrelenting ridge of night, the soft edge of their powerful glare ballooned up on themselves, making little headway into the gloom, but sat impassively back, playing home to a myriad bugs and moths who bounced off the dense glass in a series of trembling arcs.

Robert Walker moved so silently and quickly out of the shadows that Bulley couldn't be sure that he hadn't been standing just out of sight in a shroud of darkness all the time that he'd been seated there. Walker was stock-still, his features magnified hugely in the binoculars; when Bulley let them drop he was surprised to see a boy there staring up at the wall. He looked like he was searching for a way in. He walked deliberately to the spot below where Bulley was seated before he spoke. Bulley would think back to that meeting later, when his world was literally over, just a heap of smouldering ashes, and wonder if that was the precise moment of his undoing, if he'd been the one who had really let the darkness in or had he just reached out across the divide and offered a hand, like his father had taught him?

'I'm lost,' said Walker.

Everyone here is, thought Bulley, glancing back behind him at the disjointed shadows and shards of light that made up his home and the commune. Music drifted up from one of the trucks, then someone called out and it was quiet again. He looked up towards his father's house, the top windows lit, and wondered why he was out here in the ever-cooling air, the uncomprehending and unquestioning guardian of his father's estate. Why was he the last thing that stood between his father's ambitions and the outside world? Perhaps, he thought, he's testing me?

Walker hadn't moved, his gaze was unwavering, he spoke again, his voice was softer, but with no less resolution.

'I've got nowhere to go,' he said.

Everyone's got somewhere to go, thought Bulley, as he heaved on a rope and pulled the high gate back, even if this tumbledown haven was it.

Walker's black school uniform made him look like a disembodied head against the night and he appeared to unfold and form as he stepped forward and into the light. By the time he crossed the threshold of the commune he was reborn, tall and reassured. He took a startled Bulley by the hand, shaking it firmly. And then said something that surprised him.

'You won't be sorry you did this.'

Walker was weaving between the cars, trucks and trailers and heading towards the house before Bulley had even finished securing the gate. Bulley chased after him, unknowingly caught up in his wake; from here on he would always be running to catch up.

# June 1980

Some days it came down to this: poorly stacked piles of papers and photographs. Gruesome details whittled down to their essence, the very bones, the real heart of the matter, literally, sometimes, Green thought grimly. Words can't hurt you, but these ones could and did: battery, intent to kill, bludgeoned, bloodstains, fractured, broken, disembodied, bloated, beaten, the victim's throat, head, arm, ribcage, all had met with their fate and fate had been clutching a broken bottle, a handgun, a carjack, a piece of wood that had fallen from the ceiling of a burnt-out building, and fate had come out swinging.

The photos were another freak show of life suddenly stilled, large black and white shots where the lack of colours did nothing to nullify the impact of the images. Sometimes Green would sit there and, though horrified, find himself marvelling at man's ability to somehow compartmentalise their guilt and remorse over their actions and kick a ballpoint pen through the wall of another man's ear and into his brain. He had talked to killers who crowed that they'd killed, jubilant at destroying two lives, one their own, but he wasn't sure they knew that then, no one thinks they're going to grow old, not least in a concrete cube that smells of your own shit and the sun on your face is a quickly fading memory.

Some cops wanted revenge on the killers, but Green tried – and often failed, truth be told – to feel compassion for the ones caught on the spiteful hooks of circumstance and bad luck, motivated by loose, jangling nerves, striking out too hard, finding the right and wrong kind of contact with a brick in your fist in that one brief and awful moment, desperate to come out on top. Winning the battle and losing everything, Green thought, most people were brutish and dumb at times, it was just the difference between kicking in your TV in a rage or going over a pool table with a cue clenched in your fist, whaling away. As a drunk, he'd not been above settling things the way men sometimes did, rolling into the street, the sudden, furious explosion of broken glass, a gasp, a grunt: resolving things.

Men, it was almost always men – the homicidal female was more imagined than realised, and then misplaced passion, deceit and fury usually played a part; he'd seen a lover run down with their own car, a boyfriend pushed through a glass door, his top lip and nose flayed into something incomprehensible and irreparable; another time, a pan of hot oil hoisted from the stove to sear the skin off one man's face – he remembered the young woman's testimony, calm and removed, consumed by quiet shock that she'd destroyed someone's features, someone she once loved, someone whose face she'd once kissed, all in one enraged moment. At least, thought Green, telling himself lies as he sometimes did when he couldn't fully face himself, I only tried to destroy myself, which wasn't true, he'd been a portrait of unresolved anger many times, swinging wildly at strangers who often swung as wildly back. There was no self-preservation in Green then, he wanted to hurt them almost as much as he wanted to hurt himself. He didn't think that was the case with this female killer who'd taken her husband's face and life away, she'd lashed out in fear with the only thing to hand. She'd been frying food when the fight had developed, the husband had grabbed the back of her neck as they stood there screaming at the other, faces etched red with anger, and instinctively she'd grabbed the pan, let fly, and the hot oil washed his features away as surely and swiftly as a wave takes away an initialled heart carved in sand on the beach.

Green's bloody reverie was halted by another thick folder of documents landing heavily on his desk; he pulled a face as one tower of paper cascaded slowly forward and obscured the file he was poring over.

'Sir, sorry,' said the uniform standing over his desk.

'At least you didn't get my coffee,' said Green; he was doing his best to be genial, but his features remained fixed, the unblinking eyes, the tightening lips, the jaw held in a way that suggested he was about to bite. The man in uniform took an involuntary half-step back, something he'd fret about later.

'This just came in, it's related to your case; the preacher, James Bulley.'

'He's got a record?' asked Green, even though he was certain he didn't, he'd chased those ghosts down. Still, his hand shot out across the table like a snake striking out at prey.

'His father,' said the uniform uncertainly. 'Manslaughter, arson, sex with a minor.'

Green's features had resolved themselves into a look of pure incredulity. He felt like he'd just seen a magic trick resolve itself in front of his very eyes.

'His father, what was he, America's most wanted?'

The uniform missed Green's hopeless stab at humour. His voice, he hoped, reflected the severity of the situation, sombre, staid, straight-talking, there was work to be done.

'He was a preacher, he had his own commune out of Tennessee,' said the uniform; he paused, he felt like he were performing. 'He burnt it down and shot someone on the way out, someone he worked with, his kid was there, he saw the whole thing, it's in his statement.'

'He fucking what?' said Green, the folder open before him on the desk. More photographs, but this time ones Green had never seen before, pictures of things destroyed, the burnt-out wreck of a house, trucks and cars, some still consumed by the flames, a perimeter fence covered with graffiti and now partially destroyed, burnt away in sections. Someone was twisted and smeared with soot and mud, but still dressed as if for church, his legs bunched, the top of his head gone, his jacket eaten away; it looked like he'd had oil tipped on him, a smear of black across both shoulders and lapels, like he'd been grabbed by someone who'd neglected to wash their hands before they'd gotten hold of him.

He looked at the uniform and indicated the broken figure in front of him.

'Jakub Kornfell,' said the uniform, peering over Green's shoulder. 'He headed up the commune with Blue, they were in business together, I guess.'

Jakub's wasn't the only body broken and pushed down into the earth, mangled, thought Green, actually mangled. He imagined the sky falling in on these people as they looked to the heavens, hands clasped in prayer and then hell opening up behind them. There was another unidentified body, a girl as charred as meat left too long on a barbecue; her features were coal, the skin on her legs an inky black. The main house, much like the commune, was just an idea now, an old memory of what a building might have been.

Green turned the page over and there was a headshot of Alexander 'Blue' Bulley; his eyes were as wild as the recently singed hair on his head. He looked as if he'd been blown into the sky and had survived, his features too were a cruel blackface, like a clown on the wrong end of an exploding cigar, he looked beaten, a man consumed by grief at the graveside and on the verge of tears. Then there in the inside pocket of the folder, in among the other evidence, was James Bulley. Green regarded some shots of the surrounding countryside, the strange towers that stood either side of the dismantled gate, and there in the corner of the photograph sat two teenage boys wrapped in blankets. He recognised the young James Bulley instantly, thick glasses now minus one lens, his hair, like his father's, high on his forehead, like it had been blown back by the explosion that had rocked the house to its foundations, his mouth an expressionless circle like he was still taking the whole apocalyptic mess in. Shock, thought Green, that kid should be in an ambulance, not wandering around a living, breathing horror story wrapped in nothing but a blanket. He flushed with anger and his eye was drawn to the kid next to Bulley, he'd almost edged out of the photo, taller, slight, adolescent yet already handsome, as if he were waiting for his body to catch up with his ambition. He wore his blanket as if it were a cape, set across his broad shoulders in perfect symmetry, and unlike Bulley he was meeting the lens of the camera head on, staring it down, defying its power to capture him. He didn't look appalled or cowed by the world blowing up around him, he looked calm and controlled like he might have been expecting it. Green looked at the list of witnesses for names.

'Who's that kid, the one in the corner of the picture?' he asked, handing the officer the print.

There was a moment then, the scratch of pen on paper, the incessant strike of typewriter keys, someone asked which interview room and someone laughed, a car backfired and the uniform flinched.

'I think,' said the uniform, bringing the picture close so that he might scrutinise it better, 'that's Robert Walker, it looks like Robert Walker.'

Green looked squarely at him; the name had bounced harmlessly off him and rolled into a corner.

'He was fucking that actress, sir, sorry, sir,' said the uniform. 'He's always in the papers, he owns half the Upper West Side, looks like a real creep. What would he have been doing out there?'

'What,' said Green, 'were any of them doing there?'

Green spread the pictures out before him and then lifted his empty coffee cup and shook it at the officer.

'Black, no sugar.'

# May 1961

They were driving through the Tennessee countryside in a Buick Roadmaster that Walker had taken from the jungle of cars and pick-up trucks that, along with bivouacked shacks and tents, covered the ground from the front porch of the house and out towards the commune's perimeter fence. A maze of dog-ravaged upholstery, broken rear-view mirrors, deflated tyres and mottled patches of rust were scattered across blue, red and black bodywork like patterns of eczema on skin. Children hid out and played among the high wheel arches of a flatbed truck, an old Chrysler was chipped and worn, a crow sat blinking on the car's left fin as if waiting for a ride. Wheels sat heavily in grassy earth that had turned to mud and then dried out again; they were locked into place.

Though that hadn't stopped Walker roaring off the compound in the Roadmaster. He'd persuaded Bulley to clamber up into the tower and open the gate and then raced out, idled as Bulley had jumped down and turned his ankle, and then shot off as Bulley clung to the passenger seat, one trailing leg hanging outside the still open door. There was only a year between them, but it was the precipitous divide between being a kid and a teenage boy; Walker was thirteen and ripe with confidence, his eyes weren't yet dead, but still flickered with longing, they made him inscrutable, one girl had told him he smouldered and he'd laughed in her face, he was only a boy and yet people were starting not to meet his gaze. Bulley adored him, he'd read about unconditional love and wondered if this was it.

Bulley's father was caught up in his new world, mistaking some parcelled-off land and a devoted following as the roots of an empire. Blue loved his son, but he was beyond him now, he was needed for the greater good, he had taken these people in, sheltered them from the storm, saved them in some way, so didn't that make him their saviour? And so James's father pored over his Bible and found meaningful parallels to his own life's journey, all the while surrounding himself with concubines and estranging his flock, a flock already alienated by an outside world that could find no place for them. Each night an unknowing Blue would add to his own pyre, laying imagined branches and boughs across metaphorical tinder, raising it higher and higher until he was so above everything that he couldn't smell the smoke let alone see the flames that were rising up to consume him.

Walker was gunning the engine of the Roadmaster, making the car drift in lazy circles on a piece of wasteland that they'd reached by driving through someone's crops, Walker idly flicking on the windscreen wipers as ears of corn rose up and rained down on their bonnet and roof; they made a hollow sound as they hit that reverberated through the car's interior. Bulley was both delighted and terrified by this turn of events. He felt his stomach lift and fall – and he wasn't sure if it was excitement or fear that kept tipping him over into tingling shock – as the car spun around making the panorama an uneven blur of hedges, dirt, fields and sky. A rattling spray of loose stones peppered the car wing and Bulley instantly worried about the paintjob.

'I don't even know whose car this is,' he said with something like wonder.

Walker gave him a sideways glance, his fist pushing down through the gears, his foot pumping hard on the accelerator. The back end of the car tried to race away then and Bulley thought they might tip sideways or pull off into the sky; the sound the engine made was startling, as if the cogs and the teeth of the machine were turning in on themselves, eating their own. Bulley realised that Walker was trying to destroy the car, or destroy them. He saw the bird-filled trees at the edge of the field and imagined all those eyes there trained on them, these two boys and this roaring car going nowhere endlessly, the sound of strained machinery funnelling up into the air.

'Who cares whose car it is?' asked Walker, pushing up through the gears again, his words almost lost to the whine of the engine. 'Isn't it your father who's always saying that we're unified, that we're a collective, a family with one shared goal?' He was sneering, but Bulley found himself nodding; it was what his father preached, absolutely.

'But you can drive,' said Bulley as the car straightened up violently, wavered a little and then pulled off sharply down a narrow road, the back end shuddering and then true.

'My old man has loads of cars, a garage full, and I know where he keeps the keys,' said Walker, his face an exercise in concentration, the tip of his tongue jutting out over the corner of his lower lip; it made him look impossibly young. Bulley couldn't help himself.

'But isn't it illegal to drive? You're not much older than me.'

'Your father,' said Walker, choosing to ignore the question completely, 'is a bit like mine; they both preach the same kind of self-serving bullshit.'

Bulley was appalled, but consumed by the idea; he needed to know more.

'My dad writes words and dialogue for the ages,' said Walker. 'Do you know what that means?'

Bulley, unsure, shook his head.

'That's what he calls it anyway,' Walker said as he took a corner at speed, mounting the bank and spinning the car's wheels; for a moment they lifted into the air and Bulley's stomach stayed there long after the car had crashed back down to earth. Some cows looked up from the next field over; there was no one else for miles.

'I heard him talking about it to his friends one night,' said Walker; he looked completely disgusted. 'A dialogue for the ages, what a prick. You know what he really is?'

Bulley did not, but he wasn't sure that Walker was even talking to him anymore.

'He's a fucking salesman. He thinks his gift is God-given, but all he does is take the lies he's made and puts them in the mouths of other men and then they feed those lies to other men, more powerful men, and then they tell those lies to the world, so the whole world believes these things my father has said, they take them as read, as gospel. He's like a virus; he's a disease.

'I've caught that disease now.' Walker looked furious, wild.

'But that's not what they call it, he's come up with a new name for it, he's given it a brand, a global brand, but it's a taint, it's just a stain.' Walker looked miserable. 'I've got my dad's stain, you've got yours, like this God your father keeps talking about – man is made in his image and we're made in their image, we are our father's sons, we carry their traits, their features, we're doomed to carry their sins.'

Their car, as if mirroring Walker's demeanour, was now going slowly out of control. Walker was crying, the weight of his father's world pushing him slowly down into his seat. Bulley was so scared that all he could do was stare hard out of the window and hope Death wouldn't come for him.

He sat petrified and waited for the inevitable pitch and crushing roll of the car as it came free of the earth's gravity and tumbled into the nearest field. He imagined cows scattering and hoped that they didn't hit anything, he didn't want to destroy a living thing; he didn't want to accrue any more sin.

But the final full stop to the violence of Walker's rhetoric was unexpected solace as the engine spluttered, the orange needle of the fuel gauge fell listlessly sideways towards the zero and the Roadmaster made a hiccuping sound, jolted a little and then rolled silently to a complete stop. Walker lifted his astonished hands off the wheel. The anger and violence had been sucked out of the air; they were suddenly in a vacuum that contained only goodwill.

'Where,' said Walker with a smile, surveying the empty fields that rolled endlessly away around them, 'the hell are we?'

In the school where his father had sent him, Walker had talked people around before now, he had a photographic memory and a mind that grabbed information the way a crane in a wrecker's yard gets hold of a crashed car before compacting it down into an unrecognisable block. He'd disseminate these squares of compacted information and dazzle classmates and teachers alike, but it was by rote, he had no affection for the information he passed on, no feelings either way really, he was merely conducting the energy that ran through the words and numbers, the innumerable facts that when made whole conveyed an illusion of great understanding and knowledge. For all Walker cared he could have been constructing flat-pack furniture. He was playing a part, amazing and entrancing his peers and masters like a sideshow hawker; he was a conjurer, an illusionist with one eye on the exit.

After he literally had left by the window that night, he did wonder briefly why the school had never come looking for him after he'd disappeared into the woods; he assumed they'd found him as worthless as he found himself, but the fact was that they had made a desperate call in order to trace him. They went back to the man who had placed him in their charge, Walker's father. To the surprise of the school principal, one Mr David Else (who wore an academic gown deliberately traced with streaks of white chalk that he fancied made him stand out as he paced the school's corridors), Walker's father appeared to be a man quite removed and completely unsurprised by this recent turn of events.

'Get away from you, did he?' said Walker's father distantly down the phone; he was far away both geographically and emotionally at that point.

Else was frantic, he pictured lawsuits, his school and career in ruin, and he'd rather come to admire the young, always eloquent Walker – he'd imagined great things for the boy and the school if only he could have turned him to their way of thinking.

'We'll find him, I assure you, boys have run away before, they never get far, there's nothing out here.' He tailed off.

Walker's father was impassive, silent; Else mistook his quiet for brooding anger and it made him shrill with panic, but he did his best to remain outwardly calm, like a spooked cat might suddenly start to clean itself. But Walker's father wasn't seething, he had merely stopped listening, he had business to attend to, he was talking to his secretary, his hand over the receiver, his indefinable, elongated scrawl signing a sheaf of papers.

'Mr Walker?' said Else for the third time.

'Let him go,' said Walker's father.

'I'm sorry …?' said the headmaster.

'Call off your dogs or whatever it is you hunt with down there. Bloodhounds and blunderbusses, I'd imagine.'

'I assure you we won't be hunting the boy down with hounds …'

Walker's father stopped him. 'I was being allegorical, playful,' he said, sounding anything but. 'You're absolved of all responsibility, let him run. He'll show up when he's ready.'

Else imagined a quiet ditch somewhere off the highway with the young boy's broken body lying tangled at the bottom, stones and dirt in his hair.

'But he's just a child …' said Else hopelessly. Walker's father cut across him.

'He stopped being a child the day his mother died.' Then with all the forced kindness in his voice he could muster: 'You've done all you can, Mr Else. He'll be okay. As for the rest of us, that remains to be seen.'

And with that Walker's father placed the receiver back into its cradle; he was, he was almost certain, expected in a meeting soon. It might be something important.

Come in low over the hills and glide across the fields for a moment, your shadow caught as a black cross upon the land below. There they are, Walker and Bulley, two boys seen from the sky, moving slowly, traversing a field, clambering over wooden gates. A raven hopping along a wall to the right, keeping pace with the pair as if listening to their conversation. The Roadmaster was behind them now, Walker had insisted that they leave the doors of the car open, he had an idea that a family of foxes or rabbits could make a home in there. He imagined the glove compartment stuffed with yellowing grass, a vole living there as a safe and sleeping ball, the innards of the seats a refuge for coexisting wildlife; he saw the car become embedded in and then a part of the landscape. Walker often thought of the world overrun by the wild, the earth taking the cities back and consuming them. Man's crippling footprint finally wiped clean, a new world teeming with life, nature taking her course. His father's empire choked by vines, tree roots breaking through his meeting rooms, his underground garage filled with earth, his glass towers pulled down and snuffed out.

'Do you believe him?' he asked Bulley, who was staring fearfully at the darkening sky. His father had always told him that he should live in the moment more, but he was forever regretting the past and the decisions he'd made, worrying over what was to come. Right now, he was petrified of the oncoming night and what it might contain.

'Do you think about ...' Walker's voice was level, almost compassionate as he began to very deliberately push the wedge down in between father and son, to slowly prise Bulley and his dad apart, so he might eventually stand between them and study their cracks and weaknesses, exploit the fissures in their skin and the fault lines in their make-up. He liked Bulley, but to undo Blue and his little empire he had to start unpicking the boy first.

'That girl your dad's fucking ...'

'His bride,' said Bulley, flinching slightly.

'His bride,' said Walker carefully. 'Weren't you and she friends once, before your father spotted her and thinned her out from the pack?'

Bulley nodded mutely; they had been friends and he still missed her. She cooked for her new family sometimes; the three of them would eat at the same table and he would redden when she passed nearby or spoke to him directly, or touched his arm. He sometimes thought she held his gaze for too long, as if she might still miss him too, but as his father had taught him, that was just sinful pride, no one was interested in a boy like him.

'There have been other brides, plenty of others too, right? I've seen them come and go,' said Walker.

'Do you know where we are?' said Bulley; he imagined evil over the far wall, trouble at the next gate.

'How many, would you say?' Walker persisted.

'Three, four, they overlap sometimes,' said Bulley.

'And what happens to them after they've ...' Walker looked to the air for the word he was searching for. 'Expired. Once they're past their sell-by date, once they walk out of that gate – do you know?'

'They leave, I guess,' said Bulley. 'I don't know, they leave the compound, one of them stayed with Jakub for a while, that drove my dad crazy, they argued a lot then, but she left too eventually. I don't know where to.'

'Eskimos push their old people out, did you know that?' said Walker. 'When they've passed their usefulness, when they've got nothing left to give anymore, they have to go.'

Bulley's eyes were wide. 'What happens to them?' He was profoundly shocked.

'They die,' said Walker, weighing the words. 'Exposure, I guess.'

'Exposure?' said Bulley uncomprehendingly.

'It depends on the circumstances – sometimes they were killed,' said Walker, 'thrown into the sea, buried alive, abandoned. There are stories of people being left in the wilderness, or that a whole village might steal away in the night and leave the person sleeping there. But mostly, I guess, they freeze to death; they've got nowhere to go, so they sit and they wait and the snow makes drifts around their bodies and they're covered, they simply disappear into and become part of that white world.'

Bulley stopped and wondered at people simply consumed by the snow, eaten up; he'd read about avalanches taking climbers and skiers away, but not people waiting there to be swallowed up by this beautiful, slow-moving death.

'What happens to them?' he said; he was blinking back tears.

Walker was almost cheery. 'The spring comes, there's the thaw, and the animals take them, the circle of life. There's not always room for everyone in this world.' He made a small circle with his finger in the air.

Bulley was dumbfounded; they walked in silence for a moment, but Walker wasn't done turning the screw, he was digging in deep, excavating so that he might reach the foundations of Blue's empire and rattle them loose.

'What's the story with Jakub and your dad?'

Bulley was confused – all these people lying dead out there in the snow, their limbs being torn apart, their bones breaking in the jaws of wolves, and Walker wanted to talk about Jakub.

'He helped my father set up the commune,' said Bulley. 'They literally built the place together, put up fences, closed the gate, erected the towers at the entrance. They were best friends from my father's parish back in the north. But now my father says that Jakub's sinned and Jakub says that my father's lost his way, that he's strayed too far from the path, that he can never come back again.'

In truth, Jakub and Blue were in a power struggle, not dissimilar to imagined wolves feasting on frozen Inuit in the glacial north; they were two alpha males locked in a fight for supremacy. The commune was generating a steady if relatively meagre income, but everyone was expected to contribute – money, goods, fuel – and it all went upwards to Blue, bypassing Jakub in the process. Blue had the biggest room in the main house, his pick of the young women that came through too, those who were keen to graduate from sleeping in their car or tent to a real bed with pillows. Jakub found himself more and more guilty of the cardinal sins: covetousness, lust, gluttony – he even entertained murderous thoughts, saw himself standing over Blue, the hammer in his hand raised again and again. Praise him, he thought among the imagined blood, the dream of splintered bones: thy Lord's will be done.

'Jakub wanted to keep the last girl after my father had finished with her, but dad wouldn't let him,' said Bulley uneasily; he didn't want to expose his father's behaviour, his business, but he wanted approval from Walker, he wanted to be liked. Bulley was shaking his head, he felt sick, sick that he had somehow betrayed the confidence of his father – at least he hadn't related the arguments he'd heard raging through the house at night when his father and Jakub would sit and drink and talk about the future of the world they'd built.

Bulley would listen – he had no choice – to the two of them through the wall. 'Look at our Eden, Adam and Steve!' And there'd be laughter, but soon there'd be fighting and shouting, chairs thrown, tables going over. Bulley would lie still and wait for the final, thudding retreat down the stairs, the full point to their conversation. The front door to the house would swing open and stay that way, inviting the sounds of their gated world in; there'd always be a radio playing, the call and response of voices, someone would be gunning an engine uselessly and then a dog would bark and then, eventually, there'd be a bark in return and then the compound would settle like those dogs had settled and the night would finally fall around them.

'We'll get back to the compound,' said Walker; it was as reassuring a tone as he could muster. He almost reached out and touched Bulley on the shoulder.

Bulley wasn't even sure he wanted to be in the compound anymore, but it was his sanctuary, no matter how unnerved he was, at least he almost always felt safe, even with his father roaming the halls or praying loudly in the next room, invoking his God. His father and his house were blessed and when he was there with his father it was truly how he felt.

'I've got an idea,' said Walker as if it had just occurred to him. 'When we get back, and we will get back, I think you should talk to Karen and tell her how you feel.'

Bulley's face became red and flushed with panic.

'Not that you're in love with her …'

'I'm not in love with her, I'm not!' Bulley could feel the panic liquefying his insides, pushing them around.

'I know you're not, buddy!' said Walker and this time he did lay a reassuring hand on Bulley's shoulder and he drew him closer. He lowered his voice as if he were sharing a confidence.

'I think you should tell her how you feel, all that discomfort, the unhappiness, why you're shy around her. I bet she's shy too, you're both in the same bad way; she feels guilty that you can't be friends anymore too. And you were so close, right?'

Bulley nodded dumbly. He'd already forgotten about the light racing out of the sky. He couldn't see the darkness now even though it was standing right next to him, waiting to cover him up, like the ever-expanding, blinding whiteness of the snow that had once taken Inuit elders away. Bulley was staring into the void, and he didn't even know it, one step away from the eternal blackness. Walker looked at him the way you might look at someone that you're about to kiss for the first time, expectant, a mixture of longing and want, fear and trepidation.

Then the truck broke through the moment, its headlights piercing the dusk, an explosion of light in the gloom. The driver was leaning out of the window; they both recognised him from the compound.

'There you are, your father's about going crazy.'

They'd been rescued, his father had been worried about them, Bulley brightened; he felt himself bristle, get taller somehow. Then the familiar pull of dismay: the strong down-current that suddenly pulled his kite from the sky and crashed it into the side of a hill.

'He wants to know what the hell happened to his Roadmaster.'

And Bulley could only point to the long stretches of greens and blacks that now made up the fields behind him, the car too was in the past now.

# June 1980

Detective Green sat back, the spread of papers before him, drawing a mental line from a fire in the Tennessee countryside to a SoHo basement and the near-impossible reaches of the Upper West Side. People moved to the city all the time, he was a case in point; Californian kid, sunburnt shoulders, bleached hair, someone who had become as grey as the bricks of the buildings that surrounded him. But this felt like Walker and Bulley were fleeing from something, racing away as far as they could until the land ran out from under their feet. Blue was long gone, he'd died in prison, his voice was silenced forever, but the records showed that he'd killed a man, his best friend, torched his own compound, blown his world to pieces. Green understood that fleeting madness, that self-destructive streak, but what he didn't understand was why. But he did know where to find Bulley, and Walker was uptown somewhere, a very public tyrant in some glass tower. Green felt like a rope ladder had suddenly dropped out of the sky inviting him to pull himself, twisting and swaying, up towards the light.

# Summer Solstice 1980

*My name is Rose Henley and I didn't mean to die then, I was only twenty-five.*

*Look at all these people, they've no direction; they feel a sense of togetherness as they move forward, unified as a group, but that's not belonging. I found out how to belong, I found a place to be.*

*My father wanted only one thing, the one thing I wasn't: a son. He dressed me in boy's clothes in the hope that I would grow into them as a man. As he lay dying in the hospital he tried to tell me he was sorry, but I didn't want his apology, I wanted his love. I caught the footballs, basketballs and baseballs he threw for me, I chased with him through the fields, I fell from trees we climbed and as I lay there gasping in the long grass of those years – I'd catch his expression as he happened upon me lying there, taking me in from my Converse sneakers up, the disappointment in his eyes as he reached my soft hands and my thin forearms, my girlish wrists, my pretty face; my features did nothing short of devastate him.*

*Look at Detective Green there among the smoking ruins of my things. Me trying to bring life to bricks and mortar and to will that warehouse to live, only to meet my fate among the broken pieces of a thing that could not be. Green breaks his own rules briefly and touches my hair as it frames my face to reveal the bruising there, the mark that is partly the broken blood vessels beneath my skin and partly the black soot that covered the piece of wood I was beaten to death with.*

*Green is as furious as he is handsome as he bends down to stare into my mute face; there is a recklessness to him that he pushes deep inside so that it won't unbalance his thinking, so that he might always see clearly, so that he always gets his man. He wears his unsolved cases like rags; failing to solve a crime is a stain on his skin, another new tattoo of disappointment.*

*Look at Green there now: it's late at night and he's seated alone in his office, old files piled up on his desk, investigations that became dead ends; he* stares at the words, the reports, the testimony of witnesses, the pictures of a crime scene. A body pulled from a suitcase, shrunken and squared; the girl at the side of the road, her shirt and skirt torn, a leg splayed, an arm reaching out as if she's still falling. Poor Henry Willow, who was mine for a while, caught up in a tree, twisted and broken, bones piercing his skin, as if his insides wanted out, and there's my case file and there I am in the shadows, the pale light making me look monochrome. Green runs his thumb along the photograph and for a moment I imagine his hand against my skin once more before the bag envelops my body, the long zipper closing tight to bargain me away from that life to whatever this is.

I met Green once; I touched him on the wrist as I was handing out flyers on a street corner to bring people into our church. I felt the warmth in him, the warmth he didn't see in himself. He was riven with pain; it crackled through him, the anger and sadness was his misplaced life force. His face was kind though, his thin smile always questioning; he didn't want me to see him throw the flyer away, he had goodness to him mired in all that rage, but it was never allowed to surface. There we were, briefly, on that corner, I wanted to stop and talk to him, but he was forever pushing on, he couldn't be stopped. The next time he saw me I was as cold and unmoving as stone, another body found somewhere off the highway. I wish he'd recognised me, but his gaze never lingered long enough, shifting, focusing and refocusing, trying to figure out what might have left me for dead there. Death sent him racing through life, harried him on, running ever faster, black dogs nipping at his heels.

Green was briefly a father; he calls that year of his life the great crash, not that he ever talks about it to anyone anymore. He was married, a new father who understood his father differently then, but after his baby had died, mysteriously and mutely one winter night, he couldn't ever get past the surprise that you go on living long after the thing you truly loved has died, that the child in the ground didn't reach up and pull you down; he'd have gone happily into that disturbed earth if asked. He found the shock to his system unrelenting, it rang out like a bell, disquieting him each time he *thought the air had finally stilled. Life had changed in an instant, shattered into so many tiny pieces that it wasn't even visible to the naked eye anymore.*

*So he moved on as best he could, pushing hard against life, but he knew when to pause; he knew when to reach out and stop someone falling. Look at him cradling Rudy Porter in his arms, his tears running into Porter's hair, imagining the polar bear sitting alone out on the tundra of ice, a blizzard picking up, the spray of freezing water matting on his skin. Death looming across from them both, the grotesque figure of Porter's wife trapped in the limbo of her husband's longing. Porter's trembling form bent grotesquely by grief. For a moment it makes Green think of his wife and the family he once had, he wonders where they both are now, but he know what he must do and so Green is holding Rudy up, holding him together, holding on and holding on and holding on.*

*Green wants to unpick the evil that's caught around the threads of hope that knit together to make up his world. His father tells him he should move away from the city, take himself out of that life and let it go. But each time Green sees a man like Henry Willow star-shaped and strung up in a tree, or Alejandro stuck hard to the earth, or Billy broken and bloody, he resolves to make things better, but he doesn't know how; he wants to stamp hard on evil and break its neck, but there's so much wrong, it's so unrelenting. He touches the nape of Alejandro's neck, looking for where the life might have left him, and just then, like every blood-smeared scene he's attended in these last few years, he embraces the horror, pulls it into his chest, inside of him, and makes it a part of his being. Men once ate sins from the souls of others and that's Green, he wants to consume the darkness in the world and carry it until he can bury it or send it into the stars; that kind of thinking wasn't so far from a world that Walker envisaged, but both he and Green were forever marked by the things they'd seen and the things they'd done and had done to them. But whereas Walker was happy to walk on and into the darkness, Green is forever pulling the other way. He wants the light to bleach the shadows, cleanse the spirit, to save us all. And in that way, he and I weren't so different.*

*A man can unravel quickly. With his son dead, Green turned his back on his wife and, without knowing what he was doing or why, he stepped off into the black of his self-imposed oblivion and he kept falling, never reaching out to halt his descent or ask for help or to be saved. As time went on, instead of stepping back from work, he pulled longer shifts, stayed when he should have left, he stood over the body of strangers at crime scenes and cried while his men looked away and pretended not to hear his sobbing, he turned up once unannounced where they'd found an old woman who had bled out near an alleyway just feet from a busy street and he drunkenly fell through the yellow tape that was partitioning off the scene. An officer he didn't know caught him and told him to pull himself the fuck together. But still Green went on falling, scattering evidence with his feet; collapsing and tripping into strangers who were stretching their necks to see the bloody scenes unfolding just out of sight; suddenly Green was becoming the scene. By the time he'd stopped falling, his wife was gone and he was finally alone again, crumpled and bunched up from the impact. He'd gone from years spent in indifferent solitude to real love and then lost it all again. Just as he'd found that love was all and had finally tried to embrace it, circumstance and the vagaries of chance tipped his hand and in losing love he had lost everything.*

*Imagine a reel with all the cotton unwound, a thicket of knots, impossibly and accidentally complex; now imagine finding the end of one fine strand and slowly and delicately unpicking it for days and weeks until the straight line of fabric made sense again and could finally be rewound until it sat around the tiny wooden drum, a small bow holding it precariously in place. That's how he felt in those months: unspooled, a literal loose end, and then one day he was secured again and, he thought, safe.*

*Green's standing in my apartment, surrounded by my old things, his disdain for my plastic Jesus is palpable; he's wrinkling his nose, his hands pressed down on my dresser. He's holding a photo of me, I'm a child, there are birds in the trees and a bleached-out sky behind me, I can hear their call, then my father's voice telling me to look up, to hold my chin up, to stare into the lens, and I'm held there, the wind picking up behind me, the click of the camera's shutter, a murder of crows taking to the air. I am there and then I am not, but in that moment I am forever there and my father is there and Green is a* part of our world. He holds my photo up as if to get a better look, then he sighs as he replaces it gently on the dresser.

Though Detective Green loved his family, when he thinks back and tries to pull the memories together and make sense of them somehow, he can only wonder at what it was he thought he should have felt, but he was always wanting, he has a God-shaped hole and will never know it, that's the kind of thing I would have tried to tell him with a flyer in my hand, and he would have laughed at me. For a moment, when his baby had died, and his home was a box of shadows, he'd take himself drinking with men just like him, people who neither knew or cared about the other. Stilled collectively in their quiet solidarity, the mute understanding that they'd failed in different ways, burnt a final bridge, or reached the irrefutable point of letting go, they were beyond the physical now; the act of doing. So they drifted, but ever downwards, dead leaves dreaming of the power of flight again, but they were merely falling, landing gently in places like those bars where the voices were low in the gloom. Strangers who didn't want to see anymore, especially the past, and the future was never again going to be the promise of hope the young men in them might have once imagined. Green would walk home from those bars and wonder how and why happiness had deserted him and why he never thought that might happen, that perhaps he could have prepared for it in some way. But who can prepare for the darkness when they're standing in the light? Who can be ready for the end when they feel like they've barely begun? Green would kneel at his bedside as if ready for prayer and lay his head on the bed and cry until he convulsed and the crying wore him into a fitful, troubled sleep. The morning was a release from the ongoing night and a reminder of the pain he was in, it was like an elbow in the ribs each time he opened his eyes, gasping as he came up for air; suddenly, home was a place to escape from not somewhere to be.


The men in my life were really no different from each other, though they'd balk to hear that, male ego is such a funny thing, they all wanted salvation, they all wanted to be saved. Even Henry, Henry and his small swell of belly and the expanding crown of skull that shone out among the thinning hair at the back of his head. He'd self-consciously reach for it sometimes as if the wind were threatening to blow some imagined hat from his head. Maybe it was a generational thing? My father had no time for vanity as far as I could see, though that might have been different in his younger years, he was tall, broad-shouldered, thick through his chest, his hair settled into something approaching a pompadour, if you saw a photo of him from back then you'd think him handsome, that isn't his daughter talking, it's the way it and he was. There was a photo in the hallway of our house that was quietly put away on the day after my mother died. I'd later find it among my father's things, he looks strong, my mother pressed up against him. Her arm wrapped around him, he's looking into the distance, but his eyes, even in black and white, are brimming with happiness and contentment, my mother's smile is impossibly bright, I wish I'd grown up seeing that in her, in them both. Both their faces set in unremitting joy.

But I was telling you about Henry, he didn't and wouldn't, I'm not sure he could, face up to his ageing self. He'd stand there in front of my mirror, reflected in profile, tufts of hair rising like small plumes of smoke from both shoulders; he went in at the ass and out at the belly, and he'd make a face as he saw himself, sucking it in like a man taking his last breath before going into the water and he'd talk about running and hitting the gym as these loose concepts, that if you talked about them enough then they could transform your life, your shape, your wellbeing, that they could slow down life, allow you to say stop somehow and have the universe listen. This most outwardly self-assured of men, who went in for kisses too early, who touched too soon, came too fast, was already withered by age, but only in his head, his mind was filled with the dread of growing old. He'd talk about the onset of dementia, worry his bald spot until it enlarged and all the while not understand how so like a little boy he sounded.

Alejandro too, brimming with goodness and longing, a pure soul; the light shone out of him. So very far from Henry, but I never wanted to take beautiful Alejandro to my bed. I needed to be pushed, to be made to be free to let go, the insistence, Henry's persistence, I might have needed to be kissed too hard, to get past my guilt at giving in and I wanted to give in. I tried to save Alejandro and I failed; part of me drove him to that roof, I compounded his loneliness, made him want to be back among his friends at

*home more. Our group unnerved him, we scared him, I think, I know that
now, he mistook our ardour for something else. Bulley was so stained with
sin that he wanted to cleanse everyone and everything, to drive the evil out,
not least the guilt that consumed him, he was bloody like Lady Macbeth's
hands were bloody, but Walker was the hellhound that brought him down;
Bulley looked haunted because he was. Alejandro was lost before he ever
washed up on our shores, his journey across the country, hidden among the
network of rail lines, a solitary figure hitching at the side of the road, terrified
that every stranger could be death or the thing that would send him spiralling
back home. When he was finally thrown into the air and to his doom, arms
and legs paddling, trying to find some current to kick against, he thought
of his friend Guilhermo and his mother's house, her standing there in the
door, hands out, palms up, beseeching him, calling him back. They took
the parts of him back across the border in an aluminium casket so that his
family might grieve over him and wonder at the little boy they'd let out of
their sight, who had solemnly waved goodbye, told them not to worry, that
everything would be okay, and then had returned in pieces, literally shattered,
the life impacted out of him.*

*And Billy, who was nothing to me and yet everything to Walker; all
those imaginary monsters of jealousy he'd created in his own head became
Billy's very real nightmares. I can still hear his cries, his tears of confusion
as he was dragged along that terrifying path to his bleak fate. I knew that
Walker and his men had started following me around town, I'd see that
black car of his or him stepping in and out of the shadows across from our
church, a familiar profile glimpsed near a streetlight. Sometimes I'd think I
was imagining things, but then I'd recognise his driver or see him slip past
a restaurant window, his collar up. I almost pitied him then, called out his
name, invited him in to find out what was going on inside of him, but I've
learnt since then that not even he was in control of the things running around
inside his head. He subjugated the powerless and those weaker than him and
then he grieved over the things he'd said and done and he had done so many
terrible things. He made an art out of torture, of manipulation, all the while
feeling bad about it; he was one bloody paradox after another.*

*Walker, who can't help but keep returning again and again to the Tennessee countryside in order to find his true self, thinking that the real person within was made there and when he lost himself there he lost everything and forever. What Walker doesn't know is that he was marked from the day he was born and, no matter how cruel or calculating his actions, in a way he was only ever being true to himself.*

One day, and soon, Green will meet with Bulley and he'll learn the truth about everything. Dear, damaged Bulley mired in sin and grief, his whole life coloured by the fire that took his world away. Now he stands watching everything smoulder and crackle, people combusting before his very eyes, his anguish is endless, he carries his sins around with him, his life always stained by Walker, forever doomed to walk in his shadow. How Walker took the commune, his family and his home away, how Bulley's life was irrevocably changed that spring night, the glass shattering, everything splintering, now when he closes his eyes, he sees her face beneath him, the spirit running out of her as he does all he can to tether her to this life, to keep her in the light, and every time he thinks about her now all he can see is the darkness surrounding them until it swallows her up and she's out of sight.

And there's Walker, consumed by his own power absolutely. Dear Walker, I saw the boy in him, the young man he was before he waded into the lake of blood and chose to go ever onwards; I can hear his words now, echoing forever, the final moment when even his own father was in his way and rather than let the old man die a solitary death in the feeble glow of the machines that kept his heart beating, he used his power to take another life away, to snuff the old man out. Walker couldn't see the blood on his hands, but it was dense and dark and ruddy, two crimson gloves that were forever a part of the man. The hands he wanted to touch me with – at one point he thought that I might save him, but how can you save something so lost, who's even abandoned themselves?

Walker now, consumed by Green and the idea that he and I were somehow linked together, that we'd colluded against him, that we were put here to break his heart, to be his ultimate test when we were only ever starcrossed. Hell, we weren't even that. I loved Green – let me qualify that, I *loved the idea of Green. He was what I was looking for when I moved to New York; I had my faith, but I believed in the idea of a man like him, flawed yet pure somehow, but it was all too late, by then I'd met Walker, or he me. I sometimes felt that Walker might have sought me out, given how knowing he was later on, but that instant when I first met him in the park, that might have been his last moment of real introspection, of any real peace, and by then Detective Green was on another path entirely, he had staked out his own ground, his own fallow acre. As lonely a patch of earth as Walker had made for himself, two men entwined by fate, my fate, both their heads filled with noise, their eyes long dead. And they both chose to inhabit scrubland, the barren places that made up their hearts; the ground they stalked was long arid and dead. Nothing grew there because both men chose to let nothing flourish, it was better for them to keep the dirt tamped down because that way there was nothing for them to ever tend to again.*

*What Green does not know, but will know one day, and will be changed forever by it, is that Robert Walker is coming for him because he thinks that Green might be the only one who understands him, maybe even respects him. And even though he won't admit it to himself, Walker respects Green, but like everything that Walker admires it makes him wary and uneasy, it makes him want to destroy it. And as for Green, people will always want his help, for him to be their salvation, and Green will always give the best of himself, but by helping this time he will have to give everything and how much of that he ever gets back remains to be seen.*

# July 1980

James Bulley carried his sins around in a sack that he kept on his back. Imagine an unwieldy and deep bag filled to the brim with oily, black water seeping through the canvas material but somehow never losing any of its volume; its depths were endless, sloshing around each time you tried to secure it, each time you tried to make it settle across your back, the contents unstable, uncertain; try to tie it together and the weight shifted, the shape became lopsided, the centre would not hold. Each night Bulley laid the bag gently down next to his bed, praying it would not tip because then he'd lose the contents and they'd seep away and then where would he be? He'd have no duties, no penance to pay, there was no way he could ever square things away with his God if he couldn't even hold on to the sins he'd been given to carry. So each morning he would wake and the sack would be sitting there regarding him, immutable and forever; it seemed to shift around at will, stable yet fluid, malleable, distended, then a slight judder, like a disinterested shrug of the shoulders; when light shone into the sack – and Bulley had taken a flashlight to the contents many times the way a boy might struggle to read the pages of his comic book in the tent made of his bed sheets – it looked like dirty gelatine shot through with dust and detritus; he looked in there sometimes and thought he heard voices, the hollow echo of loss, saw features moving around, eyes staring back. He'd wake and dress and hoist the complaining bundle onto his back and he would walk through the streets of the city to his SoHo basement and he would sigh as he settled his load down and wonder when the final appeasement might come to free him from the endless weight of the guilt that he was forced to carry around. He wondered if Green could sense the sack sitting there between them, moving unevenly. Bulley didn't so much dislike Green as he was terrified of him; Green reminded him of Walker in a way, strong, resolute, someone who enjoyed violence for its own visceral charge. Did he enjoy it, thought Bulley, the power he held over people?

'I read the report, your story,' said Green, 'about the things that happened to you.' And then with a genuine softness in his voice,

'I'm sorry about your old man. My dad preaches too, you know?' Green thought privately that his father never felt the need to torch his congregation; he lit them up in a different way entirely.

'What can you remember about that day – is there anything that comes back to you?'

Bulley's insides constricted, he saw falling timber, he heard the screams; he saw Jakub explode mutely, the white noise filling his head. The bag of sins vibrated against his calf, the black water sloshed around, some of it fell to the floor and covered his shoes. He glanced down at Green's brogues; they were bone-dry.

'It's all in the records,' said Bulley, the cloying taste of brimstone filling his mouth, the poisonous stink of burning hair, the way it clung to him still all these years later. He'd stop on the street sometimes, at an intersection, and he'd see people in flames still going about their day, orange and red at their elbows, their hands glowing like fiery gloves, toothy smiles of welcoming recognition breaking through a mask of fire. His father had always told him that man was doomed, that we were all slowly descending into Hell and as we got closer and closer and the flames got hotter then the body would slowly burn, spark and eventually be consumed by the everlasting fire. We're all so many candles, his father would say, making it into a mantra, all waiting to ignite. Blue preached that all mankind had committed original sin and so we were all burning from the day we were born, slow-moving embers sliding uncertainly down to our fate. And it was true, thought Bulley, the more a man sinned, the more he saw the flames surrounding him. Some were listing pyres, others hurried on with a faint trace of smoke at the elbows of their jacket, the cuffs of their shirts rimmed with flames as if their cufflinks were immolating. Bulley once saw someone on the subway whose collar and hair were starting to burn and reached out as if to put out the flames, his hand frozen in space as the stranger caught sight of what he was doing and stopped him with a stare.

He couldn't imagine anyone touching Green; the detective was staring at him, his flesh was crackling with a fine film of blue flame as if he were being slowly seared; he was consumed, but looked almost comfortable in his furious, flaming skin. Bulley could almost smell the gasoline burn.

'Did you know what your father had planned?' asked Green. He had his notebook set out on his knee now; he was all work even as his skin burned feverishly, marvelled Bulley.

'Did you know he was going to destroy the commune? Do you know why he destroyed it?'

Bulley looked worn, he looked like he'd been washed up on a shore somewhere, lungs filled with water, his skin grey like the submerged stones he might have been buffeted up against. His trouser leg was damp from the sins washing up around him, the bag was tipping against his leg now, his shoe filling up with black water, his sock sodden; his laces wet.

'He was only trying to save me,' said Bulley uncertainly.

'Your father?' said Green, his voice was almost warm, calm, designed to engage. 'You could have died in that fire, James.'

Green tried to imagine the young boy sitting there among the upturned furniture and boxes as his father went to work dousing it all in gasoline, the smell all-consuming, the air riven with fear and trepidation. Then Blue standing back to survey his work, the flaming bundle of rags in his hand suddenly cast into the air, the remnants falling to ignite an unimaginable trail of destruction marked out in torched cars, burnt trucks, everything razed to the ground, lives and a home reduced to a black mark on the earth. Let the fire cleanse, rejoice, Green heard Blue say, his words defiant, triumphant.

'It wasn't like that,' said Bulley, his eyes pleading like an admonished dog's. It was still then; daylight never reached Bulley's basement office – what light there was came from an overhead neon tube that buzzed intermittently as if a fly were caught inside the fitting. It flickered out and then into life, the shadows only deepening Bulley's distraught features. To a stranger, Green might have looked like he were made of stone.

'All my father wanted to do,' said Bulley, 'was save me. And to do that he gave up everything.' His voice was stilting, small. He was lost, standing among the burning ruins of his past, the soot and shame caking his clothes, death clung to his hair, Jakub dead at his feet, unrecognisable in the way that dead bodies can be, not just his now molten features, but his limbs looked wrong somehow, one of his shoes was off, he looked unkempt, thought Bulley, the world still ringing inside his skull, his father screaming at the sky, praying that it would fall down around his ears.

Bulley looked at Green, who was looking back hard at him, trying to see in.

'I'll tell you what happened,' said Bulley, and looked beyond the low ceiling as the heavens wailed.

# June 1961

There are moments by which we are forever defined and this was his. Bulley had spent the last few weeks working up the courage to speak to Karen. Walker sat at his shoulder, assuming the voice of reason while all the while pouring poison into his friend's ear.

'She's clearly too young for him, how can she be happy? What's in this for her?'

'She needs friends now more than ever.'

'I've seen the way she looks at you, how could you not have noticed that? There's a connection there.'

Drip, drip, drip ... the sound of an endless noxious rain that wouldn't stop falling.

'Your dad casts his net wide, you know? I've watched him work a room, he's always on to the next thing.'

'He'll be looking out for someone else new soon and where will Karen be then?'

Drip, drip, drip ... Bulley looked wild.

'But he'll send her away! She'll be gone forever!'

Walker sat there, a demon of sadness; his mouth was as close to Bulley's ear as a lover's might be. He emptied the last drops of the vial of poison into Bulley's head.

'That's right, she'll be gone forever, buddy, forever; you need her, she needs you, but once she's gone, what then? That gate will close behind her and it's over. How many of your dad's wives have ever come back once they leave, huh?'

None, thought Bulley, none of them ever came back. With each step they took outside of the gates they became less somehow; they merged and faded into the landscape, disappeared into the air, some were gone before they'd even reached the horizon or the thicket of trees.

'Grasp the nettle!' said Walker; he'd actually lost his glacial composure for once, he was only goading the young Bulley on, he was his accomplice now, they were readying themselves for battle, or that was how Walker saw it, they were in this together and someone had to lead the charge.

'Seize the day,' he said quietly, surprised to find his hand holding Bulley's wrist, raising his hand above his head as if signalling that their war had already begun.

Love takes many guises, some of them imagined; Bulley's was made from impossible dreams that were then coerced, buckled, bent and – with the help of his friend – rendered into an unrealistic future. To even call it unrealised was to give it some standing or weight that it had never had or would have.

In her own way, Karen loved Blue, not that she'd ever wanted to be part of his sprawling family; she was just another runaway that had landed here in his compound. Like Walker, she'd stumbled upon the light of the compound one night and had been shown some rare kindness, had been let in, but unlike Walker she had learnt to love their God and embrace him as her own. She'd spent a lifetime adapting and surviving and this was more of the same, that's how she saw it. She'd been as surprised as anyone the day that Blue had spoken to her after service and had left his hand on hers as they talked, detailing her spiritual awakening, her growth, her place within his church. Soon they were talking long walks together outside of the compound as he spoke of his love of the place, how he wanted to expand and build, ultimately construct a city built on faith and love – imagine a utopia with only God at its heart, he'd say – and he would hold her hand a little tighter, as the passion flared up inside him, he'd rise onto the balls of his feet, some days she thought he might float blissfully away. She knew a pipe dream when she heard one, but to look into his face as he spoke was to know that he truly believed it, that he spoke the truth, or his version of it. Blue saw a sanctuary for him and his followers, somewhere they could all be sheltered from the outside world, safe from the wolves and enemies that haunted his dreams. She liked it that he believed in something, even if it was only himself; she'd been waiting a long time to see or feel that.

She'd seen girls come and go through the compound and Blue's life, girls mired in grief or lust or both, who came scratching at his door; she heard voices outside of their window some nights, but they drifted eventually. She'd ask Blue about the ones who had gone before her sometimes and he'd tell her that the wind or the current had carried them away and then he'd quiet her with a kiss or wave her away as he pored over his work, a sermon or a dense ledger anointed with scrawled figures that he and Jakub would study as assiduously as they did their holy book. She thought they were a family, the shy, awkward boy she'd befriended when she first came here, little knowing that James Bulley would eventually lead her to Blue. James had reignited the girl in her, the youthful exuberance that had been snuffed out; she found it again among the car wrecks they ran through in the land surrounding the compound. She and James would sit atop an abandoned truck and watch distant planes describe oily arcs of fuel in thinning streaks smearing the sky. She was happy in that role, but astute enough to know when she had to evolve and play the part of the boy's mother too, cook their meals, go to Blue's bed. It was an assimilation of family, she understood that, though it was more family than she'd ever had before and even if it was a facsimile of what a family might be, it was still a part she was grateful for and happy to play. She knew its impermanence, but doesn't every drowning man cling to the brief respite that is the passing piece of wood even though he knows the inevitable pull of the ocean floor awaits him? The roar of hope fills all our heads. We will all somehow beat the inevitable, transcend and be free; Blue will stop looking around him for the next thing, for someone new to sate his desires, he will settle, the moment will stay and expand and stretch into the future. Permanence was something Karen could only imagine and aspire to, though her dream that she would be Blue's last wife was about to come true.

Karen was surprised to see James Bulley at their bedroom door. He looked more fitful than usual, more nuanced fear; clasped hands, fretful, darting eyes. She worried about him, he had grown in stature since Walker had arrived, even if he did follow his new friend around so dutifully, his was a subdued happiness, but she was glad he'd met someone. Blue had exploded when Bulley and Walker had driven one of the cars off the compound and ridden it into the countryside until they'd run out of fuel, but she'd found the naïveté of pushing the car on until the tank emptied endearing, as if neither boy understood the mechanism of the machine they'd taken; they literally didn't know what made it tick. How could she ever understand that Walker was ready to push that car into a wall or over a precipice, had he found one? That he would have happily raced through a field of cattle just to feel the pain he caused, the tortured misunderstanding; the elongated fear. And now he was set to rev the engine into the red and drive it hard through her new family as deftly as if he'd caught them out on a lone road late at night with nowhere to run and with no witnesses. He was bearing down on the three of them, lights flooding the darkness, horns blaring.

'James,' she said, patting the bed next to her, 'what's wrong?'

Walker had told him not to lunge, girls hated that shit, and so, with his insides a tangle of unhappiness and dread, Bulley stepped slowly forward. He wanted his father to come through the door then, slap him warmly on the back and ask him what the hell he was up to and in doing so unknowingly save him, but there was no one here, just him and her.

'James?' She was worried about him, he looked pale and, fearing he was coming down with something, she reached out and placed a hand on his forehead to check his temperature and Bulley, who had waited for her touch since she'd first come to the compound, since she'd first said hello to him, misread what she was doing and, disregarding completely what his new best friend had told him not to do, reached out for Karen and in that moment he pushed them to the edge, causing them both to fall forever into a well of darkness from which neither could ever return. He'd never kissed anyone before, he'd made tentative approaches to his pillow when he was alone, he'd regarded his rubbery features (as he saw them) in the mirror sometimes and pursed his lips in an approximation of a kiss and then he'd regard his tongue like it was a stranger, a foreign body he'd suddenly discovered in his mouth.

His father often talked about throwing himself into things, to be in the moment, and so he did, literally leading with his head so that their skulls almost collided as Karen, now fully aware of his intentions, her thoughts flashing back to the unwanted fumblings of her teenage years, drew sharply back and his insistent forehead struck her on the shoulder, causing her to flinch and Bulley to cry out. They sprang back like two diners who had just discovered a finger in their food; it took Bulley a full second before he thought to open his eyes. Karen was standing by the picture window that looked out over the compound, she was composed, she didn't want to alarm the boy, but she was searching desperately for Blue. The night was still now beyond the glass, unmoving and featureless, though below it the compound grounds were lit up like a party; she briefly found herself wondering if Blue were out there dancing with someone new, his hand set on the small of some stranger's back. He'd told her that to think like that was a sin, but she lay in their bed some nights and those thoughts were all-consuming. She saw the way other women looked at him when he preached, how they shifted in their seats, as if by touching him then they could touch their God and if they could love him, then what – feel the true force of their Lord? And then while she thought these things, James Bulley was on her again, his voice a constant stream: an incoherent babble of pent-up longing and want.

'But I love you, I've always loved you,' he gasped, 'Robert said this would all be all right, if only you'd ...' There was a moment of silence as Bulley searched for the word and she felt her balance shift, her weight go from one foot to the other. The word came to him as they started the long fall together.

'Reciprocate!'

They went tumbling backwards together, the corner of the dresser came into focus as her head glanced off its edge and everything began to swim; she tried to push Bulley away, but he was too heavy with gravity against his shoulder and the fight had gone out of her. They two-stepped quickly backwards, like drunken dancers trying to maintain their equilibrium, and then the air was gone from the room, he felt the lights dim, the world actually spun and then there was a terrible final explosion of sound as they both embraced and went crashing through the picture window, a blaze of tiny shards of glass as fine as snowfall thrown into the air to signal this, their final reckoning.

Blue heard the noise before he saw anything, the mesmerising crack of glass shattering somewhere above his head. He looked up and tried to make sense of what was just out of reach above him: his wife and son jutting out of the main window at the front of their house, James cradling Karen as if to secure her from falling, they looked like figureheads; he imagined some once proud ship scooped up from the sea in the funnel of a tornado and dumped on the land to come crashing through his home. He almost called out their names, but realised that their pose was unnatural, they looked broken and there was too much blood, but fear had given him a sudden stammer, and then he realised that James was trying to work Karen off the piece of glass that had pinioned her to the window frame. It had entered through the soft skin at the back of her neck, snagging a ringlet of hair. Jakub said something, but he only heard one word: monstrous. Blue was quickly past him and up the stairs and into the bedroom, the blood of both the boy and the girl already on his hands.

'What did you do?' But there was no answer that would ever satisfy him or this grisly scenario.

Blue pulled them both gently inside, Jakub now screaming at his shoulder; Blue pushed Jakub violently back and both men, realising a struggle they'd both silently maintained since they'd built this compound together, suddenly fought hard in the enclosed space of the bedroom. James Bulley sobbed on the floor next to them, his hand cut from the jutting pane of glass that had bisected Karen's lip and broken two of her bottom teeth. Jakub and Blue grunted, tussling in a headlock as they pressed up against the bed; it was as unexpected as it was farcical and James let out a gurgle of hopeless laughter among his sobs, the sound reaching both men as they struggled impotently for the upper hand while James could only sit and wonder how far they were from the shattered window, how far they were from falling too. His strangled laugh travelled through the air and reached them, giving them pause and allowing a brief glimpse of the absurdity of their reaction to what was happening around them; it shamed them into stopping. They fell apart as embarrassedly as if they'd been caught in bed together; Blue pushed Jakub hard in the chest, his eyes murderous, and Jakub let him, and then Blue took the scene in fully for the first time and did all he knew to do: call on his God, quietly at first and then strong and bold as if the Lord would come and clear away this mess his son had made of his bride and this room, but there was no saviour hiding beneath the covers or in the drapes, all that remained was the taint of lust, want, sin and death.

And when his Lord refused to answer, Blue cleansed the room the only way he knew how: with fire. He collected the fuel that sat in regimented rows in the cellar and he covered every carpet and drape, sloshed the fuel down stairs, onto and into beds, books and bibles, the clothes he preached in, his zeal was uncontained; Jakub tried to stop him at the top of the stairs leading to the main hallway and he lashed out with the metal jerry can and Jakub, his jaw making a sound like an egg being stepped on, went up backwards into the air, tumbling down the stairs before scrambling through the main door below, one hand trying to hold his face together. 'Right,' said Blue, 'right.' And he busied himself with the task of destroying everything he'd ever built.

# July 1980

The swollen bag of sins groaned and threatened to tip sideways, causing Bulley to almost lean forward to right it, but then he stopped himself as he took Green in. There was no artifice now, no composed veneer, Green was aghast, his lower lip strangely slack for a face usually made taut by years of thinly veiled dismay and downright distrust. It was as if he too had been caught up in that terrible night and now the memories of that evening and of that world were flooding in on him too. Bulley, however, chose to ignore the fury emanating from Green's charged form, he still harboured thoughts of impressing the detective somehow, of befriending him, so he might find an ally who could yet help protect him from the world.

'You killed her?' said Green, the red behind his eyes now muted colours, the blue of sadness, the grey of dismay. He knew exactly what had happened, heard it clearly, processed that bloody bedroom, and yet his gut was a spiral of confusion. Part of him, as sometimes happened when he was picking over the bones of a case (all too literally sometimes), dared hope that he'd misread the report, that the child hadn't fallen from the fire escape, someone hadn't been pushed onto the rails in front of a subway train – fate, chance or circumstance had placed them there, not some hard shove in the small of the back, bargaining them away into the darkness of the tunnel, lit up by the beams that cut across the tracks. Alejandro had jumped into space, there had been no boot imprint across his back, he had chosen to escape the city the only way he knew how, but they were just lies Green told himself, a sleight of hand that would allow him to go on looking in the hope that he might see the good in any situation he found himself in. Green looked into Bulley's face, imploring him silently to turn history inside out, take Karen away from the window, leave the pane of glass intact, the rushing night stilled outside; no raised voices, no violence that was only to be met with even more violence. But like those police reports with their stories of lives being undone, in neat margins, double-spaced tragedies he pored over so often in black ink, they were vivid; unyielding markers set in time, stories of death given brief life on the page. Bulley had killed a girl, his father had razed their home and the home of hundreds of others to the ground to, what, absolve them of their sins?

'And where was Walker?' asked Green, not sure where his own question was taking him.

'I don't know, I didn't see him until the fire really started,' said Bulley, as if he too had wondered why his friend hadn't been there when he needed him most. Instead Walker came out of the flames later, like some ghoul who had waited until the buildings were buckling and windows were sucking and popping out of their frames. He appeared between two cars that they were trying to move away from the house so that they might save them, and Bulley remembered the slapping sound as Walker brought his palms down on the hoods of both vehicles as if starting a drag race. He didn't look like a young man whose world was falling apart around him.

'He asked me if I could feel the energy in the air,' said Bulley dumbly, realising perhaps for the first time what his best and only friend had wrought. 'He asked me if I could feel the transfer of power? I didn't know what he meant, all I could see were the flames and my father moving beyond the windows, I just wanted him out of the house, the fire was everywhere.'

He was quiet then, a young boy who never knew which one of life's tripwires would upend him, how he had gone from longing to devastation in a few short hours, the never-ending noise, all this sin, all his fault. And then he was a sad, defeated man again, his back bent by life, caught in time in a SoHo basement, his father dead on the road behind him; his attempts to save others with his own church here in the city had only meant that death had been visited on him again and again. Red's solitary and sad goodbye on the outskirts of the city, Alejandro snuffed out in the sky – what had led him here, dragging all this sadness in his wake?

'Walker,' said Bulley, and Green looked up sharply.

'Walker brought me here, like cattle to the slaughter, he pushed me down the ramp to the killing floor, he let me go.'

He looked so utterly distraught in that moment that Green tried to talk him around, to try and save him from himself. He could feel the maw reaching up for Bulley in that terrible moment of realisation and he leaned in to snatch him back.

'He was your best friend, you were just kids in that compound,' said Green. 'You were part of a terrible accident, remember that, your father's reaction had nothing to do with you; he lost his mind in that moment. I've seen it, I've seen people snap, they unravel, they just fall away and no matter how hard you try to reach for them eventually you find that there's nothing left to hold on to, it's just rags tearing in your hands and by then they're so far out of sight that you can't even see them anymore, you don't even hear them land as they hit bottom.'

Green stopped, imagining himself falling backward, but still reaching ever upwards for the light, the hands reaching back for him, and how he had once chosen to keep on falling and ignore those reaching out to help. He wondered if he'd even hit the ground yet – had he raised dust, pulled himself up and started the long walk back or was he still screaming through space, a burnt-out star only waiting to fade into oblivion?

It was Bulley's turn to stare. Green looked like he was suddenly engulfed in sheets of flames. Bulley could almost feel the heat on his face.

'What happened to you?' Bulley said. 'What have you seen?'

Green waved Bulley's words away and stood more sharply than he might have liked, shaking off the ghosts that clung to him in strips. The basement made him feel like he was staked to the earth. He needed air, he needed the light.

'Why don't you walk with me?' he said to Bulley, but it wasn't a threat, just an invitation. He wanted to walk a little, the city was only getting hotter and he wanted to taste the more rarefied air uptown, the kind of air that Walker was used to taking in.

# June 1961

Walker sat on the furrowed earth he'd once crossed when he'd come to the commune looking for sanctuary. Even from here he could hear the beams crack as the steep roof came apart in ragged sections like wet tissue paper, tall chimney pots crumbling inwards, ash pushing for the night sky as the roof deflated softly, almost mutely. Like a marquee coming down after a wedding, he thought. Glass popped and exploded, which made him think of shattering the façade of his father's house with the old man's golf clubs; he allowed himself a smile. The shift of sounds was seismic, he imagined the earth might rupture open and swallow the place whole and take them all down into a very real hell, and not just something from one of Blue's parables. There was shouting, confused voices; he'd expected divisive trouble, but not this happy mayhem.

As soon as Karen and James had fallen through the window and then lay suspended there, he'd run as far and as fast as he could. It was instinctual – no one knew he'd done anything wrong, but he did; he thought they might recognise something in him, not so much the guilt colouring his features, but the happy exultation he now wore. He had pushed James as hard as he could towards Karen, eager to see the outcome of his meddling, to see how he could create and then coerce a situation to his own ends (it was his little experiment), and the results had outstripped anything he might have imagined or hoped for. Fleetingly, as he ran into the darkness and it embraced him and hid him away, he thought his father might actually be proud of him for once. He'd watched the old man unpick lives and careers in a single meeting, these newly desperate men looking haunted and ashen, a solitary box filled with their professional lives as they were herded towards the elevators and then they'd disappear behind the silent, steel doors and drop the thirty storeys or more into oblivion.

'Out of sight …' his father would say and then, as if the disappeared employee weren't even worth the words, he'd wave the rest of the sentence away like so much expensive cigar smoke.

# August 1980

Walker had been here before. This still green field, those far-off trees, black knots against the blue sky of the horizon – he often came back to the same spot where he had done the most harm. I am, he sometimes thought, returning to the scene of the crime. He wondered what Green might have made of that. He wondered what Green thought about a lot of things, he sometimes wondered how it might have been if things had turned out differently, if he and Green could ever have been friends. Too alike, he'd tell himself, we'd have to cancel the other out somehow, just like we have to now.

He walked the hillside where he'd once watched Blue's world burn and disappeared out of sight over the other side of the grassy slope, down through a furrowed field much like the one he'd walked in the darkness all those years before until he came to the forest he'd once lost himself in racing away from his old school. 'My long dark night of the soul,' he sighed and crossed from the light of the day into the tangled shadows of the wood. The trees were closer together than he had first remembered, the pale sky barely penetrating the canopy of green leaves and hulking boughs. The floor was slick and he had to reach out and grab a trunk more than once as his shoes attempted to find purchase in the wet dirt. A cobweb was suddenly caught on the stubble of his cheek and he brushed the fine gossamer away as a surprised spider loomed quickly into view and then disappeared at the periphery of his vision. He laughed in spite of himself and pushed forward until he came to a clearing he recognised, the place where as a boy he'd sat and wept and felt as though the world were falling in on him. He sat and wondered where those ghosts were now, the memories and thoughts that had so petrified him that night; he wondered why he kept coming back here, why he sat alone on these hills while his driver smoked near the car and tried to understand what his boss was doing out here among all this emptiness.

I guess, thought Walker, I must have been happy here once. Before I became the great reckoning and washed all those people away. There were friends here, after a fashion; I think I must have felt safe, even wanted, once. It had been a long time since I'd felt wanted or safe. But my mantle, my way of being, he thought, has been to spread unhappiness since the death of my mother. That great wedge that had been driven between him and his father, as the only woman the two of them had ever truly loved was suddenly gone away from them forever, but leaving them with one final thing to share: their pain. It was a cliché, but it was true, he'd seen something of his mother in Rose. He snorted; maybe it was best that he'd never taken her home to meet his father then. Rose had burnt so briefly and brightly, consumed him and then tossed him away, not that she had ever really taken him in – like Alejandro he was always at the edges of her life, in the bleachers looking on. Not like that little prick Henry – he'd taken real pleasure in forcing the pool ball deep down into his throat and watching him panic and gag. He remembered the despair and horror on his face as they'd slowly beaten him to death. Wrong place, wrong time, wrong girl, said Walker as they'd cut the life out of him as he sat tied to a chair, the brown leather belt holding his wrists in place turning slowly black with blood.

Walker would follow Rose some nights; tail her in his car, instructing his driver when to stop and slow and when to go. He'd hang back at junctions and watch her disappearing in and out of the light. The click of distant heels, her jumble of hair tied up in a high knot, a plastic pin dissecting it, holding it all in place, the nape of her neck a slash of white against all that red, like a wound, he thought. Eventually, he gave up on the car and took to following her on foot; it felt more intimate that way, like it was something that they shared, just the two of them. He'd stand in the shadows across from Bulley's place and wait for her to leave, his heart quickening as she stepped out onto the street and went left. That's where he'd first seen her with Alejandro as they'd walked a few blocks together, her arm linked with his; Walker stayed just out of sight, the steely taste of jealousy and anger filling his mouth, his stomach contracting into a tight knot of unhappiness. He felt impotent and ugly as he stood on the corner watching Alejandro and Rose drinking coffee on high stools at the counter of a place called The Friendly Bean (a café he'd once resisted entering when he and Rose were together just on the name alone; she'd laughed when he'd told her that), it was a room they'd once sat in together, as she asked Walker to tell her everything. And now here she was asking the same thing of someone else, her head was tilted a little as if to take in everything that

Alejandro was saying, a spiral of hair fell on her shoulder, as Walker's pulse filled his head and turned everything into a dull roar.

Walker and his men had found Alejandro on the roof of his building, balanced precariously on the edge as if reaching for something. Walker had wanted to ask him what he was doing there, what his story was, what did Rose mean to him, but his men knew that they'd come here for one thing only, to exact revenge, even if they didn't understand what this stranger might ever have done to Walker (they rarely did); Walker's final word was always an unflinching order, the final full stop. It had been too easy, they'd literally kicked Alejandro into oblivion, pushed him off the building's edge and into the air to let him hang briefly like a star and then he was gone into the darkness below. Walker had stood and looked off into the black as if he might find an answer there; that it might reach up to him so he might finally understand what Rose saw in other men that she could never see in him. She'd once told Walker that she couldn't find the goodness in him, that there was a hole where his heart should have been and he'd guffawed and asked her if she'd heard that in a song. I laughed in her face, he thought, as she was reaching out to me, trying to find a way to let me in. She had seen the blank oblivion that he carried deep inside him and she'd faltered, it had scared her and caused her to take a step back. He sometimes imagined Rose at the top of the stairs at some cellar door, peering into the gloomy recesses below before becoming too afraid of what she might find there and so she decided against entering and closed the door shut.

And so Walker followed her, haunted her every step. Sometimes when he had to travel for work, when business took him out of the city, he would get his men to track her in his stead and note down her movements, where she went and who did she meet and what did they do. Walker would call his driver from a hotel room somewhere and he would stand by the window and stare out at some strange city and imagine them both there together, a drink in his hand, and he would listen as his driver detailed Rose's day and then feel his stomach churn when it became clear that she was on a date with another man, sitting in a bar or restaurant somewhere as Walker's gleaming black car idled a block or two away, all eyes trained on her. He hated himself, his obsessiveness; he hated the way his face burned with rage and envy as she moved ever further away from him; he broke legs, he scared people off, he left a bloody trail in her unknowing wake as he became a distant memory to her, another face in the city, another guy, just as she was becoming everything to him.

A memory, one moment in time, bloodied fingerprints at the edges of old photos – people kept family albums, Walker kept a catalogue of indiscretions (as he liked to think of them); he'd once collected Polaroid pictures, but was too shrewd to keep a paper trail of casual misdeeds for too long – bent limbs, broken men or naked girls, it made no difference to Walker, it was one more small victory to tick off and keep. He missed rifling through his array of these silver bromide snapshots, but now he only allowed himself to enjoy them for a few weeks before he threw them on the fire and sat to watch the corners curl and the naked and the dead burst and bubble and fade.

And then there was Billy, or Bill? It didn't matter so much when they were down to the bone and almost unrecognisable. They'd snared one of Rose's guys – as Walker had started to think of them – and tied him to a chair. Walker remembered the tears and the screaming, but sometimes the names eluded him. It was a familiar scenario – he liked to think that they had it down to a fine art by now, tie them to a chair, beat them up, beat them down, the pool ball and then the sudden blade, and then the slow shudder towards death. He wasn't sure what had changed this time, why Walker had snapped so hard, why it had resolved itself without its usual flourish. They held Billy in a workshop they sometimes used to house part of Walker's extensive collection of cars; it was isolated and just out of town. Walker had an array of properties like this one, old workplaces, disused factories, warehouses, he even owned an old orphanage outside of Poughkeepsie; he would tell people that those places reminded him of a better, more industrious and industrialised America. This one was a large room with high windows, most of them cracked or shattered, the space filled with metal and wooden shelving, every oily worktop covered in wrenches, hammers and pieces of wood and steel. Billy's eyes moved frantically around; the strip of silver tape over his mouth seemed to glow, amplified by the smears of blood and oil across his face. Walker leaned in so he was eye to eye with Billy.

'Now, my friend,' Walker said, picking up a long shard of glass from the floor beneath the man's seat. 'I want to talk to you, I want you to help me with something, so we're going to take this tape off you, but if you so much as even think about screaming or shouting then I'll take this piece of glass ...' He held the glass up in front of the man's face just so they were both clear which piece of glass he was talking about and then he placed the broken tip very gently against Billy's lower eyelid. 'And I will very slowly insert it into your eye until the eyeball, which can only yield so much, which has only so much give, will finally break and burst over the glass itself just like egg yolk. Imagine, your other eye will be able to see it all happening – is that ironic? Probably not.' He waved the glass around and stepped back and waited for one of his men to take the tape away.

'Do you know something, Billy?' asked Walker, taking off his coat and laying it gently to one side. 'Most people never scream anyway, they're too baffled, too terrified, sometimes they're simply in shock. And I get that – look at where we are; look at where you've found yourself.' He indicated their gloomy surroundings, the empty hall becoming shadows as night fell, the hardened faces of his men in the half-light. 'It's pretty shocking. So, tell us about yourself, Billy. What do you like to do, any hobbies? You're a fit-looking young man, I'm guessing squash, you don't look upmarket enough to play tennis. So, tell me, what gets you through the day, what gets you off?'

Walker pulled up a chair and sat opposite him.

'But first, tell me this: where did you meet her, when did you first get to know Rose?'

'This is about Rose?' said Billy softly; he kept his head down as if expecting to be struck again at any moment; he looked to each of the men as if an answer might lie there. Their still, hardened stares seemed comparatively sane compared to Walker's ricocheting personality.

'Is she your wife, is that what this is about? I'm never going to see her again, I was never going to see her again anyway.' Billy's voice was speeding up, as was his heart rate; he sounded panicked.

'My wife?!' said Walker. He sounded incredulous, hammy, as if he were playing a part.

'I'm not sure she was marriage material, or maybe that was just when it came to me? She said she couldn't see the good in me, Billy, can you imagine that?'

Billy shook his head mutely.

'It was rhetorical, Billy, rhetorical,' said Walker. 'I think my mistake was that I put her on a pedestal, showed her too much respect, I couldn't get near her; how about you, did you get near her?'

'Near her?' asked Billy; he was watching the piece of glass moving around in Walker's hand.

'You know,' said Walker, pulling his chair closer still. 'Near her. Like Henry, Hank to his friends, probably.'

'Hank?' said Billy slowly. 'I don't know anyone called Hank.'

'Rose did,' said Walker. 'Before there was a Billy, there was a Henry, sorry, a Hank.' Walker looked evenly at Billy. 'There's no Hank or Henry anymore.'

'Anymore?' said Billy; the word felt heavy in his mouth.

'They found him in a tree, someone had hung him up there,' said Walker; he'd started pacing around in front of Billy. 'You ever see a broken crow, dead and caught in the branches of a tree? You ever see that, Billy?' Billy nodded; he guessed he had. 'They're still beautiful, don't you think? Elegant somehow, even in death, the unseeing eyes, the sheen of their feathers turning slowly matte black, the head at an odd angle, the beak pointing at the sky, it's like nature placed it there as a gift, something we can all see.' Walker stopped to look hard into Billy. 'But Henry wasn't beautiful in that tree, he'd turned into something that would make you want to look away, to wish you'd never seen it. But not for Rose: maybe not for Rose.

'He got near to Rose, Billy. Did you?' Walker was staring at Billy's bowed head.

'She kissed me once, Billy,' said Walker. He had turned now and retreated into the darker reaches of the room; his voice could be heard, but he was hard to see. 'She held my face in her hands and looked up at me and you know what she told me?' Though he couldn't be sure where Walker was standing anymore, Billy still shook his head.

'She told me she couldn't love a man like me – I mean, what does that even mean? Am I a monster, Billy? All of this, is this monstrous?' said Walker quietly and then his tone became mocking, cajoling. 'I guess it is.

Tell me, Billy, what did you two talk about, did you talk about a future together, dreams, Billy, did you share your dreams, your hopes, your desires?'

'It was nothing,' said Billy haltingly, unsure of the message to send, what words, if any, could save him from a fate like this. 'We dated a few times, she meant nothing to me. I don't know what this is, why are you doing this to me?' Billy was crying now, heavy tears making small trails through the dirt and blood on his face.

'Why, Billy? Why do you all ask the same thing, why can't you accept the experience, accept that this is happening to you?' said Walker. 'And tears, Billy? Tears? Do you think she'll cry any tears for you when you're gone, when you're broken at your corners and strung up like a decoration in a Christmas tree?' Walker's voice was keening, becoming higher and tight; it sounded like it was accelerating towards a crescendo. 'Dry your tears, Billy, you're free now.'

And as Billy looked up, with one fleeting glimmer of hope that his nightmare was finally ending, the last thing he saw was Walker striding steadfastly towards him, the hammer raised high above his head, too late for him to even turn away as Walker, with an elongated and almost delicate motion of his arm, struck him across the cheek and something broke inside Billy's head and the world slid from its axis and he fell to the ground, raising a cloud of hazy dust as it landed, dust that would dissipate and be gone soon.


It was getting darker in the woods now, Walker sat in the clearing on the branch of a tree that looked like it was growing down and not up. He liked the stability of it, he imagined – and he may have been right – that it was the actual tree he had sat on all those years before when he had got lost along this way. He admired the way nature had sustained itself, how this tree had endured through all the years he'd been away from this space, how his life and the lives of those around him had risen and fallen and yet this tree had stayed here among the occasional spokes of light and had chosen to keep on living. He'd seen people crumble and crushed; been disgusted by how some of them gave in so easily. Where was the fight his father had instilled in him, where was their backbone, where was their will to live? He patted the trunk of the tree reassuringly, glad that something was still in place after all this time: that there was something he could still rely on.

Walker had been here twice before. Once, when he'd run away from school – he was always running away from something, according to his father – and then the night of the fire, after he'd persuaded Bulley to talk to Karen, to tell her how he truly felt, he had come here to wait for the first domino to fall, for the dismantling of the commune and Blue's dreams to begin. Little did he know that it would literally end in ashes, but by then he was cloaked in deceit and dismay, a teenage boy caked in the blood of girls he should have been pursuing romantically, not hounding to their death. That night had ended in a shower of sparks and the quiet flames eating away at what Walker had once considered his home. Karen and Jakub were dead, Blue ruined, Bulley changed forever, and what had it brought him? The initial, visceral thrill of power had now been replaced with a feeling that was both empty and tarnished; he felt used, but by what he couldn't be sure. Could I have betrayed myself, he sometimes thought, did I choose this gruesome path to walk along alone?

Walker's father came and collected him from the hollowed-out shell that was all that was left of the commune, and stood silently by as the police questioned his son. By then, Bulley was in mute shock – Blue had driven them off the compound only to crash their car and they had both trudged quietly back to the one place they had ever considered a sanctuary. Walker's father and the family lawyer shared a box room as the police tried to make sense of the carnage wrought in this once empty farmland. They'd clearly decided that Blue was the source of evil here, not this handsome young boy. Did he touch you, they asked him? It's okay to tell us if he did. But not even Walker would send Blue down that particular road to hell. There were lots of girls, young women, he said, but not us boys, he never touched the boys – he stammered now, as his father rolled his eyes theatrically, watching this game play out. They pulled away from the commune as the fires were finally being extinguished to drive across country and up towards their New York home. They sat mutely in the back of the car, a thin glass partition between them and the driver.

'How much of that was your fault?' asked his father.

'None of it,' said Walker, staring straight ahead, trying not to catch his father's eye.

'No, it never is, is it?' said his father and at the next roadside garage he got out of the car and joined his driver in the front. 'I call shotgun,' he said without malice or warmth, and so Walker regarded the back of his old man's head as America passed under their wheels, determined to one day smash it in.

'Never did get my hands around his throat the way I always wanted to,' said Walker. He'd been sitting alone for the best part of an hour, the tree worrying a damp patch through the pants of his suit. He'd wrestled with the old man a few times, gone for him when he had his back turned, but his father was strong throughout his body, taut legs, dense forearms, his fists were unrelenting, his knuckles blemishes of white when he tensed his hand, he wasn't above throwing a punch at the boy when he got out of hand either. Two opposing forces, one clumsy and impassioned, the other cool and remote, the father weighing the oncoming storm that was his son with a detached air of superiority and a clean right hand that knocked him clear across their library and into a high stack of book-filled shelves that shuddered with the impact. A few fell to the floor: pick those up, the old man would say and then he'd be gone, leaving Walker bloodied and bowed.

'Nice one, Dad,' said Walker. It was nearly black in the woods then, even where some light might have once got in. He could hear his driver calling his name from the edge of the copse that made up the clearing, his voice etched with worry.

'I'll be out in a little while, go back to the car,' Walker shouted, though not unkindly. He grown to at least admire and like his men – they'd do anything, they'd die for him, they had died for him.

When were things right? thought Walker, when were they good? He had a montage of images in his head that he didn't quite trust, family time at their old house out by the beach – another thing sold, got rid of after the death of his mother – the family together when he was a kid, though his father didn't appear in those memories so much. He was always away from home, always working; Walker had been raised by a string of nannies, each more exasperated than the last by his father's abruptness and outbursts. His mother, always the calming influence in their homes, would appear gentle and serene and everything would slow and still. Even his father's reddened features would soften, the lines on his forehead and around his eyes would smooth. Was that how it really was, thought Walker? Sometimes it seemed like an old film conjured out of his longing, he imagined *It's A Wonderful Life*, if they'd cast James Stewart as a megalomaniac thug – his father would have torn an angel's wings off his back, not helped him earn them. Or imagined a way he could package a deity somehow and sell him on to the world at a profit.

It was fully dark now, inside of Walker and out. He stood up with a groan and walked on further into the woods, easing past the giant timbers and the triangles of fallen trunks and the low-hanging branches. He was looking for a familiar light, but was surprised by how little his old school now gave off. He cut across the grass and stood on the lawn trying to pick out his old room and the window he climbed out of that night when he'd left for good and stumbled through the night and the forest and came upon the commune and James sitting up there alone in his tower, abandoned by his father to his fate, something Walker knew all too well and yet, thought Walker, I still had to make him my victim. I had to push life down on him hard.

Someone was walking towards him across the grounds; he was holding a flashlight and a dog on a leash. The swaying band of light played across the grass and the dog barked, but it sounded welcoming, it wasn't a threat.

'Can I help you?' asked the man. 'I look after the place while school's out.' The dog sat quietly, his tail making an occasional thumping sound as it hit the ground. 'Did you get turned around, are you lost?'

I wonder what he thinks of me, thought Walker, out here in the middle of the night while dressed for a day job in some far-off city. And am I lost? I've been lost for the longest time, my friend. Some days I thought that getting back here to this school and that window might be the saving of me, I'd hear the voices of the other children who knew me echoing down through the years, but it's just another empty building now, I couldn't even get the term time right, I'm so far off the face of the planet, the ordinary seems extraordinary. I have no right or wrong, no moral compass, my centre: I guess it didn't hold.

'Ever had your heart broken?' said Walker, though he was talking to himself now and didn't pause to acknowledge the man's brief nod. 'I mean, truly broken? In a way that felt like there was never a way back? You carried the hurt and longing with you, as soon as you woke from sleep it was waiting for you and it followed you from room to room, sat at your shoulder as you sat. I had this friend once, he carried his hurt around as a bag of sins, it's as real to him as I am to you.'

Walker sat heavily on the grass, causing the dog to step back and let out a low, keening whine. Walker's hand went quickly up, but it was to pacify the dog, to show that he meant no harm to anyone. He couldn't remember the last time he'd felt like that.

'Do you want to come inside?' asked the man; he was calmer now that Walker was seated on the ground. 'I can make you tea.'

'No tea,' said Walker, 'I just want to sit here and tell you something about myself and you'll never have to see me again, I'll disappear into those woods and that'll be it. Would that be okay?'

The man nodded that it would and, as he squatted down, the dog sat back down too.

'I've done terrible, unforgiveable things,' said Walker, but quietly, as if hoping his delivery might soften the impact of those words. 'I didn't think there was any redemption for me, but I came back here,' he spread his arms open wide, 'where I failed people and put them in harm's way.' His gesture alluded to somewhere beyond the woods and the man looked that way as if staring in that direction hard enough might let him see the horrors that lay beyond.

'I tried to be good once, but the world was indifferent, the actual entire world, imagine that,' said Walker as the man wondered if he should call someone, think about getting help; he wondered if Walker had escaped from somewhere, but he could think of nowhere nearby that might house a man like this.

'It started here and I thought that if I came back then maybe things might change,' said Walker. 'But men like me, we can't change, I was made in my father's image, and his name was fucking damnation.' He knew how hopeless and deranged he must sound. 'I thought there'd be some redemption for me in this world when I met Rose, I thought that was my way back, but it took me down a road that was darker and deeper than any one road I've ever known. Not even she could save me, she told me to my face: I was beyond redemption, I was sin incarnate, sin incarnate!'

He laughed maniacally and slapped the ground and the dog shifted nervously.

'And she said I could never repent, that I couldn't be saved, and you know what I did, I washed myself in those sins and I haunted her every step, and one night I lured her in and I followed her down to a place she imagined might be her sanctuary and I ...' Walker was crying now, the tears soaking into the rich cloth of his jacket.

'And I came back here to repent, but it's too late to repent now, it's too late to forgive or be forgiven.'

The man and the dog were backing up, headed slowly back towards the school's outbuildings. Walker was moving gingerly to his feet; for reasons he didn't fully understand, he gave a small wave, calling out to the retreating figures: 'Thank you!'

And then, as he had done so many years before, he disappeared among the trees, gone as quickly as a shadow obliterated by the light.

'You okay?' said his driver as Walker stalked across the fields towards his car.

'How long can this place keep calling me back?' said Walker, glancing back at the listless ghosts of his imagination that danced slowly through these fields and trees.

'Where to?' asked his driver.

But Walker was quiet, waiting for the roar of the engine to begin.

# September 1980

If Detective Green had been looking out of his window then, he might have wondered at the elongated limousine creeping down the street towards his door. Wondered at the figure inside as he inched down the rear window and looked up at the apartment block and directly at Green. What would Green have done then – checked his gun, called it in and ducked out of sight, or marched out to confront Walker as he exited his car? As it was, he was reading the newspaper – the headline, as was often the case, was making a line of concern across his forehead – and trying to calculate how many coffees he'd already had when the door buzzer caught him off guard. He assumed salesmen or a package for the apartment across the hall when he pressed the intercom with a gruff hello.

'Good morning, Detective Green,' said Walker; Green could tell he was grinning even through an intercom. 'Wanna go for a ride?' His tone was playful, playful in the way that a cat with a cornered bird is playful.

Green didn't even answer; he simply reached for his jacket and gun and took the stairs two at a time.


Walker's car was black and sleek like slow-moving tar, it was strangely soundless, easing through small, unhurried junctions and towns, its featureless bulk reflected in the façades of the strip malls it passed; a man looked up from his haircut and newspaper and followed its progress as it filled his window, a boy on a bicycle pulled up next to it at a red light and tried to peer in through its darkened windows. Walker let the boy's face get as close to the glass without actually touching it as he could and then rapped sharply on the black oblong of glass and watched the kid jump quickly back, his bike almost lost underneath him as he fell into the next lane.

'Shame there was nothing coming the other way,' sighed Walker as their car pulled away.

It was quiet then, the light in the car had changed; there was more of it, it was less intermittent, there were fewer buildings blocking the sky, they were past the city and heading – Green guessed – north.

'It's illegal to abduct a cop, you know?' he said, but Walker just grinned.

'You got into this car happily enough, we're just two old buds going for a ride uptown,' said Walker.

'If you thought you could arrest me for anything right now then I'd be face down in this stuff' – he indicated the carpeted floor of the car – 'cuffed up and you reading me my rights. If anything happens though, don't shoot my driver; he's just a working stiff, like you.' A thin smile. 'Why did you get in the car though? Did you think I'd spill my guts to you, that we'd have a happy little dénouement somewhere over the George Washington Bridge? I'd tell you who killed Rose, who strung Hank up like a bauble, why Alejandro had to fly...' He mimed throwing a paper aeroplane into the air.

'That you'd lead me away in chains and that Rose could rest forever and you, you could move on with your life?'

'Where are we going?' said Green, much to Walker's delight.

'Where is anyone going, really? Oh, don't you hate that shit, when people come up with that sort of crap? Where is my life leading, what does any of this mean, who am I? You're a fucking speck on the earth's surface, you count for nothing, to paraphrase Bogie in *Casablanca*, you don't even amount to a hill of beans. I bet you want to break those people's fingers – I do.' He stared across at Green.

'I bet you want to break my fingers. I tried dealing with those people once, you know? Tried telling them the truth, showing them the light. Pearls before swine, Green. Pearls before fucking swine.' Walker was suddenly quiet, staring hard at the shaded world outside.

'Anyway, to answer your question, my dear Detective Green, we are going for a drive. I want to show you something, but I want to tell you something first, something about Rose.'

He looked at Green, who looked away; now it was his turn to let the suburban streets fill his eyes, he focused hard on a car that was turning left, staring at its tail light until it stopped blinking. A helicopter's whirring fan of blades came into vision in a corner of the muted sky and he put himself aboard, above all of this. In his mind's eye, Walker's car was suddenly a distant, slow-moving oblong far below.

'There's nothing out there,' said Walker. 'All the answers are in here.' And without looking at him, Green knew that he was pointing towards his own chest. And then as he turned to face him, perhaps to agree that the answers were all locked up inside and sometimes it was better that way, boxed up and forgotten like old pieces of lost luggage, Walker was suddenly close enough to kiss him, his could feel his breath on his face, see the way his eyelashes curled almost girlishly, the thin, broken spokes of red running through the white of his right eye. And then Walker pushed a hypodermic needle of clear liquid precisely and adeptly into Green's neck, like a man who had done this sort of thing many times before, and even as Green grabbed Walker's face and tried to rip his nose off and get his fingers into his eyes, he was already stumbling towards an oblique darkness, the daylight sliding ceaselessly away.

Green came to with the instinctual feel of a caged animal; he thrust his elbows out at sharp right angles, brought his knees quickly up and waited for the first punch or kick to come, but it was quiet. It was still, there was a smear of blood on his face and he recognised the pinch of pain across the bridge of his nose; someone had beaten on him a few times while he'd been under. He sat up with a groan, patting himself down – no wallet, no gun.

There were hushed voices beyond the door, as if the people speaking didn't want to wake someone in the next room. He wondered where he was and suddenly thought about his father and imagined his home was near here, maybe in the next town over; he saw himself clambering out of a window and cutting across two or three fields, eventually hitching a ride to his father's house, his dad's surprised and elated face at the door inviting him into the kitchen, there were sandwiches and milk. Then he heard something he recognised but couldn't quite place that brought him back to the now: the clicking of pool balls connecting and then rebounding gently off the table's cushioned edge.

Sometimes after work, when he was still drinking, Green and his men would go to a bar the next street over from their precinct and play pool to shake off the ghosts of the day, but he found the game interminable, perhaps because it was a period of his life when if he was in a bar and he wasn't drunk or getting that way, then it was no use of his time at all. That's what Green was thinking as he gently pushed open the door to locate the source of the sound.

Walker's father had a pool table and a snooker table at their home; each had its own room. Typical of the old man, thought Walker, aspirational old fuck, he thought snooker a more gentlemanly sport, but in truth, the snooker table lay under a sheet most of the time, like a piece of furniture in a long abandoned house. The pool table was where the young Walker and his friends would sometimes sit and play; he'd smoked his first cigar playing pool and drank whiskey socially, as opposed to sneaking shots from his father's drinks cabinet. He liked the game even if he wasn't especially good at it, while snooker had defeated him almost instantly – the table was too long and unwieldy, the reds always seemed so very far away, the coloured balls an impossible idea that would always remain just out of reach; the complicated cue rest a problem he could never resolve.

Whereas his father's table had been pristine – one resolutely stubborn whiskey stain aside, his fault – the one Walker kept in this old bottling factory outbuilding was less so. The baize was torn and gummed over in patches; balls changed direction as if on a whim, the cushions were threadbare and worn. It had its own share of indeterminate stains, picked out by the strong overhead lights, an anomalous block in the middle of the factory floor, a few folding chairs set nearby. There was an old Chesterfield sofa off to one side, velvet and once red, now fading to white and pink, bleached patches at its corners and arms. Some rusting hulk of machinery, part of a long forgotten production line, had been pushed up against one wall, the bottles that had once snaked rattling and shivering through its complex innards on an ever-rolling series of conveyer belts to be labelled and sealed had long been boxed up and sent off to cities across the country. The whistle had long since sounded on this place.

The furthest reaches of the room were dark, a square outline of thin light indicated a boarded-up window, some sunshine tried to reach in under a large metal loading door, but for the most part it was subdued, quiet. There was no sound from outside, and inside a radio played, set to a jazz station. Green could hear the Bill Evans Trio, it reminded him of being in his father's kitchen on a Saturday morning, his dad working up his sermon, rifling through the papers for inspiration. He'd give anything to be back there now, miles from here, a lifetime of blood and violence gone, wishing that he'd chosen another path, any road but this. Green hadn't felt fear for a long time – anxiety and panic when confronted by a stranger or a gun, yes, when he felt the room suddenly shift and tilt, but not this endless sinking feeling. He always imagined a dog was racing towards him, hungry jaws agape, sometimes he wished it had just been a dog; that would have been easier to take down. In those instances, his instincts saved him, he never stiffened, he strong-armed (Walker was right about that), he coerced, he battled; he won. Sometimes, he literally gunned people down. But here, with the sparse sound of piano keys and the gentle swing of a ride cymbal, the low hum of voices and the resolute clacking of pool balls and the anticipation of what might come next, this made him scared, this made him feel small and vulnerable.

Green pushed gently through the door and made himself flat against the wall like a cat creeping among the shadows. His blood was beating loudly inside his skull; he imagined Walker and his men could hear it all the way across the room. His internal conversation was a rapid stream of enforced calm – buzzwords, things his dad had said to him – and nonsensical babbling, he wondered if he were concussed. I'm rambling, he thought, trying to locate some long-lost words his therapist had taught him to control any environment he found himself in. Own the situation, he thought grimly, that's the kind of bullshit phrase Walker and his family had built their empire on. What I am is furious, he thought, trapped and angry at having let myself get caught up like this.

Walker cut him off, silenced the voice filling his skull.

'Detective Green, join us. Do you play?' Walker was impassive, his hands set on both knees, legs splayed, he sat forward; he was all business.

Green felt spotlit and hopelessly exposed, but walked unstintingly forward, head slightly bowed as if expecting the sudden crack of a cue stick against his skull. Walker pretended not to notice, he was seated on a long, low black box; for a moment Green mistook it for a small coffin and imagined himself bunched up in there fighting for air and light.

'Would you like a drink?' Walker stood up, he was elegant, almost straitlaced, a stickler for formalities even here in this dust and gloom. He opened the lid to the dark wooden cabinet and indicated a row of heavy glass bottles and tumblers nestled in individual cubbyholes, neat rows of whiskey, a bucket of misty-looking ice set off to one side. It looked absurd in this setting, though no more than Walker, who was dressed as if for the opera even down to his white gloves. Preposterous, thought Green.

'But you don't drink, do you?' said Walker, dropping a handful of ice into a glass and then half-filling the tumbler with tea-coloured liquid; the ice cubes cracked loudly on contact with the whiskey. Walker waved the glass towards a motionless Green, the only movement as his eyes followed the ice tumbling down into the whiskey.

'What was it with you?' said Walker. 'This stuff ...' He swirled the glass around, admired it in what little light came in through the factory's soot-covered windows and then gulped it greedily down.

'Or were you more the end-of-the-bar-with-a-beer kind of guy? A few brews with your friends from the station and then they'd all drift away and there you'd be pooled in light, one bottle after another, never wanting to go home, maybe a chaser to go with the beer to take the edge off, just to put off the inevitable last order. Not that you had too many friends at the place.'

Walker cracked some more ice into his glass and refilled it nearly to the brim. The cloudy ice cubes jostling each other, intermittently breaking the surface. Green followed their lazy journey around the glass, but didn't meet Walker's gaze.

'Or were you brown-bagging it at work, bottle in the bottom drawer – we've had a few of those at my place, not least me.' Walker cackled and smiled warmly at Green and seemed dismayed when Green didn't smile back. That's not just his second drink, thought Green, and started to look around the interior of the redundant factory. Walker's men stood as silhouettes behind him, the now vacant pool table beyond them, and in the half-light there was someone sitting quietly behind that. Walker couldn't ever imagine this as a once working building filled with life; now it was airless and soulless, strangely pristine, but ultimately dead, he could smell cleaning fluid and whiskey and the unstinting musk of unhappiness. And what of Walker, what did he want? This was like being coerced by a drunk when sober, something he'd experienced many times once he'd let the booze go but had still haunted bars trying to reignite that feeling of sleepy contentment before the paranoia and self-loathing hit.

That was the voice Walker was using now; the soft edge, the slight whine, certain words almost indistinguishable, he was listing slightly, rising and falling gently on the balls of his feet, he had the insistence of a man convinced that he had something important to say and someone should listen intently to him, take him in and understand the gravity of his story. It had been Green's voice too once when he'd slowly moved from stool to stool, booth to booth and bar to bar; he imagined his movements were deft and enthralling, that people must be staring, but he kicked more tables than he could count, spilt more drinks, broke more glasses, enraged more people than he enlightened. He'd slide in next to a stranger and explain how his life, any life, was mere steps from the edge. His grasp on what the edge was exactly was an ugly mixture of metaphors and elusory language that usually ended with him drinking someone else's drink by mistake. He'd done that once and after a tortuous and protracted apology he'd gone to the bar to replace the beer he'd drunk and then returned to the wrong booth, where he gave a bemused father and son two cold bottles of Rolling Rock and clapped them both heartily on the back with a stirring, cheerleading welcome to New York. The thought of it now, of weaving through crowded bars, overstaying his welcome, blundering into people, made him bunch his fist involuntarily; the still tangible embarrassment crept up the back of his neck as a blushing spray of pink and red.

'Do you know how much this bottle cost, Green?' said Walker, who had been happily topping his glass up in the silence. 'I don't, I don't even know how much I'm worth. Is that shocking to you?'

Green shook his head, the only thing shocking about that was that he never imagined Walker to be crass enough to talk about his wealth, inherited or otherwise – he thought it boorish, he imagined Walker a much slicker proposition; he knew how dangerous and calculating he could be. He wondered if the drink tapped into Walker's own reserve of self-hatred and guilt, as it did him, if booze eventually turned all men into self-reproaching idiots who could only stare blankly inside of themselves and loathe the real emptiness they found there. Measure out their worth in markers in the road they'd made for themselves – wives, money, property, cars, even the kind of fucking dog they owned. He looked at Walker, who was leaning too far forward, as if one more inch would see him upended, sprawling on the floor; the idea didn't upset him. Walker's head was moving gently – if I took a photo of him now, thought Green, it would be just out of focus, like the subject itself.

'So if you didn't invite me here for a drink, then what?' said Green. He tried to see beyond Walker's swaying head as he said it, he didn't know if they were uptown or downtown or far beyond the city anymore. He needed a landmark to pin them to.

'You've been talking to people about me,' said Walker tonelessly, staring beyond Green's shoulder; he seemed less drunk suddenly, as if he'd found a new sense of purpose. He looked directly at Green.

'I don't know, I thought you might have taken a drink. To me, you seem like a man who might be swayed. You left your wife pretty damn quick after the kid died.' He looked at Green without pity or reproach. 'Not so much left her as ignored her, let her sit nights at home wondering where you were. It's fair to say, I think, that you only added to her pain in order to offset your own. You couldn't deal with what you were feeling and to cope with that you simply shut down, blocked everyone and everything out, including her. That's pretty unforgiveable, don't you think?'

He didn't give Green time to answer.

'Probably best the kid died, you'd have only ended up raising a boy like me.' One eyebrow went up into an arch. 'Treacherous, the kind who'd chop off his old man's head or get someone to sneak into his hospital room after dark and switch off his life support to get where he wanted to go, and no one bests you in a power struggle, do they, Detective Green? I mean, look at you, you're strong, you've got a jaw like Superman, for Christ's sake, I bet you've had those big old fists around a few throats in your time, I bet you found it hard to let go more than once. I'd go as far as to say that some of your guys had to wrestle you off some guy's back when you lost it and saw red ...'

In spite of himself, Green couldn't help but respond as soon as Walker had said the word; his head barely flinched, but he felt his skin shift, knew that his eyes flashed sidewards, and all the while Walker was watching him as intently as a snake waiting to strike. One movement and Death was there, darting suddenly forward, all-consuming, inevitable.

'Red,' said Walker again, but this time purely for effect, like someone sending a charge of electricity through a man tied to a gurney, for fun, just to see what he might do.

'Rose,' said Walker, but more softly this time. 'That was her real name, she hated it, but I guess you knew that. Her old man drained all the joy from Rose early on, took the colour out of it and her. He didn't like women much, just like you and me.'

Green looked squarely at Walker and imagined his hands on his face, his thumbs deep in both eye sockets, pushing hard until he screamed out for Green to please stop. The idea made him happy.

'Bulley,' said Walker, reaching for a fresh glass, 'thinks we're all on fire – no, not thinks, he actually believes we're all aflame, he sees it – did he tell you about his sack of sins, the one he carries sloshing around on his back? His life is caught somewhere between fire and water, which I think has a certain sort of poetry to it, wouldn't you agree? Are you sure you won't have a drink, what harm could just one drink do? Did he tell you about the commune? That place was ...'

He swirled his drink around and then dipped slightly as if he were on springs; he was moving around now, enjoying the space in which to perform. His men stood unblinking, it was nothing they hadn't seen before.

'Such a trip. Blue, his old man – hell, you must know all about Blue, you'll have read the police report, you're the inquisitive kind, you're dogged, tenacious.' Walker drew the word out; you could tell that he didn't mean it kindly; he didn't think it was an asset. 'No stone unturned, all that shit, that's you. Blue though, oh, he could raise the roof with his words, when he spoke people really listened, he was like Dr King when he turned it on; he could have changed lives. Hell, I'd have hired him just to do a sales shtick for us. But he had that dream about building his own utopia out in the countryside, he couldn't see the difference between a refuge for the great unwashed, society's fucking detritus piling up at his gates, and a gleaming city built on faith, pure fantasy, but you had to admire his ambition. I'm all for ambition.'

'He saved you, he took you in,' said Green.

'James took me in,' said Walker, bridling slightly. 'Blue was in the house at the time fucking some girl, that was his weakness, pussy. He used to preach and they'd literally flock around him, ha, they wanted to touch the hem of his garment, I guess.'

'I thought James was your friend?'

Green was already bored of this petulant, preening man-child; he wore his moods as fitfully and nakedly as a teenage boy. Arrested development, thought Green, little prick. He wanted to bang his head against the drinks cabinet until it cracked. Walker ignored his question; he had one of his own.

'Your dad preaches, right?'

He looked at Green until Green conceded that he did with a tight nod; Walker knew all about him anyway.

'He took you out of California and brought you to New York, that was against your will, right?' Green was mute on the subject.

'Why the hell would you want to leave the beach for this dump?' said Walker. 'And even he's abandoned the city now, gone upstate, I bet you miss him; you should visit him more; he misses you. Do you ever think about leaving the city, Green? I do, but where would I go? I could literally be anywhere in the world and look at me ...'

He sighed, resting his chin on the rim of his glass. 'Here in an old bottling factory with you, you're not even any fun, you won't even have a drink with me. What do you do to relax, Green? Working girls? Drugs? Beat up innocent men in custody? You don't though, do you? I checked, you're spotless – reckless temper, sure, alcoholic, absolutely, but they're old problems, you've transcended them, how dull.' He snorted derisively. 'You date, but they don't stick, do they? You keep everyone at arm's length, even the guys at work, now that you don't go out drinking anymore they never see you out of hours, no one says a word against you though, I think they're scared of you and I think you like it.'

Walker gently closed the lid of the cabinet, cradling the tumbler of whiskey close to his chest, as if to keep it from harm's way. He sat down with a gentle sigh.

'Some people say my family are self-made, some that we're gifted, and there is a strange aura around the old man, or there was, I'll admit that much,' said Walker; his voice had softened; he looked at the glass as if he wasn't sure how he had come to be holding it. 'He knew things before they happened, that's how he created a whole new language, they call it being part of the zeitgeist now, but it was more than that, he created things, he made a whole new world out of words, it was powerful stuff to be around. Apparently, it was stronger still in his old man and his before him; by the time it got to me it was the run-off, the dregs, the last drops at the bottom of the glass. If I had a kid now, he'd be pretty normal, I guess. Which isn't so bad – it's a blessing and curse, knowing what people want to hear and then finding the words to say it.'

Green regarded him, he recognised the maudlin aspects of alcohol taking hold, the dismay and the regret, the self-pity. He was surprised to see Walker so down-at-heel, so very human.

'Did Rose ever come to you in Washington Square?' he asked Green.

'I never met her,' said Green; he was almost effusive in spite of himself. 'I saw the corpse, read her story, saw the photos, tried to piece it all together, to catch whoever did that to her. And I will – what was it you said, I'm tenacious, dogged, right?'

'You met her once,' said Walker. 'You walked right by her; she touched your hand.'

Green knew when he was being lied to and as he realised he was hearing the truth something unbuckled inside of him until it jarred somewhere against his ribs.

'She gave you a flyer for her church group, Bulley's bunch, when you were walking through SoHo one day, you were kind enough not to toss it away in front of her, she held on to that. She'd seen a lot of madness and shit in this city and you seemed like some sort of hope, that's how innocent she could be, she was actually turned on, and I mean mentally, by your civility and manners. She used to go looking for you in Washington Square after that, she was looking for you when she found all those other men – Alejandro, Hank, even me. She thought we might be the path to her destiny, that we might be a …'

For once, Walker couldn't find the words. Perhaps, he thought, my magic has finally run dry; this is what it is to be like all other men? His dismay was profound, he felt like a light bulb diminishing. Finally ordinary, he thought, just like his father had always told him he was.

'I don't know – that we were a through street to get to you,' said Walker quietly. 'That anyone who showed her some sort of kindness might be on the same path as you were. She was so innocent and brave and stupid, I guess.'

There was no malice in Walker's words, he was thinking about destiny and how Red had never been his and how Green was never hers. He was sure Red prayed to her God to give her Green, a God Green never gave a damn about, never saw, would never consider letting into his life. Walker wondered what would have happened if Green had gone down into that SoHo basement one day, if the church flyer had somehow piqued his interest, if the loneliness had drawn him down those stairs, how different things would be now. Either way, thought Walker, Rose would never be his. She stayed for a while, he even thought she might have loved him for a moment, but she was only ever trying to save him and then one day she told him she had to go, that being with him was like always standing in a shadow, and with his arrogance and pride, Walker thought she meant the ever-reaching shadow of his success, but, no, she told him, her hand on his forearm, being with him was like always being in the dark when all she ever wanted to see was the light.

'If you'd just gone down to that basement then you could have saved her,' said Walker, attempting to shift the blame one final time.

'From what,' said Green, his heart beating out of his chest, his right hand a tight fist. 'A fucking ghoul like you? Someone who's never known what it is not to have power; not be the one who wields the stick, who calls the shots. Her and Henry I couldn't really understand, that fucking hard-ass, but people get lonely I guess, but you, you're some kind of malevolent force, you're poison in the well, a rain of napalm, you're death ...' Green sat back and made a sound like air coming out of an old tyre.

'You're impeccably dressed death, Walker, I'll give you that. Red was doomed from the moment she met you – no, the moment she left you. What did you do, track her movements like you've tracked mine? Compile a dossier on her the way you might a company you want to take over and drain the resources from? Crush the competition, is that what she became, was Red suddenly the competition? No, all those other men, they were the competition, that's why they were snuffed out, fucked over, wiped out.'

Green braced himself as if ready for a fight.

'So if she and I ...' He stopped, he was thinking what he would do now if he had his gun – push it hard into Walker's face, scraping the barrel against his teeth, maybe knock one loose? He shook the thoughts away, he focused on his father; he needed composure and clarity. Walker was dressed in three-hundred-dollar shoes, but they were still filled with blood; he wore the faces of other men, bones as rings on his fingers, he was decaying before Green's eyes, his flesh was rank, there were chunks of skin in his otherwise perfectly groomed hair, but he couldn't see it.

'Then what, Mr Walker – would one of your goons have forced a pool ball into my mouth and watched me stagger around ...'

'Making ceaseless revolutions to a certain death,' said Walker quietly.

'What?' said Green, fighting to stop the white noise in his head. He knew where he went from here and it would only end with Walker broken against the pool table, his men on Green's back. He slowed his breath like a therapist had once taught him, and counted silently backwards. If Walker felt the advantage sliding back towards him he didn't show it.

'It was something my father used to say,' said Walker. 'Life was just a series of ceaseless revolutions leading to a certain death. Say what you like about my old man, but he was a realist, he knew when the curtain was coming down.'

'Though you still felt the need to help him with that,' said Green.

'You think he was happy in that hospital bed?' said Walker. 'He was more a maze of tubes than he was a man by that point. It was a mercy that he died when he did.'

'A mercy?' Green was incredulous, appalled. 'Is that how you see yourself, as a power for good? You're a man who's used to the world revolving around you, you can't imagine a universe where someone might question or second-guess you, might is always right ...'

'This from you,' said Walker, suddenly vehement. 'I've watched you work, I've watched you strong-arm suspects, you might not get people by the neck anymore, now what, that you're sated, that you're clean, that you've resolved to be a better man?' He spat on the floor between them.

'You spend your time intimidating people, standing over them, bending them to your will, you're as much a bully as me, it's just that you're a cop, it doesn't matter who you break to get what you want, to go where you want to go, you've got the law on your side.'

The late September sunshine made a faint fan of milky light across the uneven concrete floor.

'Christ, you don't even know the difference between right and wrong,' said Green; both their voices were raised now. 'I obey the letter of the law, you just break it, you destroy lives, crush people, I bring people like you to their knees ...'

Walker was shouting: 'To their knees? Listen to your language, it's the language of violence, it's the language of a man who's out of control!'

He'd later see the irony in that moment, but it was when Green snapped: rushing forward and grabbing Walker by the throat, he began repeatedly slamming his head against the edge of the drinks cabinet.

'What did you do to Red?' Blood flooded into his skull, black stars popped into life at the corners of his eyes, he felt hot, I'm literally hot-headed, he thought almost whimsically, strangely pleased with himself. Walker was screaming and then he hit Green across the face with the heavy glass tumbler. Green fell backwards, and felt hands grab him, but he still swung a fist and connected with something, he heard a gasp, someone said fucking cop, but Green was close to happy, he was loath to admit it to himself, but he felt at peace among violence, he sometimes wondered if he'd chosen to be a cop as he knew he'd find himself in harm's way one day and it was where he wanted to be.

'Stop!' barked Walker, and just as quickly as the roaring violence had begun it quietened again. He was pulled into a chair; one of Walker's men laid a hand on his shoulder, pressing him down into place.

Walker and his other men had moved across to the pool table, Walker was idly chalking a cue. Then, behind them, Green's eyes picked out the seated figure he'd spotted earlier; he hadn't moved all this time. A delighted Walker followed Green's gaze.

'Oh, you've not met our other guest, this is Mr Moon.' Walker stepped back with a flourish like a magician revealing his greatest illusion yet. There, strapped into a wooden chair, was Moon, barefoot and bloody, hands and arms taped to the chair, one eye grotesquely swollen. The right side of his face was almost flattened, pushed down by some horrific force. He looked like he was pressed up against glass, thought Green, and wondered how long he had left to live. He doubted the man even knew he was in this room, which was probably some kind of blessing. Better to be ignorant of the hell he was living in now.

Walker leaned over the table and took his shot, a ball hitting the rut in the baize and veering awkwardly towards the cushion.

'Fuck ...' said Walker, and then in one seamless, almost graceful move he took the heavy end of the cue and brought it quickly around, crashing it into Moon's jaw. Moon's face made a sound like someone stepping on the shell of a snail. He didn't even gasp or shout, his head swung wildly sidewards, but the heavy chair held him upright. Green realised he wouldn't even recognise the man from a photograph now.

'Leave him alone,' Green said, but that wasn't the detective in him; that was the same kid who stepped in to stop bullies, who once almost beat a classmate unconscious for throwing a firework at a cat. He couldn't stand all the anger and hate in the world, even as his fury and violence added to it. As he watched Walker and his men torment a man to death, he didn't want to do the right thing and step in and save Moon, he simply wanted to kill them, he wanted to cut their throats, break wrists and stamp on their heads until they too were almost featureless, a mash of blood and bone, completely wiped out, obliterated.

'Red,' said Walker, 'you know I fucked her, right? She might even have liked it.'

Green's internal voice became a scream, a confluence of voices begging him to stop, to think his actions through, to find his peace and cling to it as if his life depended on it, and in a way it did. He was up and out of the chair, elbowing the goon nearest him in the throat, he reached Walker just as he was swinging the cue to meet him, the intractable collision of two forces. Green literally saw stars, bright lights speckled across the factory's ceiling as the stick caught him hard across the temple. He heard someone laugh as the room gave way, he was no longer moored to the earth, space fell through him, he was truly disembodied, made of dust, a speck in the endless strands of the universe's DNA. As he fell further and further, he saw Walker's men snap Moon's head back, pick up the green number six ball from the table as precisely and calmly as a game official might and then force Moon's mouth open and push the ball in beyond his unyielding teeth. Something made a snapping sound and even though Moon was barely conscious, he did his futile best to kick against this intrusion, this dead weight being forced inside him. From very far away, Green could smell fear, the panic, the last final, fleeting hope, and wondered what he might do when it came to his turn, how long could he clench his jaw and hope that his teeth held out.

In Bulley's dreams, New York City was on fire, finally consumed by its own sins, towers fell, people ran as panicked embers, and he stood among them appealing for sanity, some sense of understanding, but it was a misplaced call for calm. Out of the corner of his eye he could see the hellhounds gathering, waiting to take him away, to settle his debt. He'd wake and go to the window and look for the orange glow over his city, the final reckoning, but the world was mute, lit-up buildings under a black and purple sky. He sat in his basement and wondered about Green and Red and where this would finally end, what might have happened had Karen lived, what Walker had meant to him and how profoundly he had broken his heart, pushed him to the edge and sent him here trying uselessly to ever atone for his murderous act.

Bulley looked down at the bag of sins at his feet and felt the sudden fear and panic rise up through him as he realised it was now empty. It was quiet then and suddenly he could hear the baying of hounds that were on the scent of something, that were on his trail. Something was moving, and then he saw that his hand was on fire – as the city and people had burned around him he'd never seen the flames on himself, he wondered why he'd ever been spared that, and now, as far as he could tell, both hands were on fire. The flames spread slowly up his legs, wrapped themselves around his torso and raced towards his chest and face. He felt calm momentarily and then he heard the scurrying of dogs in the stairwell and voices outside, someone was calling his name, he saw the city on fire, heard the barking of the dogs and then the door burst open and there stood Walker and his men, Walker was grinning as they dragged Bulley along and tied him to his chair. Walker, a gas can hanging loosely from one hand, came in close to Bulley's face and for a moment Bulley thought Walker might speak, but his old friend just held Bulley's chin and began pouring gasoline methodically and slowly onto Bulley's clothes until Bulley finally understood that he was going to meet his fate.

# October 1980

As Green saw it, he now owed his life to Walker and he carried that burden as heavily as Bulley had hefted his black sack of sins. Green had finally come to in the factory; the only light reaching in was from a stack of bottles lining one wall that were catching the sunlight from a high, recently opened window. There was nothing else left; even the radio had gone. It was just Green and Moon and the now empty pool table making up this bloody tableau. He'd reached for his jaw instinctively, felt his teeth and wondered why he wasn't choking for air, why his teeth weren't stowed in, why he wasn't holding his head forward to stop a pool ball blocking the air trying to reach his throat. Moon was less lucky; his head was snapped sideways as if a thread of tendon were the only thing holding it in place. One eye was completely shut, his features levelled, his partially opened mouth – lips literally beaten black and blue – revealed a blood-smeared pool ball; red on green, thought Green, Walker's sending me a message.

He pushed his way outside, it was daytime, it has to be the next day, Green thought, all he knew was that they'd passed a town at some point, he remembered the kid falling from his bike as Walker laughed, the quiet indifference of that small place, the low hum of life on the peripheries – a part of him envied them being away from the clamour – and so he started walking back towards them as best he could remember. A car stopped for him within half an hour, the driver cracking his window only an inch to ask if he was okay. Green couldn't understand the hesitation and then he saw himself reflected in the car's window and understood the driver's reticence to let him in. He looked like he'd somehow survived a wreck on the highway and clambered out of a five-car pile-up, which was how he felt. His face was smeared with blood, his nose was almost certainly fractured and one side of his face was so swollen that it looked like he was perpetually working a gumball around inside his cheek. He saw that his shirt was untucked and hurried to push the tail back into his pants as if that would right this picture somehow. He had no idea where his jacket was and wondered what the impeccably tailored Walker would want with an off-the-peg suit like his.

'You okay?' asked the man in the car; his wife craned over next to him to better see this bloody spectre that had walked out of the surrounding countryside. He looked like roadkill that had come back to life at the side of the highway, got up and started walking again. Back from the dead, thought Green, back from the dead. And then he reached out a hand towards the car, causing the couple to shrink back in fear, uncomprehending and completely startled, but Green was doing the only thing he could before he collapsed: trying to hold on.

It was Bulley who was holding on now. Green stood over his hospital bed and tried to find a part of the man he'd once known. He looked like a shadow, a silhouette, thought Green, like charred wood, brittle and black. As if at any moment a piece might break away and flutter to the floor as so much greying ash. Green and Dr Brenda Bent looked at the figure in the bed the way undertakers regard a cadaver: as something to be ultimately moved on to the next place.

'Almost total immolation,' said the doctor. 'I don't know how he still keeps breathing, it's like he's in some weird state of grace.'

'He thought the city was on fire,' said Green. 'He thought we were all going to burn. He thinks we are all burning, just in different degrees.'

Dr Bent looked up from Bulley's chart, she stared at Green evenly. Placing the chart back, she adjusted Bulley's drip and regarded the sluggish flow of lines scrolling across the monitor screen. She moved past Green and towards the door.

'I'm not sure he's thinking anything at the moment,' said the doctor over her shoulder, her back already to him. 'You might want to say your goodbyes to him now.' And then she left the two men alone.

Green pulled his chair up next to the bed so that his head was level with Bulley's; there was an oxygen mask over his mouth, the rest of his face was almost featureless, it shone like oil, like the sin had melted and stuck to him, thought Green.

'Walker get to you too, James?' Green said quietly. Where was Walker, he thought? Green knew they were reaching some sort of endgame if he could ever get hold of the slippery bastard. But he still didn't know why he was alive; he'd witnessed assault and murder, he'd punched Walker hard in the face, got him by the throat, but it was Bulley who had really been made to suffer. He didn't know why Walker wanted his old friend to hurt this way. Perhaps he just wanted him to know how it was to be aflame and forever alive, to place him in his own literal purgatory and bring Bulley's nightmare scenario for all of them to life.

Bulley was looking at him. Two myopic blue eyes staring out of the night that now made up his face.

Green automatically reached for the alarm button to summon the nurse, but Bulley gave a twitch of his head, no. He indicated his oxygen mask with a downward flicker of his eyes and Green, in spite of himself, reached forward to gently remove it from Bulley's ravaged face. Bulley's eyes, once listless behind almost impenetrable lenses, were now animated with life, the only part of his that was anything anymore, thought Green, that's where all of him is now, all his fervour, that preacher's spirit, all there in those two, unblinking blue eyes.

Somewhere from deep inside Bulley came a voice, it sounded like a man trapped far below ground trying to get his cry for help heard through a fissure in the earth.

'Robert came,' said Bulley. 'He thinks I betrayed him.'

Green imagined he might; even though Walker had wilfully and clinically chosen to take Bulley's family and life apart, and then kept him close to him in some sort of quiet servitude in New York, it was, in Walker's deranged, egotistical psyche, Bulley who had betrayed him. Then Bulley said something remarkable.

'Did he hurt you? Are you okay?'

Green found his concern profound and saddening, that Bulley might actually care about another human being while he lay there waiting to fall into the abyss. It unsettled him; he suddenly saw the misplaced goodness in Bulley that he had always found hard to justify in his own father. Green's old man was always preaching forgiveness, empathy, when Green could never find it in himself for those who had transgressed, those who had strayed from the path. An eye for an eye was his way, he thought, and where had it got him, where had it got any of them? Bulley looked like he was made of oil and dust, Green had walked away from his life and family when they had needed him most, and Walker had carried his anger for so long that it had mutated into patricide and now he was running out there somewhere in the world, striking out at anyone who might come near. Walker, mad with power, lonely, angry and lost, thought Green, and what am I if not some of those things too?

'You should try and forgive him,' said Bulley quietly. 'He's only ever known pain, he's just striking back. You know how dogs bark when they're scared ...'

Doesn't mean he always has to bite, thought Green tersely; even as he was trying to contain his feelings, the black was slowly rising up inside of him.

'Walker's gone,' said Green. It was true too; they'd arrested some of his men, raided his offices, tossed his aerie-like apartment, but to no avail. His records were being pored over, but Walker had become invisible, he'd disappeared as completely as if his molecules had burst into a fine mist, his DNA unwound itself like old rope; he might as well have become of the air. He, thought Green, could literally be anywhere; he recalled that afternoon in the shadowy light of the bottling factory. Walker dour and drunk, his glass literally set at his lips. I could be anywhere, he'd said, and here I am with you.

'He's coming back, he says you and he aren't done yet.' Bulley's eyes flickered, closed then opened and then closed again. His voice was very small now; he was very far away.

'He says the three of you need to talk – you, him, Red.'

'Talk?' said Green, leaning forward to hear more, to make sense of what he was saying, but Bulley had drifted away again, blissfully unaware once again that his skin was as black and impenetrable as the sins he'd once carried around on his back, as if they had finally tipped out and fully consumed him somehow.

Walker sat with a sigh on the dusty chair and looked around him. He wasn't so very far away from New York at all. In fact, he was still in the state, hiding in plain view and out of sight. His father hadn't given him much by way of good advice, or much of anything, but he had told the boy to grab everything he could from an early age, to invest in things, to hold on to what he could, and so as soon as he had the capital he collected property with the zeal of a magnate and the ardour of a kid sat with a Monopoly board. And so through his company, and off the books, he held on to places like this one, this disused orphanage with its high brick walls, the central building an exercise in gothic hell, pointing like an accusing finger at the sky. It looked like the stuff of nightmares. And as if to compound its misery, the surrounding buildings were boxy, airless prefabricated blocks thrown up in the '60s that were too hot in the summer and bone-chillingly cold in the winter. He could only imagine the misery of kids stuck in a place like this. He rarely came here – he and his men had dragged people into this place on a handful of occasions, and then taken the bodies away for dismemberment and burial, maybe a bonfire in the grounds, but he'd never lingered before; the whole building made him feel sad in a way. He walked the decrepit halls and stopped in what must have been an old dormitory, imagining lights out, the despair of the lonely and abandoned, no place to go to but here.

'Just like little old me,' he said to himself. He'd wanted to head back to the Tennessee countryside for one last time, but he knew that Green and his men would find him there – they knew almost all of his secrets now, almost all of his hiding places.

'Except for this one,' he said aloud to the ceiling. It was arched and led to an almost impossibly high skylight; the children, he thought, must have felt very small in here.

The air had been different there in Tennessee; the place he'd once unpicked a community apart as easily as a man might fillet a fish, remove its skeleton from the inside out until it became a mere facsimile of itself, something recognisable, but forever changed. He'd been back there more than once and stood on the hill where he'd sat that night as he'd allowed Blue's dream to die – not die, he thought, more had the life choked out of it. He'd looked down at his hands: with these, he thought, with these very hands. He'd broken many people since, turned lives to dust, but the commune was his first real success, that first domino that cascaded to a terrifying crescendo of a life spent on the backs of others. Once there had been something growing inside him, like a sapling whose roots he'd decided to poison, and that poison had spread to colour everything he might have ever touched; it contaminated the well, his well. He could imagine it all now, the outlying buildings, the cars at the periphery of the high wall, the main house set back, the centre of the circle from which all the spokes of the commune reached out. He imagined a wheel coming loose, rolling uncertainly out of sight. How he might have given it a kick to help it on its way.

He'd walked onto the place where buildings had once stood, taken everything in again, the place where cars and trucks and even a school bus had once jostled for space, he remembered the front entrance and the gates and towers that had once stood there and how he stepped out of the darkness that night and called Bulley down towards him and how he had come willingly, how the pity and help had poured out of him, a true Samaritan. The fence had seemed so high then, so impenetrable that he could only wonder what lay beyond, and then he was among those people, the drifters and losers, but mostly the lost; he'd literally come through a darkened forest while they'd journeyed through their own metaphorical wood; everyone, he quickly saw, was looking for something. A way to belong, no matter how disparate the elements and strands that they had to tie together to help them make some kind of life.

Walker had always considered organised religion some kind of pyramid scheme, supposedly pulling others up along with you, but unsustainable in the end, morally bankrupt, one big empty from the top down. He wondered if the children of this failed orphanage had faith forced upon them; he could imagine meetings to talk about the good book and Sunday school and prayers before lights out. That said, he could still see why the people in the commune held on to their God, why they had flocked to Blue; he had, or so it seemed, a direction and a real vision, he didn't just live in hope, he was moving forward, going somewhere, and if these people could somehow get caught up in his wake then who knew where they might end up, on some higher, hallowed ground maybe? Initially,

Walker had felt their fervour too, but he quickly spotted the way that Blue's fallibility, ego, need and lust were to be his undoing. They were Walker's way in. Blue part-preached, he part-performed; he wasn't sure he believed Blue's exaltations of God, he could almost hear him counting the beats that might lead to a more dramatic conclusion to his sermons, they built and broke like carefully constructed songs, they had flourishes, they rose and fell, ended with a dramatic swell. Sometimes he imagined Blue might come back out, take a bow and then perform an encore.

'Your old man's smooth,' he'd once said to Bulley, who'd responded with a fulsome thank-you. Bulley was moist-eyed with ardour for his old man, he couldn't see behind the curtain to the tricks his father was playing. But then he was just a kid, which was more than he could say about some of the more ardent followers who'd tripped after Blue; the women clutched their hands tightly together when he spoke to them one on one, leaned in to hear him speak, their hand on his forearm, their eyes blazing with life, want and need; Blue didn't seem to mind that lust was a sin.

Looking back now, Walker realised that it was envy that first fed his hatred of Blue, he'd liked him at first, admired him even; as soon as he'd explained his plight – with a few suitably galling embellishments: oppressive father, abusive childhood, how he'd been driven out of his own home after his mother had died – Blue had shown him real compassion and even set him up with his own room in the main house. A viper in his bosom, Walker thought, like something Blue might allude to in one of his sermons, and how he'd sat there, idling and waiting to strike.

The commune was where Walker had first felt his gift really bloom, where he started to see and feel words differently to others, they made shapes in front of his eyes, he'd look confusedly around as letters took to the air and filled the room then resolved themselves mere feet in front of him, sudden phrases laden with meaning, tight clusters of words that pulsed with insight, that said so much. It scared him at first; more than once he tried to reach out and grab the letters tumbling before him, and once, while still dazzled with the newness of it all, it occurred to him, quite wrongly, that someone in the commune had spiked him, that he was tripping out, which both appalled and delighted him. His father had long warned him that this day would come, but without any colour, without the charm, it was a transition for the old man, for him the gift of seeing was a miserable rite of passage, not this overwhelming and sensational wave of joy.

Walker had watched Blue preach and the words had floated up and out of him, consonants of red and white trailing upward like lost balloons at a parade; vowels were fatter, rosier colours, pastels, burnt yellows that glowed; certain words had an impact all their own; 'praise' was shot through with spirals of white and blue, like an unusual chunk of seaside rock. 'Possession' came out of him black and bold as he emphasised it, as he leaned on the word a little. As the leading 'P' melted into the ceiling, Walker felt a sudden surge of panic that this was what his family was, that the Devil was inside, driving him on; it would explain his mother, the tragedy, his father's actions, the indifference – was this because of the debt they owed, had his father somehow bargained them all away to the Devil to obtain this strange, irresistible gift? He fled the sermon and sat out on the steps, the quickly disassembling words trailing behind him like party streamers caught on his clothes. This then was his lot; his father had doubted that the gift would ever come, be passed down from father to son, that he was the end of the line, but here he was sat among a haze of pronouns and adjectives, a thick cloud of letters and numbers swimming around his head and shoulders; he felt like a character in a Dr Seuss story overwhelmed by a landscape of trees, lakes and buildings built of words. He felt ridiculous and giddy and then stupidly powerful all at once.

Like Blue, he was suddenly overwhelmed by the desire to spread the word. It was the injection of his father's ego – the old man had been right: they weren't like other people, they were better somehow, as he had said to him more than once; it was simple, they were more evolved. And in a world where survival of the fittest was at a premium, it meant they were always one step ahead. So here he was now, finally beyond the pack, and out of their reach. He looked around him at the rusting cars, the broken-down people; the gap in the fence where someone had drunkenly backed their truck up and split the timber.

Everyone was smaller, shrunken somehow, fading from view. He felt like everything and everyone was in his wake, not Blue's; the preacher might have opened his eyes, helped him see, but his vision now was much more rich; Blue merely looked to the skies, Walker saw beyond the stars, touched the heavens, he heard the whispers beyond the clouds, the voices of the ages were racing down to meet him.

Walker thought about the young man he once was as he slowly paced the orphanage's corridors and halls. He wondered why his father had never abandoned him or banished him to a place like this – the school he'd sent him to back then was only meant to put him back on the path, set him true, push him towards the straight and narrow. A path that my father never chose to go down, thought Walker.

Back then he'd traced where the compound's perimeter wall once was, recalling the fencing that kept them all in and the world out, he paced a ragged circumference around a world he'd once inhabited and then destroyed. Out there in the countryside he tried to feel empathy or goodwill for the people he once knew and crushed, tried to understand their plight – he was their plight – but, as his father had once had it, sometimes Walker was just the sky falling and he didn't give a damn where he landed or on who. Only the strong survive, he'd say, all that fist-pumping bullshit, how many times had he heard that over dinner? Walker pushed the thoughts away, this confluence of ghost and demons; sometimes he looked in the mirror and his father's eyes looked back at him and that was about as much of a direct link back to the old man as he could stomach. The marrow of our bones, he thought, the blood beating in our chests, the same electrical spark prompting their synapses into life. He'd sat down among the now long blades of grass and pulled one distractedly from the ground and sat chewing the delicate stem as the sky burned around him. He remembered the cracking wood, the exploding glass, the ever-consuming fire that could never be sated, but mostly he remembered the heat and knowing that no matter how close he stood to the flames he would never burn.

It was near that very spot that he'd first met Lisa; he'd been walking out at the property's edge like a dog at the very end of its chain that wants to leave but has nowhere to go even if it could get free. He recognised her from the main house, she was one of the many young women who haunted Blue's door and were occasionally invited in; Walker had seen her literally waiting in the wings as Blue had preached, his words filling the eaves, her gaze a mixture of beatific hope, lust and want. Something had turned in her favour and then turned away again, she'd been at Blue's side momentarily and then he'd let her drift, had kept moving even as she'd stood still, or that was how it must have felt. Once he'd returned her feelings and now they scattered as they came up against Blue's indecipherable shell. Lisa looked like she'd been crying, but that, conceded Walker later, might have been a signal he wanted her to send. A rescue flare going up, he thought, but he was here to sink ships not rescue the survivors.

Walker had heard her story before: Blue's brilliant oratory had seduced her heart and mind, soon they were living in the main house together, surveying the grounds from the large windows overlooking this tumbledown paradise, content, she was still young, but womanly somehow, a wife in all but name, for a little while at least. But as more people came, Blue's attention wandered, his flock was multiplying, his people came first, not least some of the young women who gathered in groups in the front pews ignoring Lisa's murderous stares.

The comedown was inevitable, from the main bedroom to one of the smaller single rooms on the top floor of the house, until one night she found herself on the couch in the living room feigning sleep as Blue and some shyly giggling new girl stole their way past in the half-light, two embracing shadows circumnavigating the stairs. Breaking her heart as completely and carelessly as if they'd stepped on it in the dark. That strange unknotting of the stomach as everything fell through her; I'm nauseous, she thought as she lay there among all the blackness, but it was a nausea that was ever ongoing, sending her into an endless descent, the pirouetting freefall of heartache. So, Lisa Gatherar, determined to escape her pain, bargained with the universe that long night, that it might take her and this inconsolable feeling of grief away, the heavy, chest-heaving tears, the unexplainable shaking hands, the gasping, gagging hurt. In her half-sleep, she offered herself up so that someone else might live; she imagined a sick child, the hurt in the world, vague notions that her death might bring some relief to a stranger far across the country, even around the world somewhere, that she might finally do some good. But she woke again in the breaking light of a new day despondent and whole, the sound of Blue moving around upstairs only adding to her bleak, imagined scenario of what might be happening above her head. How could she have known that the universe had heard her and that even now her prayers were being answered, that she had called the sky down and the clouds were quietly gathering around her?

She had walked out into the grounds of the house and, like the day she'd first arrived here, her belongings were gathered into a long holdall draped over one shoulder in a sagging quarter-moon-like curve. And there was Walker, this strangely confident young man walking towards her, death set like two crows at each shoulder; he carried the night sky around him, he was the end of days, the long shadows, the perfect storm, and it was as if Lisa, who only hours earlier had tried to bargain her life away, was silently complicit in her fate. She took Walker's hand, as one would a lover's or a stranger invited to dance, and they wheeled silently around this strange killing floor, his hold on her an ever-tightening vice, death's very real grip. Bulley saw them both walk to the horizon together, he'd seen girls walk towards that tree-lined hill and out of his father and the community's life so many times before, he was curious, but misunderstood his friend's intentions, mistaking the evil in Walker for compassion and understanding, never knowing that Walker was the bloody messenger dispatching girls to the other side, working in a strange tandem with Blue, parlaying souls to another world as soon as the wood enveloped them and the leaves and tall trees snuffed out the light.

How many girls, thought Walker, did I take into that copse and silence their babble, still their broken hearts? Blue had caused so much damage and left him to clear up the mess. Blue owed him. That was how he remembered it now; Blue's fault, all of it, even as Walker had choked the life out of those girls, drawn a blade across their necks, turned the earth over on their ever-cooling bodies; Blue was to blame – once Walker had washed the blood from his hands he was clean.

He looked now at that distant hill, a solemn, easily discontent man, wreathed in twitching, self-delusory thinking, and wondered at the nature of good and evil, at Blue's intentions – did he know that his behaviour, his patterns, were putting these young women in harm's way? That somehow he'd have to pay eventually, that he too was indebted to the overarching power of the universe, that there had to be balance, someone had to pay; books to be balanced, Walker muttered to himself, actions and their outcomes.

And there he had found himself many times, and still he wondered why, turning the old compound earth over in his hands, working his fingers into the ground, this figure in the landscape, ruining his thousand-dollar suit, scuffing up his handmade shoes, drawing mud across his face as dark smears under both eyes. He had come here and sat just over the brow of the hillside, set back in the shadow of the trees, and he had dug and dug until his bruised and bloody fingers had hit the mother lode, the literal pieces he had left behind him all those years before, cracked skulls and broken ribcages, splayed, stone-white fingers, thigh bones, some jewellery now faded and almost colourless. They were his girls and now here they lay – he wondered how many people had passed this way after him never knowing what lay beneath, what he'd wrought there. He touched the crown of a skull and held it to his chest before leaning forward to kiss it gently.

He ran blackened fingers through his hair, he felt undone, a complete mess, when all he wanted was to feel like a kid again, to have never walked through the woods that night, to have never been gifted and cursed when another world, his father's world, revealed itself to him. He wanted to lose himself in the land, become a part of this hillside, to disappear among the long grass, walk into the woods and be no more, ended like those girls had been ended. He'd lain on his back, the skull nestled in the crook of his arm, and watched the sun idle across the sky until his eyes hurt. It'll be dark soon, he thought, and closed his eyes and tried to see Green flicker to life behind his eyelids. When he woke he knew it'd be time to meet him for one final showdown; there would, he thought with a thin smile, be a reckoning. And though he wished to see Green in his fitful sleep, it was Red that drifted through the empty rooms of his dreams, never coming when she was called, always and forever just out of reach. He woke in night's indeterminate hour and staggered to his feet, a caricature made up of crumpled cotton and silk, a face blackened with dirt, his hair a jagged abstraction made up of grass and earth. He took broken steps down the hill, moving slowly through the darkness; his car was out there somewhere and beyond that something that he thought might be an approximation of salvation. Something good. He took a long look around him into the darkness; he had, he'd decided, said his goodbyes for now and forever.

Walker was seated now in the great hall of the orphanage where the children used to sit and eat at the end of the day. He looked out across the grounds and tried to imagine them playing there, but whatever joy – if any – this building had once held had long since faded into the stone walls and seeped down the stairwells until all the colours had been washed away. He pushed the food his men had brought him away and waited for night to finally fall.


It might have been the weekend, but Detective Green sat with a yellow notepad and his pen, scratching out his thoughts with curved, uneven arrows, exclamation points; names written hurriedly in capital letters and then scribbled out in what looked like a sudden explosion of fury. It looked like the gameplay plans of an indecisive football coach. Deep in concentration, he let the phone go three times until he answered it – even on a day off he could be called in and today he was too caught up in the minutia of something and nothing; he wanted to be held by the small stuff, he wanted to solve problems and unknot things, if only in his own head.

As he picked up the phone, two things struck him, though neither surprised him: Walker had his home phone number, and even though he could be anywhere in the world he was still here with him somehow, that ever unhappy face, that contemptuous veneer, his misery all-pervading even down a phone line. But Green breathed deeply and slowed his pulse, looked inward and tried to remain still as his heart began to beat hard inside of him; he could feel its bloody repetition as the temples flared in his skull. He tried to talk, but

Walker cut across him; he didn't sound angry, more detached, as if explaining that day's plans to his PA.

'I'm coming back to town, Green, there's one more thing I need to do.'

And for a moment, Green panicked, he imagined Walker outside his building; his men crouched outside his apartment door, ready to kill, one final fire from above, his door blowing in, the sound of gunfire; the sharp stink of smoke. His attempt at calm dissipated, he was as ready for a fight now as if he'd cornered a suspect whose one way out was past him. He was, he realised, gripping the phone too tightly.

'What's that, Walker?' he said quietly. 'Stuff another pool ball into some poor bastard's mouth, tread on a few more lives; break more bones?'

He listened intently even as he spoke; he was imagining figures scratching around outside his apartment, the soft click of a gun's hammer being pulled back into place, Walker's men preparing to charge.

'No,' said Walker, 'I want to atone.'

# November 1980

The warehouse rose up out of the night, one side of its façade a network of metal tubes and wooden planks like industrial ivy scaling a giant tree. Green couldn't understand the scaffolding covering one massive wall: they couldn't rent the place before the fire had almost consumed it, but now they were rebuilding, adding flesh to the bones of the structure that remained. Insurance, maybe, he thought, too expensive to pull down, maybe? But here it was, lit with security lamps and covered in alarm warnings, rectangles of red with stop signs emblazoned across their front. Inside, the corners were lit up by industrial-sized lamps, the floor was rippled with faint grey concrete; a metal stairwell ran up one wall, the roof was almost complete now, though some night sky still got in. He remembered the last time he'd been here, broken wood underfoot, the cold night air coming through the devastated ceiling, glittering constellations hundreds of thousands of miles away sending their last light to earth, Red in the far corner, her hair spread out, exploding silently away from her head. The blood at her temple, her innate stillness, how peaceful she looked – not all crime scenes were so strangely beatific. Green remembered how he'd leant over Red's body and had a strange and alien desire to lift her head suddenly, to cradle her for a moment before they took her away; he could imagine what his men might have been saying about that as he stepped carelessly all over their crime scene.

Walker stood against the building's back wall, as shadowy as the ones that consumed him, staring at an unwitting Green there caught in his reverie. It was winter the last time they'd been here, Red too. Though, as Walker had discovered, she'd kept coming back to this place more and more. Red, wanting to save everyone and everything in this world, except him, walls talked to her, buildings said her name; the streets came alive as she passed. She was as intangible and as connected to the universe as anyone he'd ever met; Walker's father might have been magical, he thought, but Red was the girl among the stars. She'd brought this place to life once, but in killing her, Walker had killed the building too; it might now be rising again as an edifice along the highway, but it was just bricks and mortar, the soul was gone out of it. Walker might have killed the thing he loved, but he'd also killed the thing she'd loved too; he took a grim satisfaction in that.

Green felt Walker behind him before he heard him. He tensed, instinctual and predatory, a feral cat caught by the sudden beam of a lit window.

'Green, so glad you could make it. I think I've actually missed you.'

Green turned and there was Walker dressed in Green's jacket that he'd taken off his unconscious body at the bottling factory. Blood still stained one lapel; it was torn, there were no buttons left on it as far as Green could tell.

'Nice fit, don't you think?' said Walker, examining the collar before brushing it down; he shot the cuffs and smiled like an alligator.

'You went out hard and fast at the factory,' said Walker, 'I didn't take you for a glass-jaw kind of guy. You were unconscious for a while there, one of my boys wanted to skin you. I thought that was crass. It's not like you could feel anything.'

'Nothing crass about shoving a pool ball down someone's throat then?' said Green evenly, counting the breaths he made, centring himself, stilling his heart to a manageable rate; the queasiness in his stomach made him feel lightheaded as if he were on the deck of a ship and it had suddenly dipped in an unexpected swell.

'The pool ball, that's, what's the phrase, a signature of sorts?' said Walker; he was still and remote, immutable, unblemished by all the blood he'd spilt, by the blood that covered him.

'My old man used to hustle at pool long after he made his millions,' said Walker, 'he said it gave him the common touch – that was his idea of the common touch, shaking the poor down for their last few dollars.' He looked squarely at Green. 'The pool ball, that's my nod to him, the passing of the torch from one generation to the next.' He made a shape with his hand as if he were holding a pool ball between thumb and finger, as if explaining his reasoning slowly to a child.

'He was a remarkable man, the most fully rounded bastard I've ever met. Were you close to your old man, Green? Silly question, of course you were, you still are; he's like your fucking guardian angel out there upstate, wearing his faith like some cheap watch. He was disappointed in your lack of faith, wasn't he, let down? Do you think that's why he didn't come to your rescue when I was taking pot shots at your face; I ruined a perfectly good pair of gloves on you, but then I did ruin your nose too.' Walker chuckled as if the thought had just struck him for the first time.

'You don't even flinch, do you? I'm standing here pissing on your back, calling out your old man, and nothing, not a flicker. I can see you in the interrogation room, those dead eyes, pure, unreflective black, all the colour run out of you, those poor bastards trying to see into you and there's nothing to see, is there, Green?'

Walker turned on his heel as if to leave and then spun around again, walking in a straight line towards Green. Posturing, thought Green, catwalk model, fucking idiot. Walker had paused as if to gather his thoughts and was then suddenly struck by them.

'Do you know what James said to me when I turned up with my friends to see him with a can of gas under my arm?' asked Walker. 'He wanted to know how I was, he was happy to see an old friend, he genuinely had no idea what I was doing there in the middle of the night with gasoline, he offered me sanctuary, maybe he thought my car had run dry and I was looking to refuel? Imagine, Green, imagine if I had turned up at your door with a container of gas – you'd have made me drink it and then beaten me half to death with the can and then you'd have done the right thing, you'd have taken my smashed, broken-down body and then you would have processed me. That's what you do, isn't it, process people? Push them down the pipe to their doom and then move on to the next thing.'

'They chose that path,' said Green. 'I just guide them along it.'

'She speaks! I love it when you talk back, I love it when we get to talk like this,' said Walker with a grin. 'Now then, let me tell you about James: even as my boys were holding him down and I was dousing him with gasoline, he told me he forgave me, he told me he loved me, that he could save me. The gas permeating his clothes, the smell of it stinking up that room, there was no fear in him. You know what I think, Green, I think he wanted to burn. His world was flames anyway, he was just another ember to add to the eternal fire.'

'He asked me to forgive you,' said Green, his jaw set so hard that his teeth were starting to ache.

'You'd have to forgive yourself first for that to happen, wouldn't you?' said Walker. 'For all the sins you've committed, hearts and hands broken, the men you've stood on, crushed. I bet your old man would want you to do the same thing, to forgive yourself.'

Breathe, thought Green; don't let him in, just breathe. When he was younger an older boy at a swimming pool had held his head under the water until Green thought his skull might explode, he thrashed and thrashed to no avail and then relaxed and gave in to it, and when the older boy could see there was no fun to be had there anymore he let him go. That's Walker, thought Green, a lifetime of bullying, bullied by his old man and then he in turn bullied his employees, his friends, the women who tried to love him. Stand in his way and he'd happily pay someone to beat you to death, he'd happily watch it happen too; stand over the body as it faded in and out of consciousness and produce a pool ball from his pocket and force it into the man's mouth, the muffled screams, thought Green, the snapping teeth. The ever-wronged Walker taking back what he thought was rightfully his.

Walker, sensing that he was losing his audience, stepped forward, but moved quickly back as Green's head snapped up again at the sound of movement.

'Attack dog,' said Walker. 'A big, ugly attack dog. In another life I could have hired you to work for me, to protect me, but you'd have turned on me one day, bitten the hand that feeds you, and like Moon you'd have ended up in that factory trying to bargain your way back to life. He cried, you know, like a little girl, once he knew the end was coming, once we'd got him in that place.' He moved to the far wall, Green's eyes following his every measured step, and picked up a wooden chair. Green wondered if he'd placed it there earlier for a moment like this. Walker dragged it back theatrically and sat down with a sigh.

'I'd offer you a seat, but as you can see ...' Walker spread his hands out wide to indicate the echoing emptiness. 'Imagine sleeping here, imagine what that must have felt like for Rose? The last time we spoke about her you snapped, my dear Green, do you remember? Those strong hands wrapped around my neck, banging my head against the drinks cabinet, my drinks cabinet!' A chuckle. 'If I didn't know you any better, then I'd think you might have been trying to kill me. You spilt my drink.' And only in that last moment did he sound at all slighted, almost hurt, the indignant boy angry at everything and everyone.

They were both silent then; there was the slow swish of the cars on the highway off in the distance, someone shouted a girl's name, but its shape was lost before it got to them.

'Someone called to tell us that Red was here that night,' said Green. 'That was you, wasn't it? Even though you killed her, you couldn't bear for her to be out here alone, you wanted someone to come and take her inside. But you couldn't take her with you, someone had to see your handiwork, that justice was served, that she'd crossed you and that you'd settled the debt.'

'Clichés, Green, Christ! You're better than that!' Walker was exultant, suddenly on his feet, head thrown back. 'Justice served? Debts settled?' He eased himself back into the chair and crossed one leg over the other, pausing to sniff at Green's blood on his lapel.

'Do you believe in the universe, Green?' Walker stared up at the ceiling and at the pocket of sky beyond. 'Do you believe that the universe takes as well as gives? Now I'm not talking about your God, the God that you think failed you, the God that your father brought into your house one Californian summer and tried to spoon-feed you. I'm talking about a series of weights and measures strung high up there among the clouds, things bartered and bought, things owed. I'll tell you what the universe meant to Rose, but first let me tell you what the universe means to me. My father touched the universe; Rose touched it too, but in different ways. My father's life was ordered, the skies spoke through him maybe, but he needed structure, the ideas of anarchy and disorder made him feel physically sick.'

'So you brought anarchy and disorder to him?' asked Green.

'I gave him life, I took him outside of the boundaries of his own world,' said Walker with his head hanging forward; his posture was that of a broken puppet, his swept-back hair now hanging down in shining strands. 'God spoke to him and yet he lived mutely, my father built his own walls and lived discreetly behind them. I chose to break those walls down.'

Walker thought back to that final night in his father's hospital room, still amazed at the old man's final rattling exit – how much life had actually been left in him? When he'd appeared at his father's bedside, the old man hadn't even looked surprised; even as Walker prepared himself to deliver the final, metaphorical hammer blow, his father, even while taking in oxygen through a thin tube looped around his skull, told him he lacked insight, that even his desire to kill his own father was a Shakespearean cliché, that he had fulfilled his own destiny by becoming the failure his father had always imagined him to be. Walker blotted out his life as much to stop the noise as he did to take control of his father's company.

'Tell me about Rose,' said Green. 'Tell me all of it.'

'Always the detective, Green; this is my last will and testament, I'm here to tell you everything, so that we might share this moment and see where fate might finally lead us. We'll get there, but I'll tell you this: it was her fault things fell apart finally, she brought out the human in me and what ungracious vermin we are. She snared me; spat me out; said I couldn't be saved. Me, Green, as if I wanted to be saved!' He stood up and kicked his chair back so that it went skittering along the concrete floor.

Dramatist, thought Green, idiot boy, and wondered how long he would have to listen to this until he could pin Walker to the floor, break his jaw and then take him in.

'Dark thoughts, Detective Green?' smiled Walker. 'Your eyes might have died but that brooding forehead, that ever-tightening face always gives you away.

'You got away from Rose, didn't you, Green? You were the one she really wanted, but even you were beyond her reach. Look at us now, the men she touched, Alejandro, Hank, me, who knows how many others? Nothing but ashes, all of us; she stalked Washington Square seducing us, taking us in. The first time she spoke to me I never made the connection that she was one of Bulley's flock, the very monster I'd created, the monster I finally killed! Christ, if only I hadn't crossed the park that day, Green; she took my wrist, I let her touch me, she made me vulnerable, can you imagine?'

It was a rare for Walker to be out of his car or his glass-walled office, but that morning, returning from a meeting, he'd ordered his driver to go through the city so that he might gather his thoughts before he had to return and face his old man and explain once again why he wanted to push the company forward in one direction while his father still clung to the past, forever formulating words for the world to speak. I'm an antenna, the old man would say, I'm tuned into the universe – crediting the sky for his gifts, but still revelling in all their glories, happy to have their praise heaped on him and to reap the rewards. Washington Square was quiet; still, Walker couldn't remember the last time he was truly still. And then Rose was there, he saw a flash of copper hair out of the corner of his eye, long, curling tresses that billowed mutely and then she was seated next to him; he glanced furtively sideways to take in the green of her eyes and she was staring directly at him, into him.

'You look,' she said, 'like you could use a friend.' Her hand was at his wrist, just lightly enough that he could move his arm away if he chose, but he let it sit, suddenly itchy yet thrilled. She was beautiful, the focus of her face her piercing eyes, the red of her long hair framing her pale features; he couldn't see beyond her anymore, in that moment the city fell out of sight, he felt consumed. And then he shook her and it off, stalking across Washington Square looking out for his driver and car, looking to get away; he felt pursued, like the runt in the pack suddenly marked out for death. This, he thought, suddenly breathless, is ridiculous. He bought women and then gave them away, closed down any kind of feeling, hid them out of sight. How many times had he heard the phrase 'piece of shit' or something similar as the elevator doors had closed quietly and he'd smiled, happy the negotiation was finished, the contract complete and to his advantage.

'Where are you going?' Rose said, and as she stopped to wait for his reply he knew that if he turned to answer her then he had lost the upper hand; that he had acquiesced. He spent his life negotiating, dealing cards, playing the dead-eyed monster that never caved in; he always had the last word. People said he was made of stone and he liked that, liked to feel them reaching out for him only to have them recoil on contact. And so what was this? This strange woman who had reached out for him on a park bench – he often wondered later what might have happened if he hadn't stopped that day, if he'd stayed in the car, if he'd never met Rose, opened himself up like a wound and let her see him bleed, taste his blood. And so he had turned and she had smiled at him and asked his name and in giving her that he had, briefly and eventually, given her everything.

'But you knew Bulley, you must have known what the church was about, what Red was selling?' said Green; a light rain had started coming in through the corner of the warehouse where the roof remained unfinished. He watched it smearing the floor.

'I never went there, I never went inside there, I should say; I knew that was where Bulley did his work' – Walker made ironic inverted commas with his fingers. 'She talked about her leader, her priest, about him, but I never went to that basement, I'd had enough of cults and religions and people gathering in groups like cowed livestock hoping to be spared, to be saved.' He was venomous now, stung by something, he was on the attack.

'I told her she could try and save me, that I'd read her flyer ...' Walker reached into the pocket of his coat and fished out a glossy, thin pamphlet, bent and pored over a hundred times, its corners now losing their colour. 'This flyer,' he waved it weakly around. 'She said that if I read it, if I truly took it in, that maybe she could persuade me to visit the basement with her, and I agreed, but only if she'd go for a drink with me first. I thought I was playing her – what's the phrase, love makes fools of us all? If that's the case, then I was a complete fucking idiot.'

Walker was quiet then, back inside the flyer, trying to reach for some time long ago where he briefly held Rose and she him. Green watched him and finally felt some empathy for this monster, and some understanding of Red's power too. Walker had kept the flyer the way other people kept photos in their wallet, as if by holding on to something physical, something tangible, you could somehow make a two-way street out of love – send it away and someday it might come back to you. But you were just chasing empty shadows down, running into walls, forever calling the memories back, because that's all they were now; memories. And memories don't care, thought Green, that's why he strangled his; slowly suffocated them until they were gone.

'What happened to you?' asked Green; it was less the detective talking, just two men now: the night outside falling towards them. I could drink, thought Green, right now, I could open a bottle and pour it down my throat and not care about the consequences; damn the morning, damn the shape tomorrow takes.

'It was fine at first, you know?' said Walker in a voice that Green had not heard before. 'She teased that she could take me away from the dark side, bring me into the light, and for a while that was all right, the promise that things might change, that I could be the way she wanted.' He was pacing back and forth now, agitated, his shoulders hunched, he was a picture of furious concentration. The malice, thought Green, it rose up underneath him like a sudden riptide, his fingers tightened like he was holding on for dear life or strangling the breath out of someone else.

'It was good, you know, the way all these things are in the beginning,' said Walker; his tone was genial, this was the abstract, the way in which men address each other, they could have been talking sports or politics or about distant wars, there was much nodding, murmured assent, the occasional flicker of eye contact, total agreement, shared memories, they were addressing the past but here in the now with half-gestures, mute and gentle gesticulation; masculine shorthand.

'We'd go to dinner a lot, she liked Italian, seafood too,' said Walker, colouring in the outline that Red was to Green. 'She was odd, she had this whole country bumpkin shtick going on, it was a role she was playing, I guess, but she knew her power, she knew she was beautiful. If you'd only got one real look at her, got the chance to soak it all up, take it all in, it was like staring into the sun, but you couldn't look away. You only saw the hollowed-out shell, the aftermath, when the divine spirit had departed the body. That was how she spoke, "the divine spirit", what bullshit.'

Green stared at him, fascinated by the sudden rise and fall of his moods, the abrupt stabbing anger, then the strange childlike hurt in his eyes. Always on the edge, thought Green, but never able to quite let himself be free, never able to leap into the abyss of the unknown; he looked like he might cry when he talked about Red and then as if realising that might reveal too much of himself, of the man, he lashed out, but only so that his feelings might be contained, that everything be bottled up, an impassive face for an outside world trying to look in. Just a boy, thought Green, forever thirteen, always caught on the spokes of time.

'She wanted,' said Walker, 'someone just like you, strong, silent, pure of heart. Clothes maketh the man, right?' Unable to hide the smallest of sneers, he pulled at the ruddy red-black and bloody stain that covered the lapel of Walker's jacket. 'So what does your off-the-peg attire make me? Am I more of a man now, more the kind of guy Rose could be happy with? The sort of man she might take on?'

Green couldn't tell if his tone was mocking or something more fragile, as if Walker were compressing the words together and that way they might never fall apart. There was no space in his sentences to let emotion in or out, it was a hard-driven mantra, Green imagined this scenario had played out before if only in Walker's head. This was prepared, something he needed to be heard. Maybe this really was the last will and testament that he'd spoken of.

'There's a point in your life, any life,' said Walker, it was getting late, the cars passed less frequently on the highway, the unhurried silence of night moving towards another morning, a new day was coming, 'where you are the story – do you know what I mean, Green?' Green was quiet, he didn't.

'No imagination, Detective!' said Walker, but he was smiling a strangely toothy grin, a predatory, mad-eyed face filled with extremes. 'Let me tell you a story, everyone has their story, even you, are you sitting comfortably, then I'll begin.'

He looked hysterical then; Green tensed for the impact of attack, but it was as if Walker didn't even see him anymore, he was addressing the room now. 'A successful, handsome polymath, a gifted man, our hero,' said Walker, talking to the roof beams, 'meets and falls in love with a beautiful redhead, a country girl at heart all alone in the big city, she, and I'm condensing it for you here, Green, no one likes a show-off, right? Anyway, she tries to save him, but he's a guy, he doesn't even think he needs saving, he doesn't see the heartache he's caused, the pain he's visited on the world, the murderous deeds he's committed.'

Green started at the words, but Walker's fervour was undiminished, he was a man moved to impart his story, he had his tale to tell.

'Because this man, no matter what you might think, he started out as a good man, his intentions were pure, his heart was in the right place, he wasn't like his old man, he wanted to help people, not obscure their vision, not blind them to all the pain in the world, because life's pain, Green? You can't hide all your life, the world isn't black and white, it's a spectrum of colours, it's abstract, sometimes it's joy and sometimes it's just pain. Look who I'm telling that to, Detective Green, a man covered in the blood and misdeeds of others, I don't know how you carry that around with you, how you trudge ever forward day after day.'

Walker stopped then as if to take Green fully in for the first time. It was as if he could see the darkness that surrounded him, the stink of death and disappointment, the anger and dismay that soaked through his clothes until they touched and tattooed his very skin, until they became a part of him.

'Most men couldn't stay standing under the weight of things that you've seen, Green, but somehow you keep going, like a silent, steel ship churning through deep waters, you're almost eerie.' Walker gave a tilt of his head. 'No offence, Detective, but you're hard to make out, the man within is almost invisible sometimes.' Walker paused as if to collect his thoughts, to realign the ideas in his head.

'But where was I? So, our hero is desperate not to repeat the misdeeds of his dad, he always wanted to try to help people, show them the truth, but you know, Green, people don't want to hear the fucking truth, they want to be blinkered and coddled, deliberately misled. And this upset our hero more than our hero might like to admit and so he ploughed the same singularly self-serving, incredibly profitable furrow like his old man had and his old man before that. And he let something black and hard fill up the space where his heart had been.

'I was bad kid, Green, I won't deny that, but I thought there might have been redemption in my work, that I might have somehow clawed my way back, but when there's nothing left of you to save, then how could I have possibly ever been saved? Do you think karma got me, that after the evil I rained down on Blue and those people then things could never be right for me again? You can't repay those kinds of universal debts, I guess. There was nowhere to go, Rose couldn't help me, I was beyond help by the time she came along.'

Walker was quiet, assimilating and re-assimilating the roadblocks and dead ends that made up his mind. He'd spent his life running metaphorical stop signs until he'd run out of road to raise hell on. He'd come to rest, to understand introspection and what it really meant. He'd finally been able to see and hadn't liked the reality, clarity wasn't for him; he liked his vision muddied and bloody. He enjoyed the blurred, soft edges where he could get away with murder.

'That's what Rose gave me,' he said. 'A way of seeing, but it turns out I was just like those people who didn't want to hear the truth, when it came down to it, I wanted to be blind, just like the rest of them. Our hero was as scared of truly seeing himself as much as the next man, not much of a hero, I guess. I bet you don't flinch at your reflection, do you, Green? I bet you don't panic slightly every time you go to shave. And so this sweet country girl found she couldn't help our hero, she saw him for what he was and she knew there was no goodness to be found there, no way through to reach the light. Especially when there was no light.

'I have this theory, bear me out, I'll be done soon.' Walker paused. 'That thing I said earlier about being the story at a given point in your life, it goes like this. I think we're all just stories in other people's lives, and for a while people want to read that story, whether it's because they love or hate you or you've been thrown together through circumstance, people like us, Green, and those stories begin and those stories end, people stop reading you, they put you down, they riffle through your pages, but one day you're not the story anymore, that make sense? Rose stopped reading me, she put me down; she closed the book.'

Green knew exactly what he meant and wished he didn't.

'I've described an arc,' said Walker. 'The story has moved on, my story has moved on, it's ended. Once we're the story and then we are not the story, stop me if I'm getting too metaphysical for you.' There was that wild-eyed grin again.

'You and your family, you were the story; that was your narrative and then your son he was no more, and then your marriage was no more and for you that story had ended. The commune, Blue, Bulley, Alejandro, Henry, did you believe that fuck? That she would even fuck someone like him? She saw something in him that she could never see in me.'

Walker's face reddened, somewhere between loathing and loss. 'You met him – what was in there, what did she see in that neurotic lump? I was happy to hang him from that tree like a star at Christmas.'

Green couldn't help himself: 'Billy, that was you too?'

Walker was only half-listening. 'Alejandro, the pretty boy who tried to fly,' he said. 'Billy was one of ours, yes, do you know he thought she and I were married? We snatched him from the street – the confusion, the puzzlement on his face. He was on his way to meet Rose, did you know that, Detective? After Billy and I had talked it out, I went and sat outside the bar they were to meet at and watched her wait for him. I might be imagining it, but I thought I saw frustration, anger and then resignation on that pretty face of hers. Love's like that, isn't it?

'And then Alejandro always trailing behind her like a lovelorn puppy, I ...' Walker was quiet, as if now puzzled by his decision to have his men kick Alejandro from this world and into the next.

'You saw something of yourself there,' said Green. 'Waiting unloved alone in a bar, that was your place there at Red's side. You wanted her so badly, mystified that she didn't want you, that even the threat of someone else being her desperate shadow was more than you could stomach. So you made him one of your disappeared too; you're pathetic, a fucking kid who chose to strong-arm his way through the world.'

Walker flushed pink; it would have looked like blushing if it had been anyone else, but he was starting to burn now, the flames licking at his shoulders and neck, threatening to engulf both shoulders. Though his voice was even, stilled among the jumbled edges of his rage.

'I did for all of them,' said Walker. 'I was their full stop, and as for Rose, we wrote her final chapter after she closed the book on me, and now together, Green, you and me, we're writing these final words, these ideas etched on a page somewhere and who will read that story, Green, how soon will you and I be forgotten, who will be the last person to turn our page, to see these characters locked together? One's outcome intertwined with the other's, neither of us can end his story until the other has finished his. One of us has to stop, one of us has to be stopped.'

Walker looked hard at Green, the black of his pupils enlarging until they seemed to become the whole of his eyes. He was ranting now; his voice was strangled, flecks of spit traced his ever-reddening lips; he was, thought Green, as close to unkempt as he was ever going to be. His madness had unravelled him, he was upended; he looked as if he'd actually been shaken. His face was fully red now, his eyes oily pools, glassy and enraged.

'She wanted me to see the light,' said Walker. 'Her light, bathe in it, and I flew too close, like a dizzy moth around a bulb, a Greek fable falling from the sky. I got burned and fell, Rose cast me out, Green, and then my story was told and I was done.' He stopped and stared. 'And then I snuffed that light out, her story, it had to end.'

And then, suddenly, Green was looking into that light, could feel it burning his skin, it was as if the sun shone bright and fierce, like someone had tethered it as a giant balloon just feet from the warehouse roof. Hard beams of white coming through the unfinished walls and ceiling; Green imagined floodlights blossoming at an early-evening football game, his father waving from the bleachers. The light hitting the sea at the beach when he was a kid, making the water look glassy and impenetrable, he fought hard not to shade his eyes, the sunshine caught in the explosion of heavy droplets as the spray of white water scattered against the sky and into the endless reach of blue beyond that as he waded into deeper water. And then as if he'd suddenly broken the surface like a shark bearing down on its prey, Walker was there to meet him.

Later, Green would remember that moment and wonder at the loss of blood, the ferocious impact, the dull sound the metal bar made as it hit his arm and his ribs and caused a small firework display to go off at the corner of his right eye as it glanced off his temple. Though the attack was sudden, there was a clarity to that moment; he saw, he swore to himself, Red in the room, she was a blaze of light bleaching the corner of the warehouse, the place where he'd first seen her bloody and broken. She was still, her hair moving slowly, undulating, as if she were trapped underwater, its ghostly movement lifting her lilting copper coils towards the high, broken ceiling. Moments before the first blow, he'd looked past Walker, who was still entranced by his own words, by the speech he was making, and Red, he swore, turned to look at Green, she was all bleached bones and crystal green eyes and she mouthed one word to him: 'Run.' But then, as if he had also heard her instruction, Walker too was running hard and into Green, they both exhaled, the air leaving them in an explosive burst.

'This story ends.' Walker was gasping, but he was calm, his fury contained. Green knew how much harder it was to fight someone who was in control of themselves and for all of Walker's demented rhetoric, he was here now, intent on seeing this through. This is what Green thought as they grappled together, entwined figures falling quickly to the floor. Dust rose and settled on their contorted features, Green felt his own dried blood on the jacket that Walker had stolen from him, it brushed up against his face as he reached around to punch Walker in the kidneys and tried to bite him through his cheek. They were a tangle of legs and thighs, intimate in this colluded violence, heads butting at each other, each trying to find a foothold so they could somehow start to finish this, spectral fingers of the coming sun set as brands across their backs.

'Naughty,' chided Walker, but his face was pale and there was a scratch near his eye, a pulsing red trail already turning to a bloody bruise.

And there they were, these two men locked together for a moment, two stories being told then if only to the other. Green had wrested the iron bar away and now it lay like a promise mere feet from their scuffling forms. Green imagined Red standing nearby, remote now and forever removed from them both. He wondered at how he had made this so personal a vendetta; if this bloody conclusion was his way back to the world, back to feeling again. And then he thought how far he'd fallen, about the path his father had chosen, brief, fleeting moments, his wife Nancy's long forgotten face, an image he'd locked away and hidden so deeply that not even he knew where it was buried anymore. And his beautiful boy: that moment of life caught like something seen and unseen as quickly as a face flashing by from the window of a moving train, there and then gone. And in that moment, his old world falling upward and away from him, long after he'd gone as far down as he could possibly go, Louis Green decided to get up.

He wrestled one hand free and jammed both his fingers into Walker's eyes and pushed hard. He felt the give in both eyeballs, the lids trying to close around his fingers as if that might deter them, the sudden twist of panic in Walker's body, the surprised gasp.

'Cunt,' said Walker, trying to wrest his body away even as Green was clambering on top of him, pressing him down hard into dusty concrete of the warehouse floor. Green thought of Red lying here once, Walker standing above her wielding a piece of wood, his men unflinching and remote, waiting for another atrocity to be completed so they could start the car, escape the cold and make it back to the city. It had taken one blow to her head, Red spinning with a sudden smear at her temple, the blood running into her ear, a small grunt of confused pain; she saw Walker dissolve and then steady and then dissolve again, called out to the empty skies and was gone before Walker's tears had landed to stain the pale cotton of her shirt.

'You set the fire, you drew her here, you knew she loved this place, so by torching the warehouse you'd bring her back here, then you broke her heart and then you broke her.' Green was gasping, his words coming in staccato bursts, kneeling over Walker now, smashing his head into the concrete, his rage making everything sluggish and blurred.

'The fire cleans,' said Walker, but his voice came from far away, as if it wasn't his anymore. 'Broke her heart,' he said, it was a low snarling sound, the last of his anger, 'she broke my heart,' and then in among the snot and the blood pooling beneath Walker's face there came surprising tears and a wrenching sob pulled deep from within his guts.

Walker had felt their roles reversed, the sudden, unstoppable shift, like trying to reach for an already fallen object. He felt the long suppressed evil in a vengeful Green rise up before him in a ghastly wave. And then the halogen lights of the warehouse seemed to burn and dip, their outline a ghostly haze. And all the pretty girls Walker had once walked over the hill into the arms of their gruesome fate now stood before him, he imagined absolution, a slate wiped clean, but the pity, sadness and fear that had once welled up in their eyes was now turning into something unholy. He saw Rose at their head as he felt his life being choked out of him as he had once choked the life out of those girls. A faint flicker of empathy for those young bodies he'd once buried on that lonely hill swam in and out of his thinking as this parade of the damned that he'd dispatched to hell lit briefly upon him to prick the numbed ends of his conscience. Green had become a blunt instrument sent to hammer the life out of him; Walker rolled onto his back and saw the stars, and he saw the heavens, but like Rose before him he saw no God, the skies were forever empty.

Green's breathing was laboured, the sound of a man who had pushed himself as far and as hard as he could, there was sweat stinging his eyes, blood dashed across his knuckles, two of which were now almost certainly broken. His hair was matted and his jacket and pants torn from the sharp edges of the concrete floor. Though he only lay a few feet from him, Walker was an unrecognisable mess, his features pulpy and misshapen; he looked like wet cardboard, a dirty muddle of clothes, something best left outside. Green had rolled away from him when he could barely make a fist anymore, and so now he sat up; his head felt crushed, a spasm of pain spiked through his throat; he touched his neck gingerly, imagining a piece of glass jutting out of him at an obscene angle, something he'd be forced to pull free in order that he might heal, but his gently probing fingers found nothing, just the oily smear of Walker's spit and blood. His shoulder felt separated from the rest of his body and his knee had locked so that his right leg felt like it might never bend again. He felt, he thought, older than he had ever felt in his life before. He pushed himself slowly backwards along the floor, keeping Walker in his sight, though he knew that if Walker had suddenly come springing back to life, there would be nothing that he could do about it now, only watch as Walker bled the life out of him, pushed a hitherto unseen pool ball into his mouth, but Walker was still, practically lifeless, perhaps, Green considered, I might have actually killed him. Green grunted slowly backwards until he felt his back reach the pale, unfinished walls of the warehouse, he let his head drop back and saw and felt the loneliness of space millions of miles away above his head.

Had he seen Red, had she really warned him away? He was woozy and losing blood, he knew what the mind could create or call on when things got desperate, he knew he needed help and in that moment he'd called on Red and she'd come, or that's what he'd tell himself if he ever felt like telling this story again. And then he was suddenly a kid again, the Californian night was above him, because wasn't the sky that shone here the same one that had reached down to him along the beaches in California before he and his father had moved east? He was twelve and the rain was reaching upwards, retreating from the earth, and he had run outside and stretched his arms and hands high and tried to touch the cosmos and feel where the rain had disappeared to that night. He imagined travelling upwards among the spokes of rain, being lifted within the thin sheets of water, passing up towards the clouds and glancing back at his father's home as it became a distant rectangle of lights set among hundreds and then thousands of other boxes, of other acres of subdivided homes. He saw the fields and beyond, imagined his father racing into the yard to find where his son had gone, never guessing that he'd been spirited away with the weather. And then he was beyond the clouds, chasing the rain towards the heavens, never wondering how far he might yet fall.

'Where are you, Green, where's your head?' said Walker in a voice as broken as his features, his blood making an elongated black puddle around his shoulders and head, his hair sticking to the warehouse floor. 'For God's sake, come back,' he hissed, 'or we're going to die here.'

Green heard his name and thought his father was speaking to him from somewhere, he focused suddenly, surprised to find himself here back on earth somewhere, propped up against a warehouse wall on the margins of the city. 'My father,' he said, as he came to. 'I heard my father's voice, he was calling out to me.'

'Your old man's upstate, he's safe.' The blood in Walker's mouth was making him gurgle; he tipped himself onto his side and spat reddish drool across the floor. 'What are you going to do?' he asked, trying to raise a hand to his ribs to feel for fractures. 'Green?'

And Detective Green was going to do what any good cop would do.

'Call it in,' said Green as a hacking cough slowly caught in his chest, thrummed through his newly loosened teeth and threatened to rattle the life right out of him.

# December 1980

If a stranger had happened upon him, they might have thought that a group of children had been taking it in turns to colour Detective Green's face in. There was a swirl of green here, a patch of black there; his jawline was a mute explosion of purple bruises. The nurse at the hospital had joked that it was only a shame that he'd missed Halloween and he told her she should have seen the state of the other guy and she was still laughing as his half-smile turned into wincing, unremitting pain.

The sudden ring of the phone still made him flinch, something as revelatory as it was unwelcome and new since he'd literally run into Walker, or he him. Picking up the receiver too now made Green's hand ache; his fist felt like it would never fully unclench again. It was his father's voice on the telephone. He normally called his son on a Sunday and so Green was surprised to hear his low hello again on a Monday.

'They killed John Lennon.'

Green was home and had heard nothing about it: he'd been living in some kind of seclusion since that night at the warehouse. The sound of the streets unsettled him, every dark corner promised trouble, strangers glared, the sound of sirens – ironic given that it was the sound of their approach that signalled that he and Walker would live – spooked him. He felt like a skittish dog always on edge, he could hardly bear the sound of the radio now, let alone the intermittent squawk of his police transmitter. He'd hardly been back to work at all since he'd done his best to kill Walker; he was being forced to attend sessions with the squad's therapist – did he harbour murderous thoughts or intentions? Did he have a handle on his drinking these days? Had he ever truly gotten over the death of his son and the subsequent divorce? How did he feel now that Walker's lawyers were talking about suing him and the police department, Green had acted outside the law, he was a vigilante not a cop, that the case against their client was bullshit and Green was to blame? How did that make him feel, asked the therapist? Stressed, he guessed, he was almost always tired now, he couldn't hold a conversation, he'd done the best he could and now it wasn't enough, he was the bad guy and Walker the victim. And so here he was at home, staying away from the windows, rarely leaving his apartment, his knee flaring up when it got cold outside. While Walker sat in a hospital bed up at Riker's Island as his army of lawyers coerced and complained that this was no way to treat an innocent man, the real victim in this atrocity. Part of Green wished they'd both died on the warehouse floor and had done with it, it felt like there might be a sense of dignity in that, one that was missing from this.

'They killed John Lennon.' It was his father, more insistent this time.

Green realised he'd drifted away from the voice on the phone, he'd felt punch-drunk and concussed for weeks, and admitted that he probably was; tuning out of conversations was just one of the symptoms. He instantly recognised the traces of grief, anger and confusion in his father's voice, he'd heard it before in recordings of victim's reports, as people were being attacked, the call for help from family members, someone going into a seizure on the floor nearby, no matter the scenario, it always made him think of flecks of black and grey, he saw the white noise of sadness building up around their words.

Months later after the full story of the killing had unfolded, he'd think of Mark Chapman's misery and madness turning into an obsession until it overflowed and became a ruddy deluge that caught John Lennon up in its filthy wave and swept him away. He knew the old man liked the music and was appalled when – as his father had it – the small-minded tyranny of the US government had tried to get Lennon thrown out of America, but he often thought that was more about the way his old man liked to rail against the system than anything to do with Lennon's basic human rights. When his father was living in Manhattan he often said that he liked the idea of living in the same city as a Beatle, but this was more, here was his father grieving, it sounded like he was shedding real tears.

'Who'd want to kill him, who'd want to shoot him down in the street like that?'

Green wasn't sure if his father was asking if he knew more than the news was already telling people, but he soon realised that it was just the sound of his dad disentangling, trying to find an answer where there was none; it made no sense then and it never would. This was the old man he recognised when he'd had his crisis of confidence and began to doubt his God, began to think that his was a life wasted on an idea; that he'd really been preaching to an empty sky.

'You don't believe in a God, I'm not sure you ever have,' his father had said to him earlier that summer; they were seated in his father's study, it was Sunday and the sermon he'd delivered that morning had felt, to the old man at least, flaccid and uninspired. He used to preach with verve and passion, but he was always empathetic, he had no time for showboating, he was no Blue.

'I know it's still a job,' said his father, 'but you have to believe in your job and I'm not sure I do anymore. Look at you, this case with this man Walker and this girl, this Rose, it's almost taken over your life and it hurts me to see you that way, so torn, but determined, but when you lost your boy ...' He looked at his only son and could never imagine the pain and grief of losing your own family, that part of you; even now he still worried about Louis every day he wasn't at his side. 'But the job, it was what got you through, it kept you alive.'

'You kept me alive,' said Green gently, placing his hand on his father's. His father turned his hand over and they sat there for a moment, fingers linked in the quiet hush of these suburban streets, and wondered at what the other had become, what had become of themselves, these men they'd made.

'You have always had me and you always will, I'm your father, but the job was the thing, it's your way of helping people, it's how you get those things you need to do done. You want to see the good in the world and the only way you think you can achieve that is by wiping out the evil. That's the way you were made, maybe that's the way I made you, but I can see no flaws in that or you, Louis. And no matter what it takes, you'll bring that girl Rose some redemption, you won't let her be lost and tossed away for nothing. I know you won't agree with me, son, but you were put here to help and I'm proud of that and I'm proud of you.'

And his father held him hard by his shoulders and shook him a little as if he might wake him, might make him realise all the good he had done and was doing.

'I'm not sure what's going to happen next, Louis, but you'll come through this, maybe I will too, and right now you're hurt and you're lost and you can't see a way through this case, it's all bloody dead ends, I've no idea of the horrors you've seen, but you've never been cowed before, only by the bottle maybe.' He bowed his head so they were eye to eye. 'Don't let this beat you.'

And then he gently held Louis' jaw the way he had the day he told him they were moving from the West Coast to the East and the boy had cried out no, that he wouldn't go. But the old man had pushed on because then, as now, he knew that he needed his son to know it was the right and only thing to do.


Green thought about that now as his father was still talking on the end of the phone.

'Dad.' His father stopped abruptly. 'You're never going to stop preaching, are you?'

'Me? Hell no, whatever gave you that idea? People need me, even more now than they ever did, how do you make sense of something like this, Lennon had a family, you know? People need guidance and help at a time like this, it's not as if the holidays aren't lonely enough as it is. What a fucking waste, sorry, but it really is.'

'I'll come and see you soon, Dad. We'll talk it through, we'll play some of his music, celebrate his life and try not to mourn too much.'

'I'd like that,' said his dad, and then before he put the phone down: 'And how are you doing now, you still look like a clown who fell asleep in his make-up?'

Green laughed, doubling up a little. 'Don't make me laugh, ah. I'm okay, I guess. Walker's people are trying to get him out and I think they might, they're talking about a civil suit against me, but we've got enough on him outside of this that it won't come to anything. They're just making a smokescreen to hide all his other fucking atrocities. He's evil, Dad, I'm not going to let that endure.'

'Me neither, okay, son, but let someone else do the heavy lifting this time, yeah? You've done everything you can.'

Green replaced the phone and stretched out his hand and made a determined fan of his fingers. While somewhere uptown, Walker was being helped into the back of his limousine; like Green he was moving slower than he once did, both eyes were black rings and his nose had been reset, his jaw was a steel plate and he walked with a stick for support. He sat down with an audible sigh and stretched his legs out with a groan.

'Sorry it took so long to get you out of there,' said the lawyer seated to Walker's left. 'We need to go over a few papers before we decide what we're going to do next.'

Walker was staring intently out of the window and up at the snatches of sky reflecting in the buildings overhead.

'Where are we going?' he said without turning his head.

'We were going to take you home, get you settled in, make you comfortable there …'

'Do you think it's going to snow?' asked Walker, cutting across the conversation. 'It feels too early for snow, but look at the silver in the sky, like thousands of tiny needles waiting to rain down on us.'

'I didn't see the forecast,' said the lawyer, but Walker stopped his words with a sudden wave of his gloved hand.

'I want to go to the office,' he said and then he turned to look at the man. 'My dad used to be in that building too, did you know that? Down the hall a little, same floor; when I used to go and visit him when I was a kid I'd look out at that view and know it was where I wanted to be one day.'

'I was sorry to hear about your father,' said the lawyer, but Walker was staring out of the window again, waiting for the car to take the next turning and him to where he wanted to be.

Downtown, Green pushed himself up from his seat and walked to the window, edging the blinds back so he could take in the traffic and the greying sky. Snow, or maybe there's a storm coming, he thought, as he reached for his coat and a scarf.

Uptown, Walker stood in his father's old office; he could see the Hudson River off to his right and the occasional gleam of the industrial landscape beyond that, outbuildings and warehouses; he wondered if he and his men had spent any time over there. A snowflake came gently tumbling out of the steely sky and pressed itself against the window where he stood; he could briefly make out of the fine, irregular edges before the wind unpicked it from its place on the glass and made it suddenly disappear.

'Like magic,' said Walker.

He walked slowly down the corridor to his own office and leaned over his desk, reaching down to the bottom right-hand drawer, which he unlocked with a key he fished out of his pocket. Inside were two pool balls, a red number three ball and a green with the number six set inside a circle on a strip that wrapped around it. He put one each in the pockets of the long coat he was wearing like a man loading himself down with rocks who's getting ready to drown.

Green walked slowly across the park; the road was busier than he might have liked, but he'd be damned if he was going to be spooked by traffic. He was heading towards his precinct; he wanted to be around his men, he wanted to feel part of that throng, to belong. They'd caught Walker and no matter what happened now he was going to loosen his grip on this city. Green walked to the subway that would lead him across the street and hesitated at the top of the steps and peered down into the darkness and the figures moving around in there. The snow was building now, catching in his hair and settling on his face, he readjusted his scarf and stepped forward, going only down.

Walker moved some books from the shelves against the back wall of the office to reveal a safe that was hidden away there. He looked around him to make sure he was alone, opened the safe up and carefully took out the human skull that was sitting there. He kissed it softly on the crown and gently placed it in inside his leather holdall and walked to the elevator. He nodded at someone on his staff whose name he couldn't remember or never knew and entered the elevator alone and took it to the top floor. It was one flight of stairs up to the roof, but he took them carefully, afraid that he might slip and break the girl's skull he now carried under his arm. He pushed opened the door to the roof against a strong headwind that was carrying the snow in juddering waves up here and walked steadily towards the roof's perimeter. He stood alone for a moment and held up the skull as if to take it all in.

'I put you in the ground,' he said quietly as the snowstorm built around him and clung to his clothes; the wind made his coat-tails straighten and snap, he could barely see more than a few feet in front of him. 'I can't make good on all those things I did,' he said, the sound of the storm becoming louder and louder in his ears, 'but I can follow you down.' And Walker took Lisa's skull and he threw it as hard as he could into the face of the storm and out towards the snow-filled horizon and he quickly stepped out after it, his hand reaching for one final embrace as they both fell into the dazzling sky forever.


As Green hobbled painfully out of the subway and up the steps to the street above a sudden flurry of snow blew in towards him, making the interior of the stairwell suddenly bright. He instinctively reached for the glowing mass, making a fist around a handful of flakes, and then stopped with a jolt as the snow pulled back and started to rise upwards and away into the sky. He looked around him, but like the night the rain reversed, no one else was there to see the sky fold up in on itself. He followed its upward trajectory, taking the stairs uncertainly like a man who's suddenly exited a dark room and is struggling to see in the unfamiliar light. He opened his fist and stared at the quickly fading crystalline stars in his palm, he tried to still their watery decay with a useless intense stare and found himself thinking of Mr Porter clinging to the body of his dead wife, like all the things he had once tried to cling to, and like Porter he could only go on living now and the things that he had once held were now so much water simply running through his fingers. He stared hard at the shallow pool of memories on his hand.

Then the sky fell inwards again and wrapped itself around him until he was lost in the white, his features disappearing in the sudden maelstrom, then he and Red were standing suddenly alone among the flakes, two hazy columns of colour among the nothingness, then the sky sucked hard and he imagined her hand in his as the sky retreated one final time and then the snow was falling normally again, the street lights flooding through the white haze, cars moved, someone brushed against his shoulder, he sidestepped a crack in the sidewalk and picked up his pace. He pulled up his collar and bunched both fists down into his pockets and kept on walking, hoping that as both hands dried the memories would diminish too, that the colour of those thoughts might finally fade and disappear forever, that the spectrum might fragment and become so much dust, that he'd get past this, that the intangible pull of need and want might finally set him free. And he repeated small words of hope to himself and kept on walking until he became a speck against the city and the snow kept falling until it was hard to see him anymore.

# Thank You

Thank you for helping with the heavy lifting: Grant Moon (have you tried changing this...), Piers Leighton, Mikey Evans, Dai Edwards, Neil Lach-Szyrma, Andy Bass, Alexander Milas, Sian Llewellyn, Tanya Slater (now stop going on about it!), Zaki Boulos, James, Nicky and Sean Manic, Geddy, Nancy and the Wassermans (thanks for sharing the lake with us), Alex and Neil (we'll always have R40). Pegi Cecconi, Jeff Gorin (for taking the manuscript on holiday to Hollywood), David Miller, Andy Hunns, Sahra 'Welsh' Goodall, Laura Jones, Ewely, Paddy (I love you, Brighton), P, Dylan and Ravioli. Sylvain forever. The good people at Unbound who picked Red up when I thought I'd put her down for good. And for the inscrutable, beautiful girl who quietens my insecurities and keeps me standing in the light: I love Lauren Amy Archer.